THE ACCIDENTAL MERMAID

DAKOTA CASSIDY

COPYRIGHT

ISBN: 9781720223597

Imprint: Independently published

ACKNOWLEDGMENTS

Darling, amazing readers,

Thank you so much for grabbing another Accidental! Can you even believe it's number sixteen? Me neither!

Either way, I'm glad you've stuck around and I'm thrilled to finally bring you a mermaid. Over the course of almost ten years since this series debuted, many, many of you have suggested a mermaid as an accidental, but it took me a while before a story struck me enough that I had no choice but to finally write it.

That said, as always, I've taken serious artistic license with mythology/folklore and made it my own, as I'm wont to do. Also, a note to any lovely residents of Staten Island: the locations where this adventure takes place are entirely fictional and created to suit my own story purposes—because I think we all know there are no mermaid pools in SI. Or are there? LOL!

Anyway, I hope you'll forgive my fast and loose

geography/bodies of water and just roll with it—and as always, with me. I'm a native New Yorker, born and bred, and I'd never want to disrespect my people!

Anyway, you guys are fantabulous, and I love that the girls and the accidental friendships they've made along the way have become as much your family as mine. With that, I so hope you'll join me for Marty's journey hopefully in later winter of 2018, and *The Accidental Unicorn* (yes. You read that right!) coming soon thereafter.

Until then—Nina wanted me to tell you not to wear yellow. She says it's not in your color wheel—even if you're a mermaid. LOL!

Love,

Dakota XXOO

THE ACCIDENTAL MERMAID

BY DAKOTA CASSIDY

CHAPTER 1

"On the real?" the dark-haired, eerily pale woman—wearing a hoodie and a T-shirt that read "Not Today, Satan" with slim-fitting jeans—asked her very pregnant friend. Who, by the way, dressed like Grace Kelly and smelled like a luscious rose garden.

"Yes, Nina. On the real."

"Like a tail, and scales, and one of those little beaded B-cup bras?"

The pregnant woman sucked in her cheeks, her nostrils flaring. "No beaded bra, but definitely a tail. It's quite beautiful, in fact. I mean, as tails and scales go."

"So lemme see, Wanda," she insisted with a pleading tone that held a hint of strangely malicious glee. Her beautiful eyes gazed curiously as she peeked over her friend's shoulder from the hallway leading off the changing rooms.

But Wanda put five pale-polished nails to the

woman's shoulder and shook her head. "Only if you promise not to stare and make rude jokes."

"Don't be a moron. Of course I'm gonna stare and make rude jokes, Wanda. She has a fucking tail, dude. She's in the middle of a public pool floor, under the stairs to the diving board, no frickin' less. Who *wouldn't* stare at that shit?"

"*Nina…*" the woman said with a warning tone, her high cheekbones turning a pretty pink.

Wanda and Nina—both very nice, solid names. It's always pleasant to have a name to attach to the people talking about you and your "predicament" as though you're not even in the same room…while you're on the floor…literally flopping around, looking for cover.

Nina, holding an equally beautiful dark-haired little girl with curly hair and the cherubic face of an angel, wearing the sweetest purple tutu swimsuit with ballerinas on the chest, pushed her way past the pregnant Wanda at the entry to the pool. She looked down to the blue-tiled surface of the flooring where Esther Williams Sanchez lay.

And then her mouth fell open.

Immediately afterward, she clamped her mouth shut and her shoulders slumped in a pouty way. "Is this another wormhole, Wanda? Like Shamalot? I don't wanna go back today. I have shit to do, and it always takes days for me to readjust to the time zones. It's like fairytale jetlag, dude."

A woman with long, glistening blonde hair, styled

similarly to a Kardashian's, skidded into the pool area on a pair of burnt-orange heels so high, Esther thought surely she'd pitch headfirst into the pool. And then she thought what a shame that would be, because all that beautiful fake blonde hair would undoubtedly turn green if the pool's chemicals were to touch it.

"Ho-lee fucksticks!" the blonde shouted, her words echoing in the chlorine-scented air as she stopped just short of the tall dark-haired Goddess, who grabbed her by the arm to steady her and keep her from falling into the pool. "Is she a...?"

Nina, obviously recuperated, said, "No, Marty. She's not. This is all just a big fucking joke because that's how we roll at Mommy and Me swim class. We prank each other all the time. Last week, we fucked with all the moms by telling them we found Nemo in the pool."

Marty rolled her sapphire-blue eyes and let out a ragged sigh, cupping the back of her neck and massaging it with her fingers. "Shut it with the sarcasm, Dark Overlord, and tell me what happened. I have a headache the size of your mouth and I'm tired. It was a long day at Bobbie-Sue." Leaning over, she dropped a kiss on the baby's forehead and smiled. "Did you find something awesome at swim class, Charlie Girl? Who's Auntie Marty's favorite genie princess?" she asked the baby.

The baby answered with a squeal of joy, holding her arms out for her aunt to take her from her mother. Which Marty did, pressing kisses to the baby's chubby fists, making her coo with delight. Then she looked at the women named Wanda. "Her tail is spectacular, don't you think? And that hair! I'd kill a bitch to be in this kind of humidity and still have it fall all down my shoulders in those luscious rainbow curls."

Wanda eyed her tail and fins, the iridescent scales shimmering in a pale yellow and melting into shades of aqua and teal, and nodded. "It truly is magic."

"It's fucking yellow," Nina muttered.

Marty smiled distractedly at Nina before her face became serious. "So, what do we have so far, girls? How the heck did this happen?"

Esther squirmed uncomfortably. Well, she tried to squirm uncomfortably, but her tail (her tail!) made it almost impossible to move due to its heft and length. Also, if she moved the wrong way, her suddenly luxurious rainbow-colored hair would reveal her very naked breasts.

Wanda, with the swollen belly, dressed in a light blue maternity dress and conservative yet fashionable low heels, shook her head. "We don't know. I tried to talk to her, but she clammed up." Then she looked to Esther with her soft brown eyes, made up quite tastefully in pastel eyeshadow colors. "No pun intended, of course."

Clam up. Hah! Well, if nothing else, they had a sense of humor. Esther had a sense of humor, too. Which is one of the reasons why she'd agreed to take the Mommy and Me class for first-time swimmers—the only class they had available at the Y at this time of year, now that summer was over and fall classes had begun.

She'd taken it at the urging of her friend Juanita, because Esther was thirty-two years old, couldn't swim, and she was tired of hearing her friends tease her when they went to Mexico for impromptu vacations and she sat on the beach all alone due to her fear.

Marty eyed Esther with a critical glance. "Any idea why a woman of her age is taking a class at Mommy and Me?" She paused and then gasped. "Wait! Is there a child involved here? Where's the child? Oh, hell. Please tell me there's not a baby in the mix, Wanda."

Wanda shook her head and picked invisible lint from Marty's sharp beige suit before straightening her dark brown and rust scarf. "No children involved in the making of this…this…whatever this is. I mean, I know what this is, but you know what I mean. I did manage to get that much out of her before she stopped talking to me. So, I'm not sure why she's at a Mommy and Me class."

Marty sighed, now massaging her forehead as she looked to Nina. "Did Big Mouth scare her? How many times have I told you when you find yourself in a position where someone is afraid, don't make them *more* afraid, Nina?"

The beautiful Nina pushed her hoodie from her head and flicked Marty's arm, taking the baby back. "Shut your Botoxed lips, Blondie. I haven't said jack shit. I was handing off Sam to Heath when all this went down. Speaking of, we better send him home with the kids so we can spend the next nine frillion hours of my life listening to the fish cry and carry on about how awful this is."

Wanda looked up from her phone. "I just texted him. He was in the parking lot waiting for me. And please, Nina, don't be so crude. You'll make her think we don't care. Plus, it's not like you don't have nine-frillion hours. You, my dear, have eternity."

Sam must be the baby with the strange complexion Nina had been carrying around in the pool along with her little girl Charlie. He was quite small, in Esther's opinion, for a swim class. But then, who was she to talk? She was in her thirties and still afraid of bathtub water deeper than four inches.

A tall, devastatingly handsome man with dark hair and gorgeous eyes, wearing a casual navy-blue pullover shirt and low-slung jeans, appeared behind Nina, carrying Sam. He put a hand to Wanda's waist and asked in a husky tone, "Trouble, honey?"

She patted his cheek lovingly and smiled, pressing a kiss to the baby's cheek and nuzzling his button nose. "Or something."

"Remember what we discussed, okay? Please?" he reminded her in a tone that spoke of a serious conversation they'd had.

Wanda smiled coquettishly at Heath and batted her eyelashes, rubbing her belly. "Promise, no heavy lifting today. I have to watch out for junior. He's my first priority. Always."

"First, that's my *daughter* you're carrying around. And that's not what you said when you picked up the car to collect Sam's teething ring, young lady," he teased good-naturedly.

Picked up the car? Like, the car-car or a toy car?

"Oh, stop. The SUV's not that heavy. I certainly wasn't crawling under it with this belly, and that's Sam's favorite teething ring. How could I leave it there until you got back from your golf game? And this?" She pointed to her belly. "Is a boy, Heath Jefferson."

Okay, So Wanda had picked up a car-car. Not a toy car.

What the fresh hell?

Standing on tiptoe, Wanda kissed her husband's lips. "You take the children home, would you, please? I promise to be very careful. No heavy lifting. Okay?"

Nina nudged Heath's wide shoulder. "Don't worry. I got her back. We won't let her do anything she shouldn't do. Text Greg before you leave and he'll come get Charlie from you. Carl'll worry if she's gone for too long, and Calamity'll have a cow if Carl gets upset." Nina plopped kisses on each baby's forehead and waved them off.

"Stop being a worrywart, Heath. Would we, in a million years, let anything happen to Wanda and baby Jefferson? Never. We got this," Marty said, blowing kisses to the babies and waving to Heath before she turned around and narrowed her gaze on Esther, like she had a purpose and Esther was her mission.

Esther, who still hadn't spoken a word, fought a cringe under Marty's scrutiny.

As a general rule, she liked to observe people, situations, life, more than she liked to interact. At least at first. Her job as a divorce mediator required she pay close attention to body language and inflection and all sorts of things. But right now, after what had happened when she'd been the last in the class to climb out of the pool, she didn't have any words left to offer.

Instead, she'd just sit here under the diving board until this *thing* attached to her like some sort of colorful, yet, admittedly beautiful growth went away. It *would* go away, right? It had to go away…

On a sigh, Wanda slipped her arm through Marty's and they made their way the short distance to the diving board.

Marty sat on her haunches and looked at Esther with the prettiest sapphire-blue eyes Esther had ever seen. "I'm Marty Flaherty. What's your name?"

"Swear to fuck, if it's Ariel, I'll piss myself," Nina cackled, coming to stand behind her friends.

Marty reached behind her back and swatted Nina's leg without even looking. "Find your inner marshmallow, Elvira, and show some empathy," she ordered, as though the order made any sense at all.

Now Wanda gazed at her, genuine concern on her finely boned face. "You're frightening us, honey. Please say something. We want to help. I promise you, we can help if you'll let us."

Yet, Esther cringed, attempting to inch farther away. After everything she'd heard, she was convinced these people were either all part of some weird cult of unbelievably pretty people who believed they had superpowers, like super-strength, or she was having a nightmare. A stone-cold, really real, scary-AF nightmare.

"Fuck, Wanda. Am I gonna have to haul this chick out to the car?" Nina complained, as though she hauled chicks with multicolored tails every day. "Because I'm tellin' ya, Marty's gonna have to move that shit-show of Bobbie-Sue crap out of the backseat. Her car's the biggest one we have, and we'll never stuff her ass in there with all that lip gloss."

Suddenly, and quite without warning, Esther found her voice. "Bobbie-Sue? Do you sell Bobbie-Sue?" She'd sold Bobbie-Sue once, in order to pay for college.

She'd been about as bad at it as a breast implant salesman at a porn convention, worse at trying to put all that makeup on her face, let alone anyone else's. All that talk of color wheels and blend, blend, blend was not her gift.

Marty smiled warmly, her eyes lighting up. "She speaks! Yay! Now we're getting somewhere. And I *own* Bobbie-Sue, honey. I'm an honest, reputable business-woman. And my husband owns Pack Cosmetics. We're in the process of merging the two companies right now. Which is why I missed Mommy and Me class tonight with my little girl, Hollis. But now you can see, you have nothing to be afraid of."

Tentatively gazing at the women, Esther confessed, "I tried to sell Bobbie-Sue to help pay for some college courses."

"Yeah, and you bought what with that pile of cash, a pack of pencils? Some Ramen noodles for a week?" Nina asked on a cynical snort.

"Actually, it was a loaf of bread and a bottle of mustard from the Andes. Did you know they even had their own mustard in the Andes?"

Marty shook her head and clucked her tongue. "Sounds like you didn't work the program… What's your name?"

"I'm not sure I want to tell you because I'm pretty sure you'll laugh." After that Ariel crack, she *knew* they would.

"Aw, they won't laugh," Nina reassured her. "I will, for damn sure. Trust and believe. But these two sensitive snowflakes would rather die than hurt your fucking feelings."

Giving them all a sheepish glance, she winced even before she spoke. "It's Esther…"

Wanda leaned in, her eyes questioning. "Esther…?" she coaxed with a hopeful glance.

She swallowed, smoothing her hands over the long length of her new locks. *Just say it and get it over with. You've lived with it all your life, for pity's sake.*

Well, sure I have. But that was just a bunch of lame jokes about being named after a famous synchronized swimmer and not actually being able to swim.

It wasn't because I had a tail with a fin.

"Esther Williams…er, Sanchez. Esther Williams Sanchez," she finally blurted out.

There was a short silence while each woman processed who Esther Williams was as the lights from the pool played against the ceiling and the floor continued to dry around her.

"Like the famous synchronized swimmer?" Nina crowed, holding her belly before she doubled over at the waist.

And then they all began to laugh.

Wanda was the first to recover, sputtering against the back of her hand and using her thumb to wipe tears from her eyes. "Ladies! Stahhp!" And then she choked out another string of hyena-ish giggles before she straightened and cleared her throat, composing herself. "Girls. Knock it off! There's someone in need. Also," she said, her eyes imploring Esther's, "please forgive me for behaving so poorly. I'm given to fits and spurts of all sorts of crazy emotions since I got knocked up. I wasn't laughing *at* you."

"But I wasn't laughing," Esther protested, catching a glimmer of her yellow and aqua tail under the pool lights before briefly clenching her eyes shut.

Wanda bit her lip to keep from laughing again. "Okay. I was laughing *at* you. But you have to admit, it's kind of funny, your name being…and you ending up a mermaid." Wanda shook her head as if it would help clear it. "Never mind. My apologies for being so rude."

Esther watched this all play out, but simply said, "No sweat."

Marty plopped down on the ground, holding her belly after laughing too hard, then she reached out a hand and placed it on Esther's arm. "I'm sorry, too. Now let's get down to business, Esther Williams Sanchez. How did this happen?"

"I'm *not* sorry, 'cuz that shit's funny, but yeah. How the fuck did this happen? Like, how do you have legs one minute and a tail the next?" Nina inquired.

Esther stared at the length of her body, and then she looked up at the ladies, all expectantly waiting for her to answer. The pressure to explain became intense. "I…I don't…"

Tears began to form in the corner of her eyes and panic swelled in her chest. Her heart raced, crashing against her ribs until she thought surely it would burst through the wall of her chest.

Nina rasped a sigh, planting her hands on her hips. "Fuck. Here we go, girlies. Meltdown in three, two—"

And then Esther screamed.

She screamed loud. So loud, it reverberated around the Olympic-size swimming pool, swirling and swishing as it wended its way into one ear and out the other.

And she didn't even care if she came off as some hysterical, screeching shrew—something she despised in most women.

She had a tail.

A fin.

A whateverthehell you wanted to label it.

She had it and it was attached to her and she didn't know how to get away from it.

So, she gulped in a fresh breath of air and screamed again.

Even louder.

CHAPTER 2

"Shut the fuck up, Rainbow Brite!" Nina roared at Esther, hiking her up on her shoulder as she stomped her way out the back door of the Y into the early fall air. "You're killing me, for fuck's sake!"

Still, she struggled against this woman who had to be as strong as Thor, her grip was so tight.

Then there was a hand on her bare back, soothing, warm. Wanda's voice wafted to her ears. "Esther! Listen to me. Stop screaming. You're going to draw attention to us, *and* you, and I'm thinking you'd prefer not to be seen this way just yet. Also, I don't relish the idea I'll go to jail for aiding in the kidnapping of a mermaid. Now, I swear to you, we're going to help, but you have to stop screaming."

"Wanda? I swear on my GD blood supply for the next year, I'm gonna sock her in the mouth if she doesn't quit squirming! She's damn slimy! I'm gonna end up dropping her headfirst if she doesn't knock it the fuck off!"

"Esther!" Marty yelled into the near-empty parking lot, putting a hand on Nina's shoulder to thwart her movement. She took hold of Esther's face with both hands and lifted her head until their eyes met. *"Stop. Struggling. Stop. Screaming.* Understood? I've had a brutally long day. My head is pounding, which is crazy because I'm a werewolf and we don't get headaches. My feet are tired, my eyeliner's running, my back hurts, and my Spanx are too damn tight. Now, knock it off, shut your face, and let us help you!"

Whatever it was in Marty's tone, whatever words she used, or maybe it was just that she was disgusted with herself for screaming like some hysterical, out-of-control girl, Esther instantly stopped struggling and blew out a breath, letting the cleansing, cool air of early fall seep into her lungs.

"Okay," she murmured as they stopped in front of an enormous black SUV with tinted windows.

Marty patted her cheek and smiled a weary smile. "All right then. Now, let's get you in the back of the car, and very calmly, you're going to tell us what happened and how this came to be while we get you somewhere safe. Okay?"

She took in three or four more gulps of fresh air and nodded with a bit of difficulty, due to the weight of her new hair. "Okay."

"No more screaming?" Marty asked as she pulled

something from the back of the SUV and put the backseat down.

Esther shook her head, so heavy with hair, her body trembling violently. "Not a sound."

Throwing a blanket around Esther's shoulders, Marty opened the back of the SUV. "Nina? You push her through the back, I'll pull her in, got it? Wanda, turn the car on and turn the heat up, please."

Wanda sighed a pretty, delicate sigh. "I *can* help, you know."

But Marty shook her head, along with her finger, her bracelets clacking together. "No—no you cannot. Bun in the oven means nothing arduous. Heath would plain eat our faces off if we let you get hurt. Or are you forgetting our last OOPS meeting, where he threatened to tie you to a chair and have Arch force-feed you so much of his delicious food you'd be too fat to walk, let alone chase after a client?"

OOPS? What the hell was an OOPS meeting? Some kind of acronym for a weird addiction?

Wanda chuckled, a sound so light and as pretty as her sigh; it almost made Esther smile. This Heath wasn't just handsome, he clearly loved his wife, and she hadn't seen that kind of love since her grandparents.

"I remember the conversation well. Didn't that happen while I was stuffing my face with that insane smoked brisket he made on the Fourth of July?"

Marty's nod was sharp as she tucked the blanket tighter around Esther. "It was, and OMG, that brisket.

It's still slathered on my thighs. Now, please start the car."

Wanda made a face at her friend, but she smiled as she did, and it was warm and fond. "I rather feel like we've switched roles, and you're suddenly the one with a level head on her shoulders and I'm the one who needs direction and patience."

Marty tweaked her cheek. "Well, don't get used too it. There's only so much nice I have in me before Nina Hulk smashes it right the hell outta me."

"Hey! Yippy and Yappy? I'm carrying a fucking mermaid on my back like a sack of GD potatoes from the Shop Rite down the road. Get your pats on the back out of the way before I beat your asses with her tail."

Nina stalked her way to the back of the SUV and let Esther slide down the front of her body until they were eye to eye.

"You're strong," she commented. Yes, it was a silly thing to say in light of the situation, but now that she was mentally mostly back in the saddle, she couldn't help but mention it as she stared at this woman with eyes so black, they looked like coal.

"I'm also deaf now, too."

"I'm sorry. It just hit me all at once, and I lost it."

"Well, pay attention. I'm gonna hit you and your yellowness all at once if you scream like that again. I have sensitive ears. You feel what I'm puttin' out?"

Esther's breath shuddered in and out, condensation

creating small puffs of clouds that escaped her lips. "I do."

And she did. This woman was formidable. Everything about her—her strength, her body language, her piercing gaze—all said she was a force Esther didn't want to reckon with.

"Good. Now, I'm going to turn your sparkly rainbow ass around and shove you in there on your side like I'm stuffing a sausage back into its casing, and Marty'll haul you inside. One peep out of your big-ass mouth—one peep—and I beat the shit out of *you* with your tail. I'm not gonna end up on Cell Block D, fighting my way for top-dog status and making shower shoes out of panty liners and duct-tape, because I tried to do the decent thing. Understand?"

"We have simpatico," Esther agreed, then biting the inside of her cheek to keep from crying out. She wanted to ask where they were taking her, but at this point, she was beyond hysterical and well into shock.

It almost didn't matter what they did with her.

Nina nodded, her swirly hair falling around her glowingly pale face. "Good. Here we go." Repositioning her so that Esther was literally tucked under her arm like a 2x4 length of wood, Nina put her upper body into the back of the SUV, laying Esther on her side before rolling her onto her stomach with a grunt.

Marty crawled into the driver's side and reached over the top of the seat, her cheeks red, a bead of perspiration on her lip, and grabbed her upper arms, pulling on them as Nina latched onto the lower half of her body. They lifted and shoved until Esther was almost all the way in.

"Marty? Hold up. Problem," Nina said, and Esther heard the concern in her tone.

Marty blew a strand of hair from her face, the SUV lights revealing tired lines around her eyes. "What's wrong?"

"Her fin's hanging out the back of the SUV, dude. She's too damn long to fit. We can't drive around Staten Island with her fin hanging out the back. People will think we're batshit."

They didn't already think that? Surely, with all this talk of werewolves and lifting cars, someone had labeled them crazy at least once.

Rising to her elbows, Esther tried to make herself as small as possible and scrunch upward, but the weight of the tail made it almost impossible to move the lower half of her body.

But Wanda had an answer as she held up something Esther couldn't quite see. "Tarp. Nina had a tarp in the back of her car. We'll wrap it around her tail and bungee the back shut."

That settled, they made quick work of things while Esther stayed as quiet as promised, afraid to ask what was next—because really, what *could* be next?

A gig at Sea World?

Tamping down another wave of rising panic, helpless as a newborn kitten, she still didn't say anything as Marty roared the engine and shot out of the parking lot, with Wanda in the passenger seat and Nina in her car, following behind them. The exposed part of her tail and her fins flapped like flags in a hurricane, but the women had done a pretty decent job of disguising her.

"Where do you live, Esther? Can we get you into your place relatively unnoticed?" Wanda asked as they drove away from the lights of the YMCA.

Now hold on. Whoa and Nellie. She wasn't bringing these people to her house. Where she slept. Wasn't that akin to suicide?

But then, what were her choices? For all the kooky conversations they'd had around her about werewolves and such, they appeared to know what they were talking about. They'd swept in and taken charge and she'd hardly said a word.

Besides, who the frick did you call when you suddenly had a tail and fins? *Who*? Who exactly was in charge of that department? Disney?

Not to mention, *how* did you call when you couldn't move out of your own way?

But Marty assuaged her unspoken fear. "Esther? It's okay to bring us to your house. We won't rob you, or sell you to the government for scientific research purposes and a new Maserati. Or worse, give your story to *Inside Edition*. Oh, and we won't murder you. I know this is all happening very, very fast, but if we can just get you somewhere you feel safe, where we can have some privacy, we're going to help you. And you'll understand why and how women like us can help you, but it's going to take a certain amount of blind faith."

The words fell out of her mouth before she could stop them at the thought of seeing her small cottage on the beach, of being around her things, and her dog Mooky and cat Marsha. "I live near South Beach—in a small suburb called Oyster Hollow. In a cottage that used to be my grandparents' before they died. Ironically, right on the beach."

Wanda leaned forward, her slender finger hovering over the navigation system. "Your address?"

"But wait! I don't have my key or my purse or—"

Wanda held up Esther's purse and smiled. "You mean this? I took the liberty of grabbing it from your locker. I hope you don't mind."

"But I locked that before..." She shook her head. If the woman could lift a car, surely she could pop a locker. Duh.

As Esther spewed her address and said a silent prayer these people were only superficially banana-pants, not deep-seated-crazy psychopaths, Wanda typed in her address and sat back, the streetlights flashing over her classically beautiful features.

Marty looked into the rearview mirror, her bright eyes sparkling. "What do you do for a living, Esther?"

"I'm a freelance divorce mediator."

"Oooh, fun times, I'll bet," Marty murmured, twisting a strand of hair around her finger.

Or not. Divorce mediation was a sad, sometimes exceptionally ugly job. She often wondered why marriage had ever been invented, for all the torture people put each other through over ridiculous things like leopard-spot ottomans and silverware.

One couple had fought so long and so hard over a single picture frame before they'd agreed to settle, Esther had come close to threatening to drop the stupid thing at the dump and set it on fire.

It was disgraceful—which was why she wasn't a fan of marriage, other than that of her grandparents, who'd been married for fifty years until her grandmother, Consuela, had succumbed to Alzheimer's. Her grandfather had died of longing for the woman he'd loved for over half a century.

But their love was rare, and almost inconceivable today, with so many things like the Internet and social media interfering, keeping people apart in worlds they've created on a computer rather than inspiring them to spend time together.

"It's challenging. That's probably a better word."

Wanda threw her head back and laughed. "I can only imagine. I've been divorced. Years and years ago, mind you, but I just can't understand all the fighting over useless things. I say just kill them and then you get to keep everything."

Esther clamped her mouth shut, a shiver of fear running along her arms.

There was a short pause, where Wanda's words hung in the air like ticking time bombs, before Marty laughed out loud. "She's kidding, Esther. Promise. Wanda's got a case of raging hormones these days. She just says whatever she thinks lately, but we're all very happily married, I assure you."

"Good to know," she muttered.

As Marty took a sharp right on what felt like two tires, Esther didn't budge, the weight of her tail holding her steady. When the surroundings became familiar, and she saw the lights of her tiny white beach cottage, set far apart from her neighbors, she almost cried.

Home was good. Home would at least make some of this better. Mooky and Marsha were there, and there was some leftover lasagna in the fridge from last night, and if they could make this tail go away, she'd send these people home and cuddle on the couch in front of a fire with her furbabies while she watched *The Big Bang Theory* reruns.

As Marty pulled to a stop, the women looked around, scanning her small front yard with potted mums she'd purchased last year and wind chimes hanging from the maple tree.

"Looks pretty quiet. How far away from your neighbors are we, Esther? Can we get you inside without them seeing?"

"Mostly everyone's gone, now that summer's over. The Reynolds are my closest neighbors, and they packed up and went home after Labor Day. I think we're okay."

And thank God, too. Little Stacy Reynolds would have a field day if she saw Esther had a tail and hair like a mermaid. Stacy loved a Disney princess almost as much as she loved vanilla ice cream with rainbow sprinkles.

Marty nodded her head and popped the car door open. "Then let's get you inside. You good, Wanda?"

Wanda smiled an affable smile, holding up her hand and spreading out her fingers to examine them. "Oh, I'm fine. I thought maybe I'd do my nails while you and Nina do all the work."

Nina knocked on Wanda's window, her eyes blazing hot. "Knock it off, Wanda, and stop being a pissy bitch! We're not treating you like the good china because we like it. We're doing it because we want you to have a healthy baby. Now quit feeling sorry for yourself and haul your big ass out here and do what you do. Nurture. Listen to her cry. Pat her on the back, bake her some fucking cookies."

Wanda lifted her middle finger at Nina and stuck out her tongue, but she popped the door open and hopped out of the SUV, stalking past Nina to Esther's front door with her purse tucked under the crook of her elbow.

Marty, who'd come around the car, looked at Nina and blew out a breath. "She's a lot these days, huh?"

Nina snorted her commiseration. "No shit. I swear, some days I wanna wring her dry of all these hormones flooding her brain cells like some kind of mad cow fucking disease. Maybe it's because she's half vampire, half werewolf?" Nina shrugged her shoulders. "I dunno what the fuck it is, but Christ in a bikini, I don't know if I'm gonna make it to the end of this pregnancy."

As Esther watched this all unfold, again, the words she was hearing—words like "vampire" and "werewolf"—fought to terrify her, really seep into her brain and make her lose it all over again.

They thought they were werewolves and vampires. Like, seriously creatures from mythology? No way was she letting these people into her house

Aw, hell no.

That was when she opened her mouth to scream.

Again.

CHAPTER 3

Almost as if Nina sensed Esther's discourse, her fear, she craned her neck in Esther's direction and gave her that death-ray stare. Esther clamped her mouth shut as fast as she'd opened it—because that woman was terrifying.

And then she went about self-soothing.

If she looked logically at what had happened to her, if she gave realistic credence to her new tail and fins, how could she discount werewolves and vampires?

Yet, how was she going to live with the idea this was all real? Were there more of them? How could she tell? Were there more of *her*? Was she really a mermaid? *Forever?*

She didn't have time to think much more on the notion as Nina grabbed hold of her tail and pulled her from the SUV, tucking her back under her arm like she was no heavier than Wanda's purse.

The wind howled as the ocean water she so loved to

look at from her wood-framed windows rushed to the shore. It was so much cooler here, especially now that fall was on the way. The taste of the salt in the air was different, the tang in her nose sharper somehow.

In the distance, Mooky, her half wire-haired terrier, half Doberman, barked at the unfamiliar voices and noise from behind the front door.

"Mook! Knock it off, bud!" she yelled as Wanda jammed her key in the door and popped it open, running her hand over the wall to find the light switch.

She heard Mook's nails on the bleached hardwood floors as he ran for the kitchen, where he'd try to make himself as small as he could under the kitchen's dark gray quartz peninsula until she reassured him it was safe, but she only caught a glimpse of Marsha, curled up on her favorite chair, fast asleep on a red-checked throw.

As the room became enveloped in the soft lighting from the recessed bulbs in the ceiling she'd personally chosen when she'd remodeled, Esther almost sighed in relief.

She loved her little cottage on the beach, with its comfortable seating and bits of red and turquoise accents for color, her reclaimed dark wood coffee table, and a big fireplace done in white brick with a rustic wood mantle.

It made her happy, swell with pride that she'd picked everything out, and done a lot of the renovations herself.

But then she shivered. Now she had to find an

explanation for these women as to how this had happened, and sound like a complete moron when she revealed she had no idea how she'd gone from limbs to fins.

"Ohhhh," Wanda breathed, her eyes scanning the living room, open to the small dining room and kitchen. "It's beautiful, Esther! How warm and inviting. I love, love, love the fireplace and that bleached-wood clock over it. I'd kill to have that over my mantle. Beautiful!"

That's when she stiffened in Nina's arms and attempted to crane her neck upward. Were they scoping out her house so they could dump her and steal all her worldly possessions?

Wanda bent down and looked her in the eye with a hint of laughter on her face. "We're not here to steal your things, Esther. I promise. I'm just commenting on how lovely it is because I'm a decorator at heart, too. There isn't a Home Goods store I haven't tapped every corner of. Please relax. Oh, and I love the pops of red and turquoise in the pillows, and the watercolor painting. Beautiful."

"Hey! DIY Diva, she's no lightweight," Nina complained, hoisting her higher against her waist. "Where do you want her?"

"Put her on the couch, Nina. It looks like she'll fit," Marty ordered, pointing to her beige sectional with fluffy red and turquoise pillows in various textures and sizes.

As Nina unceremoniously dumped her in the midst

of her throw pillows and cushions, she brushed her hands together. "So, what's next? Do we blow-dry her?"

"Blow-dry me?" Esther squealed, trying to sit up.

"Yeah, dude. If we dry you out, you'll get your legs back. Like Ariel. Didn't you ever see *The Little Mermaid*?"

Oh my God! She hadn't even thought about that. "My blow-dryer! It's under the sink in the bathroom. Let's try!"

Marty ran a hand through her hair and frowned. "You don't think that'll really work, do you? It seems a little farfetched and fairytale-ish."

Nina threw up her hands and said, "Well, *Splash* was the same damn way. Remember Daryl Hannah in a tub? Fuck if I know, but what else you got, Blondie?"

Wanda crossed the room and went down the short hall to her master bathroom. Esther heard another vague "Ooooh," probably stemming from her new white-and-gray-marble bathroom, before she reappeared with the blow-dryer and handed it to Nina, who plugged it in and began running it back and forth over her tail.

Marty sat on the chest of drawers Esther used as a coffee table, moving her candleholders and a pot of succulents out of the way, and said, "So explain how this happened, Esther? Just tell me about the incident—who, if anyone, was present, and we'll go from there, okay? Why were you at a Mommy and Me class anyway if you don't have children?"

Speaking of children. Damn, she'd forgotten about

Mooky and Marsha. "Mook? C'mere, buddy. It's okay. C'mon, pooky!" she called, watching him poke his Doberman-like head with the crazy mix of wiry hair from beneath the peninsula, but he hesitated.

Nina handed the blow-dryer to Wanda and sat on her haunches to peer under the peninsula, patting her thigh, her tone soft and sweetly pitched for someone so crusty. "Who's so handsome?" she asked, as Mooky cocked his head. "I'm Nina, Mooky. Cool to meet you. Come say hello, dude." She patted her thigh once more and waited.

Mook considered, much in the way he always did when he met someone new, and then he was in Nina's lap, licking her face like he'd always known her, his excited whimpers drawing Marsha's interest. Nina scratched the unusually long length of Mooky's neck and whispered encouraging words that made Marsha curious enough to hop off her favorite chair and saunter toward them with a cautious stride.

Nina took one look into her green, marble-like eyes, and like magic, Esther's caramel and white cat jumped into this strange woman's lap and purred, rubbing her face against her arm.

As Nina gathered them into her lap, petting and cooing, and Wanda diligently blow-dried her tail, which wasn't going away at all, Marty asked again, "Esther? We need to know how this happened? I really need you to talk to me. Some things you might not find terribly concerning could actually be of great concern. So, let's do this, *please*?"

That was the million-dollar question. How had this happened? One minute, she'd been in the pool with Maurizio, her sexy Italian Mommy and Me swim instructor. The next, everyone had cleared the pool and she was lingering on the steps, marveling over her bravery for actually attending the class and getting in the water all the way up to her waist—when *wham*!

She had a tail with fins. And it was beautiful; so magnificent, she almost couldn't believe it was attached to her. When she was done accepting the reality that this tail wasn't budging, she'd panicked, afraid to call out...afraid to move...*afraid*.

And she relayed as much to Marty, who'd taken over the blow-dryer while Wanda went off to the kitchen in search of tea bags.

"I swear, I was just sitting on the steps of the pool in the shallow end, being one with the water and all that jazz Maurizio taught us today, and *kaboom*! I almost drowned trying to get out of the pool. Between my Rapunzel-like hair and my tail, I gained what feels like fifty pounds. Thank God for upper-arm workouts, because I hauled myself out of the pool and managed to pull myself to the diving board before I realized I had no idea what to do. Who to call. Like, who do you call when you have a tail? Sam and Dean? Mulder and Scully?"

Marty worried her lower lip as she paused, pinching the bridge of her nose before she asked, "Did anything unusual happen in the pool? Did you feel anything strange? See anything strange?"

Esther shook her head, pushing her flowing locks away from her face as more of that panic swelled in her gut again. "No! Nothing. Though, I admit, I was terrified to get in the pool—really terrified. I can't…well, I can't swim. I know, that sounds ridiculous at my age, but I can't. I took the class at the urging of my friend, who's good friends with the instructor. I did it because I want to go on a cruise with some of my girlfriends this winter, and I didn't want to be odd man out again. It just happened it was the only class they could fit me into. I figured, who better to take swim class with than a bunch of kids, right? At least I could keep up."

"You live on the beach and you can't swim?" Wanda asked, moving around her kitchen and opening cabinet doors.

Esther cringed at the question, even though she heard no condemnation in Wanda's tone. But the reasons behind her reaction were still as raw as they'd always been. Twisting a lock of her hair, she began to fiddle with it, wondering how she'd ever get it into a ponytail and still be able to hold her head up. "I know it sounds silly, but I love the water. I grew up around it. I love looking at it, hearing it at night as it rocks me to sleep. I love the smell of salt in the air, and I love a good storm. I even love to build sandcastles. In fact, I won a competition here two years ago during the summer for one of my sand castles. I'm just afraid to get into it."

But she'd done it tonight. Okay, she'd only gone to her waist, but she'd done it, and she'd like to think her grandfather, Salvador, would be proud she'd at least partially conquered her fear—a fear he'd often soothed as he'd rocked her to sleep after a nightmare of that horrible night.

Wanda rifled through her antique-white kitchen cabinets and found some tea bags, then set about filling her teakettle. "So, you can't remember anything unusual happening before you suddenly had a tail? You're sure?"

Now she felt like the accused. Why would she lie about something like that? Suddenly, it was all too much—too overwhelming. She struggled to sit up straight, pushing the pillows on the couch out of the way. She decided to divert the spotlight off her, something she did often with couples in mediation.

"Here's a question for you guys—who *are* you? And why do you care what happens to me? Why are you here right now, helping me at all?"

They all stopped what they were doing and looked up before Nina sighed and muttered, "Here we fucking go. Wanda? Find some hooch in those cabinets. She's gonna need it."

~

A half hour, two shots of tequila and the absolute most terror she'd ever experienced in her life later—barring one incident—and Esther had to admit, Nina was right.

She did need the hooch. She needed *all* the hooch.

As she stared at these three women, two of them now redressed in their "people" clothes, as they plucked each other free of hair, as Mooky and Marsha stared stoically at them, Esther tried desperately to untie her tongue.

Putting a knuckle in her mouth, she prepared to bite down hard to check and make sure she was really awake. As her teeth hit skin, and she bit, everything remained the same except her finger hurt.

She still had an effin' tail, and Nina had fangs, and both Wanda and Marty had patches of hair sprouting from various parts of their bodies.

She held up a hand and inhaled as Wanda set a steaming cup of tea down next to her on the end table. "Let me get this straight. You, Wanda, are half werewolf, half vampire. Nina, you're half vampire, half witch…and Marty's just plain old werewolf. Am I correct? Because when it comes time to identify you, I don't want to be an insensitive shlub and mislabel. With society the way it is these days, you can never be too careful."

Marty looked at her thoughtfully, deeply gazing into her eyes as she placed her scarf on the arm of the couch. "Are you sure you're okay, Esther? I know it's a lot when you first see all the commotion and snarling and hair and teeth. There's lots and lots of hair and teeth, but we're really no different than you."

But Nina swatted her on the back, jolting Esther forward with her strength. "Aw, she's fucking fine, Marty. Right, Esther? Took that shit like a total champ.

If we gave out awards, I'd give you one for best non-freak-the-fuck-out in a real-life performance."

Rather than fill the shot glass again, Esther grabbed for the whole bottle of Cuervo and took a long slug, letting the heat of the alcohol warm her from the inside. "Do I get a trophy?"

Nina cackled, tucking her fangs back into her mouth and slapping her on the back again. "See? She's fucking fine. She's got chops. That's good. You'll need 'em."

Wanda took Esther's hand and began rubbing it to warm her cold fingers, while taking the tequila away from her, handing it to Nina, and replacing it with the warm tea. "Esther, you can tell us if you're not okay. You can also ask us questions, if you'd like. Nothing's too risqué or off-limits."

"*How?*" She squeaked the word out. How had all these women come to be?

Marty stretched her arms up toward the ceiling. "Long story short, an accident. Probably something similar to yours."

"So, chemical spill, nuclear power plant explosion, bad pharmaceuticals?" she joked.

Wanda chuckled softly and smiled warmly. "No, but we can tell you the stories, if you'd like. It happens in all sorts of ways. An accidental biting, a scratch, you name it, it's happened. But that's why we do what we do. Because we had something life-altering happen to us and we didn't know where to turn. Now we help people with the same sensitive issues."

Now Esther, her mouth falling open, breathed, "There are other people like you? Like me?"

Nina cracked her neck by rolling it from side to side. "If you only fucking knew. Listen, let's get on with this shit already. We need to find your people so we can hand your ass off to them and they can take care of you so we don't fucking have to. We have enough of you crazies running amok to last more than ten eternities. I don't think we're going to be able to rent a fucking hall big enough to hold all of us for barbecues and bullshit if we add someone new. Especially if the dragons come. Shit gets real when the dragons come. Something's always goddamn on fire."

She was just going to flat-out ignore the reference to dragons for now. Vampires and werewolves were plenty to process, thank you very much. "My people? I don't have any people. I mean, my parents and grandparents are gone, and my uncle Gomez, my father's brother, died a few days ago. I have no one..."

When she said those words out loud, she realized for the first time just how alone she really was. There was no one left but Mooky and Marsha and her.

Just her.

Not that her uncle's passing had made a big difference in her life, unfortunately. He'd never been interested in communicating with her. She'd hardly known him.

Emptiness settled deep in her chest, poking at her vulnerability and making her swallow hard. She had friends, and Mooky and Marsha. That was plenty, and she'd damn well be grateful.

Noting her hand trembled, Wanda squeezed it tight. "I'm so sorry about your uncle, Esther."

She shook off the despair threatening to take over and squared her shoulders. "No, no. It's okay. We were never very close. He was a little kooky. A nice enough guy, from what I understand, but very introverted with his work. He was a scientist we hardly ever saw." Apparently, according to his suicide note, a very depressed scientist. But she couldn't dwell on that now, and she didn't want to offer TMI.

After her grandparents' deaths, she'd tried to get her uncle to meet her for lunch or maybe even just some coffee or a drink. The hope was, they'd at least connect on some level and neither of them would be all alone in the world. But he'd been as introverted as her family had always said he was. He'd never returned any of her calls, and aside from the few colleagues from the lab he'd worked for and herself in attendance, his funeral had been a desolate one.

Her perspective on losing her uncle felt more as though she were on the outside looking in. It was almost as if she'd come across his death by overdose in a newspaper article, and she had fleeting feelings of sympathy in the way she would if he were a complete stranger.

In fact, she'd only actually been in his presence three times in her life. At her parents' and grandparents' funerals, and once at a family barbecue. But her grandfather had always spoken of Gomez with such pride, she'd attended his funeral out of respect for him.

When his attorney had notified her of his death, he'd told her Uncle Gomez had left instructions to notify his closest living relative, whoever that was at the time, and that he'd left his worldly goods to science and his funeral arrangements were all pre-planned. All she'd had to do was show up.

She hadn't asked many questions because, in her mind, there wasn't much to ask. But now she was vaguely curious about how he'd come to that point in his life.

Nina sat at the edge of the coffee table, scooping a bewildered Marsha off the floor and rubbing her chin on the feline's head. "But you do have people, dude. You must. Otherwise, how the fuck did this happen?"

Esther shook her head. "Maybe I'm just tired, but how could my people be the ones responsible for this?" She waved a hand down the length of her tail. "I don't have people who are mermaids. I have people who were immigrants from Venezuela who came to this country for a better life and ran a shoe store for almost fifty years before they retired."

Nina shook a finger at her, waving it under her nose. "I mean your *new* people, Esther Williams Sanchez. Your mermaid fucking people. Believe me, they're out there, and I don't GD well know how or when, but you can bet your sweet, slimy ass, they're gonna show up sometime soon. They always damn well show up. Now, they could be good people or they could be bad—"

"Nina!" Wanda chastised with a stern tone—just like the ones the nuns from Catholic school used. "Don't frighten her. For the love of Pete, let her adjust."

But Nina scoffed, now scooping up a stiff Mooky, too, easing her magic hands along his back until he relaxed. "Please. Adjust. Hah! We all know how that fucking goes, Wanda. Let's just tell her the truth and stop easing her into it. It's better than fucking sprinkling that shit with sugar all the time. Her life's going to change in a big damn way. Some good. Some bad. Probably a whole lot of bad before it gets good. So lay off the bowl of sunshine with whipped cream on top and—"

Her doorbell rang, interrupting Nina's tirade about sunshine and sugar and shit and a lot of words Esther couldn't process for the tequila she'd consumed.

"I hope that's Arch," Marty murmured as she rose to answer the door. "I texted him about an hour ago now. Darnell, too. We need to find some information on merpeople and who can help us get Esther's legs back."

But Esther, suddenly petrified it could be a neighbor, cringed, pulling the blanket from the back of the couch and attempting to cover her tail with it.

Which was rather like trying to cover a beached whale with a hand towel, but whatever. "What if it's not the people you texted?" she asked, terrified.

Nina smiled at her with confidence, rolling her

shoulders as she set Mooky and Marsha down on the floor. "Then we'll fucking handle it, of course."

As the door swung open, and the cold wind rushed in, a very large, very good-looking man literally pushed past Marty until he was almost inside the cottage.

But Marty, clearly offended, shoved a hand into his shoulder and frowned disapprovingly. "Excuse me, but who the hell are you and how dare you push your way in here like you own the joint?"

"Is this where Esther Sanchez lives?" he asked in a very distinct but light Australian accent that, under normal circumstances, would have sent shivers along her spine—because sexy. Very sexy.

Instead, it wrought panic and fear in her.

"Who the fuck are you and why the fuck do you want to know?" Nina asked, bouncing from foot to foot like a jazzed-for-fight-night boxer.

"I'm Tucker Pearce, and I need to speak to Esther Sanchez immediately," he insisted, his square jaw clenching.

Nina instantly went into attack mode, sidling up to him and giving him a wild-eyed stare. "Yeah? Well, I'm Hits First Asks Questions Later, and if you don't back the fuck off, *mate,* your intestines are gonna be the shrimp on my barbie."

And then he saw Esther, her fins draping over the end of the sofa, her hair falling down along her lap, and his eyes—his beautiful hazel eyes, with just a fleck of gold in them—went wide.

That's when he said, "Well, fuck all."

CHAPTER 4

Yeah, fuck all.

As the gorgeous man stood frozen on the spot, quite out of the blue, Nina paused for a moment then threw her head back and laughed. "Oh shit, dude! Ding-dong, Esther's people calling!"

And then Marty began to laugh as well, her chuckle hearty and rich to Esther's ears. She slapped Nina on the back and nodded. "Oh my God! I bet you twenty and a pint of blood, you're right! I can't wait to hear this one!" she said on a sputter before she collapsed against Nina in a fit of hysterical laughing.

Esther looked helplessly to Wanda, the only sane one of the bunch because she was currently the only one not laughing. "Wanda?"

Until she was.

She doubled over and laughed, too, eloquently, of course—and all this while Esther and Tucker stared at them and then at each other, perplexed.

"Well, don't just stand there, dude. Get the fuck in here before your mermaid mama catches a cold," Nina instructed, her nostrils flaring.

The man looked at her, a question in his eyes, but Nina broke from laughing to say, "I know you're a merdude. I can smell you, man." She pointed to her nose then resumed laughing.

Tucker took two long strides, his thick thighs bulging beneath his jeans, placing himself by the kitchen's peninsula as he openly gawked at Esther, who'd suddenly become very aware the only thing between her and total upper-body nudity was her hair.

"What the hell…?" he muttered.

She hauled the blanket up over her chest and gave Tucker a sheepish glance. "Um, g'day, mate?"

And that made the women laugh all over again—laugh until tears fell from Marty's and Wanda's eyes and Nina dry heaved.

But Tucker didn't laugh. He didn't even smirk.

He ran a hand through his chocolate-brown hair and began to approach her, then clearly thought twice because he took a step backward. "You're Esther Sanchez, yes? Gomez Sanchez's niece?"

She nodded numbly, unclear why he seemed vaguely familiar. He was incredibly good-looking in a rough, edgy kind of way, but everything before tonight was a total blur at this point. She was having a hard time remembering anything before she'd inherited a tail.

But she answered with caution. "I am. Actually, it's

Esther *Williams* Sanchez. Who are you, and why are you here?"

"As in—"

She held up a hand to stop him. "Yes," she snapped "As in the synchronized swimmer, okay? Now, who are you?"

His strong jaw twitched. "We met briefly at your uncle's funeral the other day."

Huh. She frowned. Why couldn't she remember that? Certainly a man like this stood out in a crowd, and there hadn't even *been* a crowd at her uncle's funeral.

"And?"

"And I have some questions for you."

The lingering laughter in the air evaporated instantly as Nina strode up to Tucker and eyeballed him with clear irritation. "Hold the fuck up, *mate*," she sneered. "You have some questions for her? For *her*? That's a joke, right? Correct me if I'm wrong, but you *did* this to her, didn't you?"

Tucker's nod was curt, but he didn't back down. Instead, he stared right back at Nina. "I think it was in fact me. So, to answer your question, yes."

"Then slow your roll and use your fucking words, pal. Apologetic words. Like, oops, I'm sorry I turned you into Tina The Tuna. My apologies. How can I fix this?"

Inhaling deeply, Tucker held up an enormously wide hand. "Allow me to begin again. I'm Tucker Pearson, and I met you at your uncle's funeral. We brushed up against one another, and…"

"And?" Nina prodded, crossing her arms over her chest.

"And that's how this happened," he confessed.

Esther's hair stood up on the back of her neck and arms. She didn't remember brushing up against anyone. Especially not someone as good-looking as this man. "I don't remember that at all, and believe me, you're not hard on the eyes. I'd remember brushing up against you. You're at least seven inches taller than me and the size of a bulldozer. How could I forget you?"

Crossing his arms—his big, bulging–with-muscles arms—over his chest, Tucker sighed. "I *did* brush against you when you were getting up to leave the pew in the church, at the service. I rose from my seat out of respect for a lady, and because I'm a rather large man, and the pews were crammed together quite tightly, you faltered, I righted you, we brushed against one another."

Esther's eyes went wide in disbelief. He'd only brushed up against her? But…she brushed up against people all the time. In a crowded elevator, a busy street. Would she turn everyone and everything she bumped up against into a mermaid?

"So, what happens if you actually *touch me*-touch me? Do I turn into the Loch Ness Monster?"

Now Tucker smirked. "No. You won't turn into Nessie, but there's a strong possibility you could turn into Willy, as in Free."

"Hah!" Nina barked then rolled her eyes when Wanda hushed her with a frown. "What? It was fucking funny."

But Marty wasn't laughing anymore. She planted her hands on her hips and popped her lips. "Are you seriously telling me that all you did was brush up against Esther and she turned into a mermaid? Seriously?"

"I'm quite serious, Miss…?" He held out his tanned hand to Marty and smiled for the first time, and it was a doozy. All teeth and dimples and sexy-sexy.

"Marty. Marty Flaherty." She put her hand in Tucker's and lifted her chin, narrowing her gaze. "Explain the science behind this, please? I'm not sure I understand how brushing up against someone can turn them into a mermaid."

Esther struggled to sit up in order to address Tucker in a manner that at least hinted at some sense of authority, but as she did, she slid to the floor, knocking the handspun candleholders on her coffee table to the floor.

Her tail reacted, flopping awkwardly with a thud, nearly wiping out Mooky and Marsha. "Oh!"

Mooky and Marsha scattered as though a bomb had gone off, but surprisingly, Tucker was the first to help her get back on the couch. "Allow me," he offered when Nina reached down for her, stepping in front of Nina and scooping her up as though she were lighter than air.

And that was when she remembered brushing up against him at the church.

She'd been trying to get out of the pew to take an urgent phone call from work, a difficult, very high-profile divorce case she'd been mediating for almost two months, when she'd stumbled in her heels and fallen into him. She'd only looked up for a mere moment before she'd been looking back down at her phone.

But his scent, a slight whiff of something woodsy and fresh, had obviously stuck after their first encounter. She recognized it immediately now.

"I do remember that day," she whispered as Tucker repositioned her back on the couch, tucking pillows around her to keep her upright. "How did something so small turn into this?"

Tucker eyed her as he straightened, his hard face not emoting a single expression. "Sometimes, when emotions are heightened, things happen."

"What the fuck are you talking about, dude?" Nina asked, her face riddled with skepticism. "Things happen? *Things?* You better get explaining, buddy, because I have little time for this shit."

But Tucker didn't waver under Nina's penetrating gaze. "It was a sad occasion. Sometimes when a merman—or mermaiden, for that matter—is at the height of a particular emotion, it plays with the chemistry of their bodies, and scales can pop out. Unlike mermaids, mermen also have bands of scales around their wrists. They're meant to protect us in underwater battles—"

"You have underwater battles?" Esther gripped the blanket, that dark fear returning.

"No. Not in this day and age. Though, back in the day of the Vikings, I hear the wars were quite something. The point is, we've evolved, and they're just a byproduct of who we are as mermaids now. But when they scratch someone...well, this is the result. I'm sure you must have noticed a small scratch on your wrist, Esther?"

He said it all so matter-of-factly, it almost made sense. But not quite. Though, as she looked at her wrist, she noted the faint scratch that had now begun to heal—one she thought she'd gotten from Marsha and had hardly paid any attention to at all.

"Okay, big guy, first things first. Where are my legs, and are they ever coming back? Because if they aren't, you're in for some lawsuit. A big, fat, ugly lawsuit."

He conceded by nodding his head with amused eyes. "That'll certainly be one for Judge Judy, won't it?"

"*Where are my legs?*" she yelped, frustrated from sitting on the couch. Never mind the fact that she had to figure out, if she'd always be like this, what the hell she was going to do.

"They'll return shortly, I promise you," Tucker assured, as though they were talking about a dog that had gotten out of the yard. "Sometimes, as a first-time mermaid, it takes a bit longer to return to your human form."

"Wait. So you've done this before?" Esther asked in disbelief. "You've turned other women into mermaids?"

Tucker shook his head. "No. But children are prone to this issue. When they become old enough to think about having a tail and fins, they begin to struggle until they learn otherwise."

"And my hair? Because I gotta tell ya, there isn't enough product in Walgreens to make this manageable." Esther held up a thick, wavy lock and shook it at Tucker.

"That too. You'll be good as new, shortly. It just takes time for your body to simmer down. The more you allow it to happen, the faster you'll have your legs back."

Well, humpf. Okay then. What to be angry over now? Oh, wait. Just the rest of her life spent as an effin' mermaid! What would all the other little mermaids say when they learned she couldn't swim? They'd make a mockery of her—and why wouldn't they? What the hell kind of mermaid couldn't swim?

Her anger began to swell, but she somehow managed to keep herself in check. "Good to know, Tucker."

"You can just call me Tuck."

"How generous of you," Esther said, her tone rife with sarcasm "You can just call me Out For Blood. Now, about how I'm supposed to live like this... Can you change it? Fix it? Make it go away? I can't be a mermaid today. In fact, had I been given a choice, I'd have chosen unicorn for the obvious reasons, of course."

For the first time, Tuck's face went gravely serious, his hazel eyes clouding over. And he didn't mince his words. "I cannot. You're a mermaid for life."

"Is that so, Tucker Pearson?"

"That is so, Esther Williams Sanchez."

"Then you know what, Tuck?"

He cocked his beautiful head full of shiny chocolate hair. "What's that?"

"I'm going to kill youuu!" she shouted, red-faced and wild-eyed as she made an awkward lunge for him.

~

As Esther flopped to the ground with a thud that shook her small house, attempting to get at him by wiggling her way along the floor like some mermaid's imitation of the worm, knocking over everything in her path, Tuck winced with remorse.

Thankful the women intervened, he tried not to panic.

But man, had he really fucked up.

He'd been so intent on getting a word with Esther about her uncle, he hadn't been thinking clearly. Her uncle was the only tie he had to help him out of the dodgy mess he was in. Yet, when he'd seen her in all her mahogany-haired, olive-skinned, generously curved, crimson-lipped glory at her uncle's funeral, he'd fumbled like a damn guppy at his first reef dance.

Quite literally, she'd stolen the breath from his

bloody lungs, and he hadn't been lying about heightened emotions. Indeed, his emotions had been heightened, but as much of a shit as it made him feel like, it hadn't been sadness that had fueled his reaction.

It had been lust. Thick, murky, forbidden yet undeniable lust. She was a beautiful woman. A beautiful woman who, under normal circumstances, he'd have asked out without a moment's hesitation.

But that wasn't why he'd attended Gomez Sanchez's funeral. He'd attended because he wanted answers, and he'd figured some of Gomez's relatives would surely be there.

Little did he know, Gomez Sanchez only had one surviving relative, and he'd only been able to find out she existed due to the scientist's obit in the paper. He'd had to do some digging and call in a favor or two to find out her name. At the time of the funeral, he didn't even know the sexy woman he'd brushed up against was Gomez's niece.

Also, he'd had no idea he'd actually scratched her with an errant scale until he'd seen her tonight.

As if it wasn't bad enough, having been kicked out of his pod, now he'd turned a human into a mermaid.

The coral would surely fly if his father found out about this. But his sister would help.

Now, as the women restrained Esther and hauled her back up on the couch, he had to find a way to make this right while getting what he needed from her.

"Esther!" he said with force, taking note not to yell. "Please, calm down or your legs won't return."

But she struggled against the women, her deep-brown eyes flashing angry and hot. "*You* calm down, you Outback maniac! Look what you've done to me! How the hell am I supposed to live like this?"

He held up his hands and offered his best apologetic face. "I'll help you, Esther. I promise I'll help you if you'll just calm down and allow me."

The dark-haired woman, who's name he hadn't quite caught, cupped Esther's jaw and made her focus on her face. "Dude, get it the fuck together and let us help you deal. Hear me? Suck it up and let's figure this out. What's happened to you isn't the end of the world. If I can fucking adjust to never stuffing another damn Ring Ding in my mouth for all eternity because I have to drink blood, *you* can damn well swim around and be pretty. Don't go off the rails now, kiddo."

Drink blood? Did the dark-haired sheila say she drinks blood? What kind of madness was this?

Esther appeared calmed by the snarling vixen, as odd as that sounded—she didn't even cringe about the mention of drinking blood. What she meant by that blood reference, he didn't know. He didn't want to know.

But Esther gripped Nina's slim wrist. "You'll stay until we do? Until we figure it out?" she asked, hearing her shaky words then hissing a breath of obvious aggravation. She appeared annoyed that her voice had faltered.

Nina stared back at her and nodded without hesitation. "Count on it."

"Of course we'll stay, Esther. Of course," the pregnant woman assured in soft tones, easing her hold on her arm. "I told you that. This is what we do, honey. Now, please. Deep breaths, and let's get your legs back, all right?"

Esther began inhaling while Tuck looked on, unsure what to do next. Obviously, he was a dipshit and he had to fix what he'd done. He just wasn't sure how to go about that without upsetting her further.

And who in all of fuck were these women helping her? Her friends? And what did the pregnant one mean by this is what they do?

Knowing he needed to do something, Tuck kept his distance but sat on his haunches and gazed at Esther, even more beautiful in mermaid form than she was as a human. "Esther, I swear to you, on my life, I'll help you join our community right here in Oyster Hollow. I'll teach you everything you need to know to live your life here, right here in your cottage, and still live as a mermaid. If you'll let me, that is. You can still do all the things you've always done. Work, play, whatever it is you've always done. I promise."

Her wild-eyed gaze had softened now, her fists, once clenched into tight little balls, relaxed and her heavy breathing slowed. "Okay."

He held out a hand to her, his hazel eyes sincere. "Shake on it?"

As she let him envelop her much smaller hand, as she watched him like a hawk, that swell of lust swarmed his body once more, and he had to yank his hand away to keep her from knowing he desired her. And she'd surely know, or learn to know that feeling, now that she was a mermaid. It was instinct, a natural reaction when you met someone you found attractive.

"Then let's begin by getting your land legs back. You'll learn to do this with ease as time passes, but for now, please close your eyes and take some deep breaths," he instructed in his husky tone.

As she did what Tuck instructed, as she settled back into the cushions of her couch and breathed, her body began to melt and twist.

And just like that, her limbs were back—long, graceful, beautifully shaped.

Wow, were they ever back.

"Marty?" Nina called with her infamous cackle. "We need a bigger blanket!"

CHAPTER 5

Esther's heart crashed against her ribs as she pulled on some yoga pants and a ratty old NYU sweatshirt, trying to parse the day's events without crying hysterically. One look in the antiqued white bathroom mirror, her luxurious rainbow locks now gone, replaced with her shoulder-length brown hair, her legs just the way she'd left them in the pool back at the Y, told her this was not some nightmare.

This was real. She really was a mermaid and there was a hot, gruff Australian guy in her living room who was a merman.

A merman.

As Nina said, this was some fucknuttery. She had a million questions, a million thoughts, but for right now, she was just happy not to be flopping around like some literal fish out of water. Her limbs were intact, and if she'd learned anything being a mediator, she'd learned to tackle one item at a time.

That meant food in her stomach, and a good Tucker Pearson interrogation—she needed answers. She'd think about the heightened-emotions thing and how Tucker had known her uncle later.

If Tucker had been her uncle's friend, she'd like to know. Maybe he had some perspective on who he really had been.

Pulling her hair up into a messy bun, she reached for the tap—then realized she was too afraid to wash her hands. She almost felt like those rubber things you got in your cereal when you were a kid, and when you put them in water they expanded. She did not want to take a chance she'd expand again. So, she wiped them with a Wet-Nap and popped the bathroom door open, forcing herself to go back out into the kitchen, where Marty and Wanda were heating up some food for her, chatting the entire time like this was a dinner party rather than a paranormal crisis.

She had to trust that they were telling her the truth about this OOPS hotline they ran. Anyone could have a website with lots of glitter and a toll-free number. That didn't mean they knew what they were talking about—or even what they were doing. But that website had some pretty wild tales, and instructions, and people to call if you needed paranormal help. So she'd gone with it.

She only knew that for the moment, these women were all she had, and after that crazy display in the living room earlier, where she'd sat terrified and awed at the same time, she'd rather have them here with this Tucker Pearson than not here at all.

If nothing else, they were clearly capable of taking care of themselves, and while Tuck was a big guy, these women were formidable foes, especially with Nina as their head-savage-in-charge-of-all-eviscerations.

That comforted her in a way that only a day ago it might have actually frightened her.

As words like vampires and pods and fins swirled around in her head, Esther let Marty sit her down at her small dining room and place a napkin in her lap.

Wanda scurried in with a bowl of steaming-hot soup and a sandwich and set it in front of her with a smile. "Eat. It'll help. It always helps me," she said on a tinkle of laughter, rubbing her belly.

Nina pulled out a chair next to her and cupped her chin in her hand as she peered at Esther. "So, I guess that's not a tuna sandwich, huh? Would be considered like eating your friends?"

Marty and Wanda both gasped their dismay from the kitchen counter where they sat on stools. "Nina—too soon!" Marty chirped.

But Esther found herself chuckling as she took a bite of sandwich and waved it under Nina's nose. "You know what, Nina?"

Nina's eyes glittered as she cocked her head. "What's that, Little Mermaid?"

"You're fucking funny. Just thought you should know."

"See, you bunch of sensitive fucking Nancys? Chicken of the Sea thinks I'm funny."

As she took another bite of her sandwich—an egg salad, rich and creamy, served on soft, doughy bread—she eyed Nina. "So, you do this often?"

"Do what often?" she asked, scrolling her phone.

"Help damsels in distress."

"We've helped a couple dudes, too. This accident shit happens more than you think."

"Really? Like to who or what?"

Nina looked up from her phone and sighed. "Like demons and cougar-shifters and bear-shifters and the Goddess of Love, familiars and dragons, and a princess in a real-live fairytale."

Sipping her soup, Esther digested that bit of information. Trying to keep her responses cool and level-headed, because again, there was no denying what she'd seen in her living room. "But no mermaids yet?"

"Nope. To date, besides our dragon buddies, you're the freakiest thing we've come across. Well, I dunno, maybe you tie with Jeannie our genie. That was fucked up and just as sparkly."

Esther held her sandwich mid-air. "A genie? Like Barbra Eden, blink-your-eyes genie?"

Nina chuckled and nodded. "Just like that, only with evil djinn and shit. Also, I have a familiar named Calamity. She's off in the realm, visiting her familiar friends for a week."

"What's a familiar?"

"A pain in the ass. A loveable one, but still a boil on my damn butt."

Esther's mouth sagged open, a question in her eyes.

"She's a talking cat, who, when I was turned half witch, showed up to 'guide me' in the fucking witch world. She's mine forever—except for this week, because she's—"

"In another realm," Esther repeated.

Nina nodded and grinned. "Exactly."

"Do I want to ask what this realm is, or means, or even *where* it is?"

Her deadpan expression gave Esther a moment of pause. "You probably don't."

"So, this genie…" That fascinated her even more than vampires and dragons.

"What about her?"

"Pictures or it didn't happen," Esther taunted teasingly.

"I don't have a pic of Jeannie on my phone, though I do have a kid because of her. But you wanna see a fucking baby-dragon?"

"Like a *Game of Thrones* dragon? Shut up!" Esther crowed, her eyes going wide when Nina showed her a picture of the most angelic little girl with wings, sitting next to a full-on dragon. "You could have Photo-shopped those. I call bullshit."

"Was what you saw earlier bullshit?"

Esther wrinkled her nose and rethought her words. "Okay, you win that round."

Tucker, who'd stood quietly in the corner by the

pantry while they chatted, scrolling his phone, cleared his throat, his face still quite serious. "Ladies? I hate to interfere in a good gab, but my sister will be here at any moment—"

Esther's doorbell rang again, making Mooky bark, but Nina grabbed him, cradling him close, and held her palm up at Tucker. "You wait there, Sharkbait. I'll answer the door."

Tucker didn't fight her on it. Instead, he swept his hand toward the door and backed off, leaning against the pantry and crossing his long legs at the ankles.

"Why is your sister coming here?" Esther asked, wiping her mouth and pushing away from the table to approach Tuck. She wasn't sure if she was ready to meet another merperson right now.

His dark eyebrow rose as he tucked his phone in the back pocket of his tight jeans. "I thought it might be helpful to speak with an actual mermaid. As with human men and women, our differences can be vast. You'll like her. Everyone likes her. She's smart and tough. Look, I'm just doing what I promised. I thought Jessica might be able to help."

"Are you in the market for a medal?" Esther quipped, smoothing her hair back, feeling self-conscious of her messy appearance.

If his sister looked anything like he did, she'd probably hit the gene pool lottery jackpot, too.

Tucker looked down at her, his eyes amused, but his sharp jaw twitched. "No. But I wouldn't turn down a tiara."

"Tuck?" a soft, lyrical voice called out as a sultry dark-haired woman, lovely and composed, walked into Esther's entryway, arms hooked with a good-looking gentleman who had a very ugly black eye. She pulled a black fringed wrap from around her shoulders and put it over her forearm. "What's going on?"

Tuck smiled at her with clear affection and held out an arm, crossing the room and pulling the tall, delicate woman close, planting a kiss on her sharp cheekbone. "Jessica? This is Esther Sanchez. A brand-new mermaid."

Jessica blinked, then she blinked again, looking from the beautifully dressed man to Tucker, her wide dark eyes fringed with thick lashes. "Sorry?" she responded in the same light Aussie accent as her brother.

"He said, Esther's a mermaid and it's all his fucking fault." Nina held out her hand to a dazed Jessica, who took it with great hesitation. But Nina pumped her hand up and down anyway. "Nina Statleon, by the way. Nice to meet ya."

Tucker held up a hand. "First, this is Chester Morning, Jessica's boyfriend. He works in IT for my family's company. Good to see you, man," he said, bumping shoulders with him.

"Yeah, you too, buddy. This whole thing," he spun a lean finger around in the air, "sucks. Sorry it's happening to you."

Tucker nodded. "What happened to the eye?" He pointed at Chester's very blackened eye.

"Went a round with an underwater pier. Never saw it coming," he joked charmingly.

"Hah!" Tucker laughed out loud, slapping his friend on the shoulder.

Pushing her short dark hair behind her ear, revealing a large silver hoop earring, Jessica looked to Tuck in confusion. "Stop bromancing and explain. I don't understand. How can she be a brand-new mermaid…?"

Chester cleared his throat and rocked back on his heels, trying not to smirk at Tucker.

And that's when a light bulb must have turned on in Jessica's head. "Oh, *Tuck*…you didn't? Did you? Say you didn't! Without protection? With a human?"

"Oh, he fucking did, lady. Yes, he did," Nina crowed, looking to Mooky and rubbing noses with him. "He did, didn't he, Mook? He's been a very bad boy."

Feeling incredibly awkward around this woman, dressed in a slim red wrap dress and gleaming black heels with a statement necklace in silver. Esther wiped her palms on her yoga pants, feeling frumpy and disheveled. Still, she stepped closer, held out her hand and introduced herself.

"I'm Esther Williams Sanchez. The brand-spanking-new mermaid. It's nice to meet you both."

Chester saluted her with a smile, his handsome face bright and open as he clearly fought laughter.

"You too," Jessica murmured, sending signals of distress to her brother with her eyes as she took

Esther's hand and patted it. "How did this happen? Are you all right, Esther?"

Chester snorted then covered his mouth with his hand and looked at the painting on the wall beside the entryway, studying it as though it were a van Gogh.

Esther sighed and scratched her head. "Well, we had a hinky moment or two when I didn't think I was ever going to have legs again, but I'm okay, I guess. As okay as anyone can be when they have no idea mermaids really exist, but someone turns them into a mermaid and proves them totally wrong."

"She's cheeky," Tucker commented, rolling his tongue along the inside of his mouth as he crossed his thick arms across his chest. "Very cheeky."

Jessica held up a hand to shush her brother, obviously annoyed with him. "How are we going to tell Father about this, Tucker? Aren't you in deep enough already?" Her eyes sought his, but almost as quickly, she looked back to Esther. "I'm sorry. I don't mean to be insensitive, but Tucker's not exactly on the best of terms with our father right now. Of course, that's not your fault at all, Esther."

Sucking in his cheeks, he seemed to dismiss the idea of his father. "Are either one of us ever on the best of terms with Father?"

Jessica's eyes glittered as though she were amused. "The *tyrant*. And I maintain to this day, he's a sexist pig. He'll never leave the ways of old behind."

He gave her a lopsided grin. "I'll deal with Father. Right now, I just need your help with Esther, Jess,"

Tucker said, thus sweeping her comment entirely under the proverbial rug.

Esther didn't want to pry into his private affairs, so she chose to leave the comment about his father alone. Though, she had to wonder what their beef was about.

Yet, Jessica didn't feel quite the same way Tucker did, as evidenced by her next comment. "But you do know you'll have to speak to him—tell him about Esther, don't you? We have to integrate her into the pod, Tucker. You can't just leave her hanging out to dry, and you can't integrate her without telling Father. This isn't a small event."

Chester turned around after giving her painting a good, long study and looked to his friend. "She's right, Tuck. You know she is."

"Are you going to be in some kind of trouble for doing this to me? It was an accident. I'll tell your father that, if you'd like," Esther offered, looking to the siblings.

At those words, Chester nudged Tucker with his elbow and chuckled, low and husky. "An accident, eh, mate?"

"I wouldn't exactly call this an accident, Esther," Jessica said, pushing her hair from her face with nails painted in a shimmering black polish. "Well, maybe his scales sticking out was a mishap, but that's the only part of this that's an accident. I don't mean to be indelicate here, but he did sleep with you while knowing the risks."

Esther's mouth fell open, but she managed to sputter, "*Sleep with me?* He didn't sleep with me! I've known him for all of an hour at best. We just officially met!"

Jessica's smile turned cynical, and so did Chester's as he put an arm around her. "You two aren't going to try to use that line of denial when you tell Father, are you? He's been around the block a time or two. I don't think he's going to fall for it, Tucker."

"Hold the fuck on, lady. She didn't sleep with your bro. She brushed up against him at a GD funeral. *That's* how this happened," Nina said as she stared down at Jessica with angry eyes.

"Who the hell are you?" Chester asked, straightening his square shoulders and taking a step in front of Jessica.

"Ooooh, wait. Hold on!" Marty cautioned, moving into the living room, her finger in the air. "Cute shoes, by the way," she complimented Jessica.

"Thanks!" Jessica replied with a smile and motioned to Marty's neck. "Love your scarf!"

Marty pointed a finger in the direction of the kitchen and looked at Nina, who slinked off—then turned back to Tucker and lifted her chin, a smirk on her lips. "Didn't you say heightened emotion can make your scales stick out? I think I know what that means. You weren't *sad* at her uncle's funeral. He was horndoggin' you, Esther!"

Esther blanched uncomfortably. Under normal circumstances, she'd be all sorts of flattered. He was definitely very sexy. But Tucker didn't just think she was attractive, he'd turned her into his mermaid bitch because he couldn't keep his scales to himself. No *bueno*.

"Horndogging?" she squeaked, because she didn't know what else to do but play dumb.

Chester nodded his sleek head. "Definitely horn-doggin'." And then he laughed.

Tucker closed his eyes and sighed a ragged sigh. "She's right, Jess. Sort of. We did not sleep together, and we *did* just meet. The truth is, I did think Esther was quite attractive, and when we brushed up against each other at her uncle's funeral, one of my scales errantly popped out on my wrist—"

"Her uncle's funeral?" Jessica asked in disbelief, her eyes darting from her brother to Esther.

"I told you I was going to attend Gomez's funeral, Jessica," Tucker reminded her, as if they had some kind of secret about the event.

She nodded her head in understanding, her shiny hair glistening under the recessed lights. "You did, and I totally understand. It was such a tragedy. I would have gone, too, if it hadn't been for that grueling schedule Father's put us on."

You know, she hadn't once stopped to wonder *why* Tucker had attended her uncle's funeral. She'd been too caught up in the "OMG, I have a tail" business.

But now she was suspicious. "So, why were you at my uncle's funeral anyway, Tucker Pearson? How did you know him? I think it was pretty evident from the low attendance, he didn't have a lot of friends. Were you his friend?"

"I'd never met him in my life," Tucker said with stark honesty, his gaze steady.

Esther scratched her head again before putting her hands on her hips. "Is it a mermaid thing? To just randomly go to strangers' funerals then? Should I make sure I keep my black tail and fins handy at all times so we can funeral crash with the pod?"

Jessica smiled as she winked at Esther. "Oh, she is cheeky. I like that in a girl. Also, Esther, I'm so sorry for your loss. We valued your uncle greatly."

Her dumbfounded look made Tucker respond. "No. It's not a mermaid thing, Esther. Your uncle did some work for us in his capacity as a scientist. He'd done so for years."

Okay, so? Something was off in his tone, his vibe, his *everything*, and she wanted to know what. "Is this where you're being intentionally vague or you're hiding something? Because I don't get it." She looked at Tucker and the two newcomers, waiting for an answer.

Tucker's sexy lips thinned. "Your uncle tested our water for us."

"Like your special mermaid water? The water you swim in? Your pool water? Your dog's water?"

Tucker barked a laugh, shoving his hands into the pockets of his jeans. "I don't have a dog. I have two cats. Freckle and Fran."

She lifted her chin and wrinkled her nose. "Okay, so this *is* the part where you're being intentionally vague, and even obtuse."

"No. I'm just telling you I don't have a dog. Though,

I love them. Freckle and Fran were part of a stray's litter. Their mother was killed just before I found them."

She melted on the inside a little. That he was a nice guy with a kind heart was beside the point. "What water did my uncle test for you?"

"My company's water, of course," Tucker responded, as though she should know. "My family owns H2O-Yo."

The bottled water? No way.

Marty piped in then, her eyes aglow. "Shut the front door! I'm Marty Flaherty—owner of Bobbie-Sue! My husband, Keegan, owns Pack Cosmetics. You provided bottled water for our convention just last year," she gushed.

"I knew you looked familiar!" Jessica said, her excitement evident as she clapped her hands together in glee.

"Of course she does," Tucker chided teasingly. "What brand of makeup *don't* you have? Better be careful, or Father's going to cut you off."

"Amen," Chester breathed.

She made a face at Tucker before looking back to Marty. "We must chat about that new moisturizer you've come out with, Marty! I can't tell you how amazing it is on my skin. I mean, mermaid, right? Dry skin for days! It's so creamy. How do you get it—"

"Hey!" Esther finally yelped. "Business Owners of America—*mermaid* here! I don't want to interfere with your meeting of the ultra-successful minds, but I have a tail and fins I don't know the first thing about! So could you table the discussion on dry skin until after we help me figure this out?"

Marty shook her finger in admonishment. "You won't be saying that when your skin's dry and flaky because you spend so much dang time in the—"

"Shut the fuck up, you two hens!" Nina scolded, pushing her way between Jessica and Marty and heading straight for Tucker. "Stop with the yapping and let's get to the point. I want to go the fuck home, and I can't do that because I made a promise to Fins over here that I'd stay until she feels comfortable. I don't break my promises, *ever*. Now what the hell is next, and how do we teach her how to be a mermaid?"

Esther jumped up from behind Nina's shoulder and said, "Yeah! What she said. What do I do next?"

Jessica's face fell. Her perfect features instantly sympathetic, she reached for Esther's arm. "I'm so sorry, Esther. My deepest apologies. Of course I'll help you get settled with the changes your body is going through and explain the ways of our pod."

"I'll help, too, if I can," Chester offered with a handsome smile.

Esther breathed a small sigh of relief before she looked to Tucker again. "Thank you. But first things first, why did you go to my uncle's funeral if you didn't even know him?" That was just plain curious. Lots of subcontractors died, but their business ties usually sent a fruit basket or flowers, they didn't attend their funerals.

"Out of respect. I never met your uncle in person, or his assistant, Armand, but we communicated via email quite frequently," Tucker provided, again, without embellishment.

And another thing... "Okay, but why did you come here to see *me*? Was it because you felt guilty for turning me into one of your people at the funeral?"

Now he stared her down, dead on. "I had no idea that had happened, Esther. That's the truth."

"Okay, so why did you come here? To pay your respects? Because I'm going to be honest. My uncle was as reclusive with me as he was with everyone else. I hardly knew him, and I don't know anything about his death."

Tucker didn't even blink when he said, "I came because I wanted to ask you some questions about him."

"Tucker! Stop. Stop right now," Jessica intervened, putting a hand on her brother's arm. "He just died, for goodness sake, and whether Esther was close with him or not isn't really the point. She has enough on her plate, thanks to you."

And Chester apparently agreed. "Let this be, Tucker," he said, his warning clear. "It's the wrong time."

Wanda, who'd somehow managed to fall asleep during this latest interaction, sat up straight, shaking off the nap she'd been taking on the chair in the living room.

When Tucker didn't acquiesce, Jessica said once more, "*Please*. Let this be for now."

But Esther didn't mind a bit. Now, she was curious. What could he want to know about her uncle if he'd only shared emails with him?

"No, no. It's okay, Jessica. I don't mind answering questions, for all the good it'll do you. I don't know much about my uncle Gomez."

Tucker nodded his head in curt fashion. "Good enough. Then can you possibly answer this—why did your uncle take his own life? And why did he do it after he approved the testing on our newest brand of water —water that made hundreds of people sick and killed an innocent old man?"

CHAPTER 6

Pumping her legs harder, Esther gripped Mooky's leash and ran, trying to pace herself and remember she couldn't run away from everything that had happened if she ran faster.

The idea that her uncle had taken his life because his work had hurt someone, astounded her. But she wasn't ready to address that just yet.

Last night had still been quite clear in her mind this morning when she'd awakened to find not just the women in her house, but two more people added to the mix. A zombie named Carl, the sweetest soul ever, who'd thumped her on the back and given her an awkward hug. Then she was treated to the best eggs Benedict she'd had in her life, made by Archibald, who, according to the ladies, was some kind of master chef wannabe and, surprisingly, human.

And if his eggs Bennie was any indication, he had her vote for chef of the universe. She'd eaten the decadent treat as though she hadn't eaten in a week, and thanked him from saving her from another bowl of tasteless oatmeal.

Now, as she took her ritual morning run with Mook, she finally had a moment alone to think about what to do next. Because what did you do when someone told you your uncle screwed up some tests he'd allegedly done for years and had somehow made a bunch of people sick?

Tucker had spat those words at her last night as though she knew thing one about what her uncle did or didn't do, but Nina, sensing how tired she was, had sent Tucker and his sister and her boyfriend on their way, and instructed them to come back tomorrow, when they could all sit down and iron out the details of her mermaid-ness.

But he'd had something to do this morning, and Jessica was in an important meeting about this issue with their water.

So, she'd decided to take a run to help clear her head.

Stopping to catch her breath, Esther stared off into the choppy water and asked Mooky, "What do you suppose Grandpa would say to this, buddy? He'd probably laugh that his only granddaughter is now forced to literally sink or swim, huh?"

Mooky sat beside her in quiet reverence, leaning against her calves—which in doggie speak meant, "Whatever you say, Boss. Just keep the canned food and pizza crust coming."

Her grandfather had tried everything and anything to break her fear of the water. He'd taken her to a swim class when she was twelve, only to have the teacher tell him Esther was uncooperative. He'd even paid for private lessons, to which Esther had responded by playing hooky.

She wanted nothing to do with the very water her grandfather and her father loved so much. Both swimmers in high school, her father Eduardo had almost made the Olympic swim team.

In fact, as outrageous as it sounded, her father had chosen her name because he'd literally had a crush on Esther Williams as a kid. When everyone else was hanging up Janet Jackson and Paula Abdul posters in their rooms, Salvador told her, her father's teenage crush was Esther.

The day was gray and full of a heavy mist that hung low over the ocean, leaving her hair plastered to her head. As the tide rushed in along the shore, she skipped backward, trying to avoid the swell of frothy water.

But then she remembered what Tucker had said this morning when he'd dropped by to check on her. "You only have to worry if you're fully submerged in water —like in a pool or something. You can still take a shower, get caught in the rain, etcetera. The movies make it something it isn't. Not totally, anyway."

As her dreams of going on a cruise with her friends went down the drain, and she'd listened to him tell her the very basics of her new life as a mermaid over a cup of coffee, she fought the intoxicating scent of his cologne and her body's reaction to how attractive he was—maybe more so in the cold morning light, if that were at all possible or fair.

Though, as quickly as he'd arrived, he left, telling her he'd see her later. Now, as her head swirled with information and fear and wonder, she considered her uncle and his death.

According to the police, her uncle had definitely committed suicide. The proof, they claimed, was in an identical email he'd sent to his assistant and two of his colleagues, a vague and very brief email. Though, when the police had informed her of his death, they hadn't given her any further information and she hadn't asked.

It had almost felt like she was invading his privacy to ask to see the email, she knew so little about him, and when the police asked if he'd shown any signs of depression, she couldn't answer because she didn't know.

And now Tucker was saying her uncle had approved water for them that was tainted. She knew little about Gomez Sanchez, but she did remember her grandfather telling her how meticulous he was in everything he did.

Sighing, she decided it was time to go back to the cottage and face the music. And somewhere in there, she was going to have to tell hunky Tucker she didn't know how to swim.

Turning, she meant to take off, but lost her footing when her sneaker sank in the wet sand. Of course, she did this just as a wave rushed to the shore, knocking her feet right out from under her.

As the freezing salty water hit her tracksuit, she fell forward, still clinging to Mooky's leash as the tide tugged her closer to the water.

In an instant, that same panic, that same flood of helplessness from so long ago assaulted her, and she began to flail, not even thinking about the fact that she was now submerged fully in the ocean. The icy water sloshing over her body like stinging pricks to her skin. As she reached out toward the shore, another wave crashed over her, the water invaded her mouth and eyes and made her lose her grip on Mooky, who barked playfully.

Anxiety settled in within seconds and Esther forgot everything but the fact that she was in water—cold, harsh, unforgiving. Her heart began to race as it engulfed her, swishing over the top of her head and knocking her around until she swallowed more of the salty brine and lost her breath.

When the tide pulled her back under again, swallowing her whole, she began to flail her arms as she tried to think about what Maurizio had said yesterday in that class she took—about how she had to move *with* the water, not against it, but her terror took hold, preventing her from remembering much else.

So she began to scream, sputtering and coughing as her lungs filled with the ocean. "Mooky!" she managed to yell, her pulse pounding in her ears in time with the roar of the waves. "Get heeelp!"

Mooky knew the water well. He loved the water. He loved to play ball in the water. If nothing else, he could draw attention to her, but she couldn't see him anymore.

And then it happened, that heavy weight replacing her limbs, dragging her lower body down, down into the murky depths of the ocean. Her head suddenly felt heavy as the length of her hair flourished, the heavy ropes only making everything that much weightier as it twisted around her body and covered her eyes.

She began to sink with the heft of her tail, coupled with her hair, and the more she panicked, the more she knew she was panicking, the harder it became to keep her thoughts clear.

Just as water began to fill her lungs, someone latched on to her, someone with a grip like steel, and dragged her upward.

"Esther!"

She heard her name, felt that someone was trying to help her, but in her panic, she forgot those were good things, and she began to thrash against the very hands that served to save her.

Hauling her upward and dragging her body a short distance through wet sand and water, someone yelled again, "Esther! Stop fighting me!"

She stiffened as a wide hand she could just see through the wet mass of her hair, pushed the thick strands out of her face. That's when she realized it was Tucker.

"Esther! Are you okay?" he huffed, his jeans and

jacket soaking wet as he pressed her body to his and pulled her to shore. "What the hell are you doing?"

She began to cough, not caring that she was naked from the waist up or that she was in the middle of a public beach with a tail. Tears stung her eyes as she gasped for breath, heaving and coughing.

Tucker flopped down beside her, pulling his wet jacket off and gathering her to him. "Cam down. What were you doing out here?"

Running a shaky hand over her face, she pushed more hair from her eyes and fought to catch her breath. "I suppose you'll never believe I was surfing."

He threw his head back and laughed. "No. But boogie boarding? Eh, maybe."

"Sunbathing?"

"Still cheeky," he said, obviously fighting a chuckle, from the looks of the deep grooves on either side of his mouth.

"Oh, fine. I tripped, and then a wave rolled in and knocked me down, and I was out so far I couldn't get my bearings."

"Out so far?" he asked, tucking his jacket under her chin and peering into her eyes.

She made a face and coughed again. "Well, yeah. Didn't you see? I was in pretty deep."

He nodded his head, the overcast day making his skin ruddier as droplets of water glistened from the ends of his dark hair. "Esther?"

"Yes?"

"Look up."

She did as instructed, following the line of his finger to the sand at their feet. "What am I looking at?"

"The shoreline."

"So? What about it?" she asked on a violent shiver, the wind picking up and clawing at her upper body.

"You were, *tops*, two feet from it when I scooped you out of the water."

Oh.

Shit. She'd panicked. She'd done that before on more than one occasion. Hell, she could panic in a puddle.

Esther let her head hang, though she didn't have much choice because her hair was so heavy. But she felt very defensive now that he'd put her on the spot. This was a sore subject for her—her inability to swim—and today had proven she was going to be the suckiest mermaid to ever suck.

On a sigh, she gave him her guilty stare. "I'm sorry. I don't know *why* I should be sorry. I mean, you're the one who did this to me in the first place, but I'm sorry you got all wet saving me."

Tucker stared at her as though he were thinking before he said, "Care to tell me what that was about? Why were you fighting as though your life was on the line in a foot or less of water?"

"Nope," she responded, her teeth chattering. Nope, she sure didn't want to tell him what a complete fool she was, or what her reasons were for being one, either.

He put a hand on her shoulder, a hand that made

her tingle. "Esther, you must be more careful. If you reveal yourself to humans, who knows what could happen to you. I don't want something to happen to you."

Humans. She almost snorted. "But I *am* a human, Tucker Pearson."

He eyed her critically and nudged her with his broad shoulder. "No, you're *half* human now, and you have to be very, very aware that not everyone thinks a real live mermaid is just a pretty creature. If someone who wished you harm got their hands on you, they'd turn you into a government science experiment. But you wouldn't just risk your own life, you'd risk the lives of those in the pod."

The pod. Who and where was this pod? Every time she heard that word, all she could think of was *Invasion of the Body Snatchers* and pod people. She loved a good horror movie. She just didn't want to play a part in one.

"Hey! Chicken of the Sea, what the fuck?" she heard a husky voice call.

Nina came to a halt in front of them, her hair whipping in the wind around her pale face. She threw a blanket at Esther and knelt, wrapping it around her tail and up along her shoulders, handing the wet jacket back to Tucker. "What the hell are you doing? I thought you were going for a run?"

"I tripped," she murmured sheepishly, which sounded ultra lame even if it was true.

Nina's eyes held skepticism when she tilted her dark glasses downward to get a good look at Esther.

"You tripped, huh? You could've fucking drowned, you moron! Jesus, look at you. You're gonna freeze to death. C'mere," she ordered, rubbing Esther's arms.

"Drowned?" Tucker repeated, his brows pushing together in a frown.

But that's when Esther realized she didn't know where Mook was. Immediately, she tried to stand, forgetting about her tail. "Where's Mooky? I have to find Mooky! I lost his leash when I was in the water. Mooooky!" she hollered into the wind, terrified she'd never find him.

"He's fine," Nina reassured, tucking the blanket around her waist. "He's the one who let us know you were out here splashing around."

She breathed a sigh of relief on another shiver. "Oh, thank God. Now," she waved her hand at her tail—her beautiful, shiny tail, poking out in places beneath the blanket from her couch. "What do we do about this?"

"We wait," Tucker said, crossing his broad arms over his chest.

"Wait?" she almost screeched, then covered her mouth with her hand, lowering her tone and looking around to make sure the beach was still deserted. "We can't just sit here on the beach and wait, Tucker. What if someone comes and sees us?"

That panic she'd felt earlier set in once again, making her stomach threaten to heave the lovely breakfast she'd had less than an hour ago.

"We'll tell them you two like to fucking role-playing," Nina cackled, pulling out a bottle of sunscreen and applying some to her nose.

"So…vampire, eh?" Tucker commented, gazing at Nina. "Can't say I've ever met one before."

"Half vampire, half witch, to be exact," Nina corrected with a saucy smirk. "Wish I could say I'd never met a merman, but here the fuck we are."

Tucker didn't appear offended at all at Nina's words. Instead, he nodded. "I can certainly understand that. We don't make a point of announcing our existence."

Esther reached a trembling hand out to Nina, touching her arm with concern. "You go back inside. It's pretty cold today. I don't want you to get sick because of me."

She shrugged beneath her hoodie, tucking her hands inside the pockets. "Doesn't matter, I can't feel it anyway and I don't get sick. You just shut up and think about your freakin' legs. I'll stay till you Free Willy," she joked with a grin.

Esther's heart warmed. She felt safe with Nina—with all of them—and right now, as precarious as things were in her life, safe was good, and they were all she had.

Just then, someone called Esther's name from behind them—an unfamiliar voice with a heavy New York accent. "Esther Williams Sanchez? NYPD. I have some questions for you!"

CHAPTER 7

Esther's heart began to pound as the officer drew closer. She looked to Nina, terror gripping her throat. *"What are we going to do?"* she whisper-yelled as her glittering aqua fins flapped in the chilly wind and she froze on the spot.

"Stay calm, Esther. I'll handle this," Tucker assured her with a confident smile and a squeeze to her hand, pulling his phone from the back pocket of his jeans. He held it up and pointed it at her, pressing a button. "That's it, Esther, just like that. You're beautiful, babe! Now, give me your best look of fear, as though someone's just exposed you as a mermaid after you washed ashore during a terrifying hurricane." He reached down and pulled the blanket from her tail to expose her, snapping pictures on his phone one after the other. "You're lost, alone, afraid! C'mon, baby, work that lens!"

Nina sent her a message with her eyes that said

play along—or at least she was pretty sure it said play along. Maybe it said shut the fuck up, but she knew she had to get it together enough to make the officer believe she was pretending to be a mermaid for some crazy modeling shoot, and Tucker was her photographer.

So, she looked into the phone Tuck held up and grabbed her throat, mimicking a clutch-your-pearls moment, as though she were in grave danger, which *duh*. She was in grave danger—of being discovered. It wasn't much of a stretch, but she was going to work that camera if it was the last thing she did, like her life depended on it.

"Gorgeous, Esther!" Tucker encouraged, yelling the words in an over-expressive tone, thickening his accent. "Can you hang on a sec, officer? I don't want to miss this shot. It's too good. The sky is perfect, wouldn't you say, mate? Now, give me coy, Esther. C'mon, kitten, I know you have some vixen in you."

When the officer finally reached them, out of breath and red-faced, he held up his badge. "Are you Esther Williams Sanchez?" he wheezed, his jowls shaking when he spoke.

Esther turned her chin into her shoulder and gave Tucker a seductive but shy smile. "I am Esther Williams Sanchez, officer, but I'm a lil' busy right now, as you can see. I'm trying to earn a living. Can we talk at another time?"

Out of the corner of her eye, she saw the officer look at a small notepad. "Actually, it's Detective Johns.

And it says here you're supposed to be a divorce mediator, not a model."

Esther flapped her hand at him and giggled like a giddy schoolgirl. Nina frowned at her over-exaggerated laughter and ran a finger across her slender throat, but Esther ignored her warning and plowed ahead. "If only that paid the bills. I model part time for extra money, Detective. Oyster Hollow's not cheap, you know. A girl's gotta make a living somehow. It was either this or the stripper pole, and I'm an epic fail at bikini waxes and keeping rhythm to 'Pour Some Sugar on Me,' so..."

As the wind lifted the hem of his wrinkled dark blue suit coat, he stared down at her tail. His tiny eyes, buried deep in his doughy face, registered surprise. "That looks so real," he said in awe as it sparkled even under the clouds.

"Damn right it does, buddy. I made it myself. Nina's the name. Costuming's my game. Sewed those damn yellow and turquoise scales on one by one. Show 'em your fins, Esther. Show 'em how they fuckin' flap."

Esther lifted her hips and waved her fins at the Detective, who backed away for a moment and shook his head. "How...?"

If only she could tell him how much she could relate.

Nina nudged him with an elbow and tipped her glasses back up on her nose, leaning into him as though she had a secret. "It's rigged. But I can't tell you how or I'd reveal all my magic."

Detective Johns blustered and gave her a curt nod. “Of course. Listen, Miss Sanchez, I need to speak to you about your Uncle, Gomez Sanchez. Can you give me a minute of your time?”

But Nina saved the day again, linking her arm with his. “C'mon up to the house and we'll get you something warm to drink while they finish up. Shouldn't be long now. The whole crew's inside. They'll hook you up,” she said in the pleasantest tone Esther had heard her use since she'd met her.

“I'll be right there, Officer Johns!” Esther called out, winking at him as she turned her fact back to Tucker.

When they were far enough away up the beach, she looked at Tucker, her panic returning. “Good thinking. But now what?”

Tucker draped the blanket back around her again, sitting on his haunches. “Now we get you to relax. Just breathe and let your fear go. Your legs returned last night, there's no reason they won't today. I promise you.” As he spoke, his voice hushed and reassuring, he rubbed small circles on her back with the palm of his hand, and she found herself relaxing.

She also found herself some other things, too, but she was trying like hell to keep her thoughts focused on getting her legs back so she could find out what this detective wanted.

“What do you suppose the detective wants? I didn't even know my uncle.”

“You said that last night.”

She turned to look at him. “Well, it's true. I don't

really know him at all. He never visited my grandfather here at the cottage. Grandpa always went to see him in the city—so did my father. My dad told me little children overwhelmed him, which was I guess a nice way of saying he wasn't too interested in his brother's only child. I tried reaching out to him after my grandfather's funeral, but he never returned my calls. I don't even know where he lived other than in the city somewhere."

"Your parents are gone?" he asked, continuing to smooth his palm over her back.

"Yes," she managed without even a hitch in her voice, looking down at her fingers before clenching her eyes shut. She shook off the mention of them. "You do know how they say my uncle died, don't you?"

His palm stopped moving over her spine when he looked at her with somber eyes, the gold flecks in them deepening. Jeez, he was hot. "I do, Esther. It's why I came here to begin with. To ask you about his death."

She forgot all about what he said when she felt her toes return as though shot from a cannon—they sprouted back into place like they'd never left. "Look! Oh, thank God!" she yelped, wrapping the blanket around her and struggling to stand.

Tucker helped by grabbing her around the waist with a strong arm and pulling her upward, bringing her tight to his chest when she faltered upon the awkward residual feel of her legs' return.

Oooooh was the first thing she thought. The second

was oooooh, too, but the third thing she thought wasn't fit for polite company.

Then she brushed it off. She knew all about this kind of bonding. People in the height of a divorce did it all the time. She couldn't count on her fingers and toes how many times parting spouses came to a mediation with guilty looks on their faces after a passionate night spent coming to terms with the end of their marriage, only to realize it had been a mistake made due to their heightened sense of fear of being alone.

Ironically, it happened most often after cheating spouses found themselves in the middle of a divorce, and it was called hysterical bonding. When a traumatic event drew two people together during stressful times.

And indeed, this was a stressful time.

Yet, as their eyes met, and Tucker smiled down at her, his luscious lips saying something she totally didn't hear, Esther felt a tug. A sharp, distinct tug in her belly. A tightening of her chest, and the buttery soft give to her knees.

She'd felt it before. Maybe not quite this strong, but certainly similar.

And it was the last thing she wanted at this particular time in her life.

Do. Not. Want.

It was the last thing she thought before she said a quick thanks and made a stumbling run for the cottage where, if nothing else, something safer than this feeling waited.

~

"So you say you didn't know your uncle very well?"

"She said that three fucking times, dude," Nina crowed from the corner of the living room, her face hard, her fists clenched. "Are you the best NYPD has to offer? Because you're a few sprinkles shy of a cupcake, buddy."

Detective Johns squirmed in his chair by the fireplace, everyone else plunked down around him to hear what he wanted to talk to Esther about. He ran a finger around his tight shirt collar, preparing to speak.

But Esther held her hand up to prevent Nina from saying anything else. She needed these women, and especially Tucker, to know she wasn't completely helpless, and all she needed was a little support until she could get back on her feet—or fins. Whatever.

Changed into a fresh pair of yoga pants and a clean, warm sweater, she felt more in charge when she answered.

"Yes, sir. That's what I said. I didn't know him very well. In fact, I've met him three times in my life, total. My father told me he didn't much like children, so it wasn't like I even saw him around the holidays. But my grandfather went to see him in the city all the time."

Detective Johns' forehead wrinkled. "Did your grandfather ever tell you if Gomez was depressed?"

She had to think about that for a minute. Her grandparents had always been so proud of her uncle.

Often, her grandfather would tell her about the important work Gomez was allegedly doing as a scientist, but he never got into specifics, and he certainly never mentioned depression.

Esther shook her head. "I can't remember him ever saying much about my uncle, other than his work was important and he was proud of him, despite the fact that he didn't come to visit. I grew up thinking of him curing sick children somewhere far, far away, locked in a hut, sweating over some beakers in a jungle somewhere. I know now that's not what he did, but you have to understand, Detective Johns, he wasn't a part of my life at all."

Detective Johns sat forward, taking a sip of his tea as he watched her. "Yet, you went to his funeral."

She looked back at him, unflinching. "Of course I did. Whether he was close to us or not, my grandfather loved and respected him. I went out of respect for my grandfather. Wouldn't you do the same?"

But he didn't answer her; he simply asked another question. "So, he never spoke to you about his depression? Never hinted he'd thought of taking his own life?"

"What about this shit don't you get, Starsky? She said no. She told you she hadn't talked to him. Like, what are you fishin' for here?" Nina asked, her tone full of barely contained anger.

But Esther wanted to know the same thing. She sat forward on the cushions and asked, "Listen, what's going on here? I was told his death was a suicide. Are you suspecting foul play? Because if this is about money or the research he's done or whatever, I didn't get a single penny from him, and I have no idea what he was working on. He left everything to science and his funeral was prearranged and paid for. All I did was show up."

Detective Johns tucked his pad back into the pocket inside his wrinkled jacket. "No, ma'am. I'm just tying up loose ends."

Loose ends? Interesting. "So you drove all the way here from the city to ask me things you could have asked me over the phone? Is this an official investigation?"

"No, it's not, but we like to be thorough," was all he offered before he was up and moving toward the door, his large body quicker than one would anticipate.

"Wait!" Esther said, sliding off the couch, where she sat between Tuck and Wanda, the latter of whom was dozing beneath a blanket Esther's grandmother had crocheted. She strode toward the door. "Can you tell me what was in the emails he sent? I know it sounds macabre, but now, since you came all this way to ask me questions about something I thought was pretty cut and dried, I'd like to know why he committed suicide. How he was feeling before he..."

His eyes scanned the room for only a second before they settled on her. "I can't reveal that information, Miss Sanchez. It's classified."

What an odd word to use about a suicide. Unless her scientist uncle was involved in something bigger than she was aware. "Classified? You're an NYC detective, not some FBI agent. How can it be classified?"

Detective Johns looked over her shoulder when he said, "I meant *private*. I can't show you an email he sent to other people. It's against regulation. Now, if you'll excuse me, I have a long trip back to the city. Have a nice day, folks." And with that, he popped her front door open and left.

Esther turned to face the group, each of whom had the same expression on their faces she was sure she had on hers. "Did that seem odd or is it just me?"

Nina popped her lips, setting Marsha on the ground with a scratch between her ears. "Dude, fuck yeah, it was odd. I don't know what, but I can tell you, some shit ain't right."

Then Esther turned to Tuck, who sat very quietly on the couch. "You seem to have known my uncle better than I did, even if it was just through email. Care to tell me if he seemed depressed?"

Tucker rose from the couch, removing Mook from his lap and setting him next to Wanda, who was lightly snoring. As he approached, his tall frame looming over her, he said, "Actually, in all truth, I was going to ask you some of the same things the detective did, Esther. But you've made it clear you didn't know Gomez well enough to know his state of mind."

"Why were you going to ask me if he was depressed? What do *you* care if he was depressed? Am I missing some kind of link here? You said you'd never met and only shared work emails. I don't know about you, but when communicating in a professional capacity, I don't usually go deeper than common courtesies. Also, I'm pretty sure you can find someone new to test your water, can't you? What made my uncle so special?"

Tuck looked past her and shrugged. "He'd been with us for years, we trusted him. It was so sudden."

"But it's like you said, he approved a test on some water that killed someone and made a bunch of other people sick. That he was depressed, and feeling responsible for someone's life because of his tests, doesn't make it seem so sudden. It means he had a heart, even if he didn't show it to his family."

Which stung a little, in light of the fact that her grandfather loved him so much.

His expression went stony. "That's a fair assessment."

But Esther waved her finger under his nose. "Nuh-uh. Don't give me six syllables and call it a day. You know something, Tucker Pearson. You know something, and I want to know what it is. The fact my uncle killed himself would kill my grandfather if he were still alive. He loved Gomez, made excuses for his absence in our family all the time. Why don't you tell me what's really going on here? Because I don't believe it has anything to do with your respect for his work as a scientist. You may well have respected his work, but because he approved some tests for your bottled water, he killed someone. That makes for bad PR, buddy. What are you after? And you'd better quit skipping around the mulberry bush about it or I'm going to lose my shit all over you!"

Nina slapped her on the back and grinned. "Proud of ya, Guppie—way to sniff out a snake. I think our work here is done, ladies. Looks like the newb's got a handle on this all on her own."

Esther would take pride in the compliment, coming from a woman so fierce, but she wanted answers right now. So she lifted an eyebrow at him. "Well?"

And he refused to bow down. "I think it's best we stick to mermaid lessons for now."

Nina set Esther behind her and jammed her face in Tucker's. "I don't give a shit what you think is best, Flipper. If she's in some kind of danger, which I'm suspecting she is, because every fucking newb we've ever come across *always* is, I wanna know *now*. I'm not fighting paper dragons, buddy. I'm here to look out for her, just like I said I would. Now spit this shit out!"

As much as she appreciated Nina's protection, because really, a vampire on your side can't be a bad thing, she was no slouch when it came to sticking up for herself.

She stepped in front on Nina and gave Tucker the stink eye. "What she said."

Tucker ran his hand through his thick hair, no worse for the wear after all that saltwater. When he finally spoke, his words chilled her to the bone.

Gripping her by the shoulders, his expression became grave. "I don't believe your uncle committed suicide, Esther. I think someone killed him."

CHAPTER 8

Hashtag mind blown.

Killed. Someone had *killed* her uncle?

Why would someone kill her uncle? According to her family, a meek, mild-mannered scientist? Had Tucker sucked the air from her lungs, she couldn't be more breathless.

Her heart began to pound in her chest with a heavy thud. "*But why*? Why would someone kill him? Do you think it was the family of the man who died? Because they were angry his tests failed to catch something in your water? What the hell was *in* the water, anyway?"

But Tucker shook his head with a firm movement in the negative. "*No*. No one knew the identity of the scientist who did the tests other than the police. We did everything we could to prevent his name being released, and we took full responsibility for the illnesses and the death of that man."

"And he died of what?" Marty asked from the couch.

Tucker's face went grim, his eyes distant, almost sad. "A deadly bacteria. Due to his age and a heart condition, it killed him."

Esther reached for Nina's hand, needing something to hold to keep from trembling herself right out of her fuzzy slippers. "Then *who*? *Why?* Why would you think he was killed?"

"To shut him up," he literally ground out, as though he were angry with *her* because her uncle was dead. His jaw twitched and his teeth clenched, yet still, she didn't understand why her uncle's death or alleged murder made a difference to Tucker if he didn't really know him.

"Okay, enough with the small sentences, Tucker," Marty said angrily, hopping up off the couch and throwing her finger in Tucker's face. "Spill the whole story and spill it now. My head is killing me. I'm tired. I'm trying to merge two businesses from a goddamn phone via text message and Facebook. Stop with the song and dance and get to the fucking point!"

The last words roared from her mouth, and one of her incisors elongated, dripping with a gleaming drop of spit.

Nina, the easily ruffled, was suddenly unruffled and cool as a cucumber as she grabbed Marty around the waist to keep her from going for Tucker's throat. "Werewolf, chill. What the fuck's gotten into you? Nobody's got their head on straight anymore. Wanda's either crying about absofuckinglutely nothing or drooling while she's passed out in a corner somewhere, and you're either full of sage wisdom and advice or on GD fire. Your pendulum swings fucking wildly, werewolf-san. Everybody, chill the fuck out! And you, Fishman, talk or I'll let Blondie here loose. You do not want me to let her loose!"

Marty tried to struggle out of Nina's grip, but Nina gave her a good shake. "Promise me you won't eat the man, Marty. At least not until he spits out whateverthefuck the problem is."

But Marty grabbed at Nina's hands with angry swipes, trying to pry them from her waist, her cheeks beet red, her face furious. "Get off me, Dark One, and put me down!"

Nina pulled her close, her lips at Marty's ear. "Not until you promise you're going to get a grip on your shit and turn down the volume. You know I can kick your ass—don't make me do it in front of people and embarrass you. Now...breathe, baby, or I'll take your ass outta the game."

Marty surrendered, her lightly tanned skin going pale as she sank back against Nina. "I'm breathing. Put me down. Please. I have a massive headache and your death-breath isn't helping it."

Nina nodded, seemingly not offended at all by Marty's poke. "Better. Go get some aspirin and a cold pack and sit this one out. Maybe go find Carl and have him read you a story or something. He's in the backyard with Mook. But we're not going to get anywhere with everyone at each other's throats. And that *I'm* the one to tell you people that should scare the fuck out of you."

Marty shook Nina off and took her leave, her pear-scented perfume wafting to Esther's nose as she huffed her way out the back door of the kitchen.

Nina turned to Tucker, planting her hands on her hips. "Speak. Tell us what's going on, and tell us this fucking instant, or I swear to Jesus, I'll make you beg for your life. If Little Fish here is in some kind of danger because someone thinks she might know something about her uncle's death, you can't keep hiding it—because if you want *anyone* in your corner, it's us."

Then she looked to a sleeping Wanda, sprawled out on the couch, and Marty in the backyard, massaging her temples.

"Okay. It's good to have *me* in her corner. Just me. Do it. *Now*. Why do you suspect someone murdered Gomez?"

Tucker ran a hand through his hair again, then over his chin covered in dark stubble. "Because Gomez was accurate. He was always accurate. I can't tell you how many times he did testing for us—how many disasters he saved us from because he was meticulous. And I don't use that word lightly."

Esther rocked from foot to foot, crossing her arms over her chest. "So that to you means murder? Because he made a mistake? Everyone has one to their name, Tucker. At least one."

"No. Not because he made a mistake, but because those tests weren't just done by him, but approved by me. *Allegedly* approved by me, that is. Everything about this new bottled water we've developed has been a disaster from the start. From the difficult location we culled it from, to the testing, to production, and whatever else came in between."

"Swear on Mook and Marsha's lives, if you say you culled whatever you put in the water from Atlantis, I'll die. Right here before your eyes," Esther threatened, and she wasn't even joking.

Tucker actually smirked before he covered it up with another serious expression. "Not Atlantis, exactly. Australia, actually."

Interesting… "So how do you guys manage to live with people and still be mermaids? How do you keep from being caught?"

"Have you heard of Atargatis Lake?" he asked.

"The private lake community with security guards at the gate?" She'd driven past it a million times and just assumed rich people lived in row after row of the gorgeous houses.

"That's the one," he confirmed, his gravelly voice low.

Her mouth fell open. "Shut up! You guys own that lake, don't you? OMG—so everyone in that community is a mermaid? Like right here in Staten Island?"

"Named after a Goddess, and yes, right under your cute noses," he confirmed, finally smiling again. "And we didn't cull the water from the lake—that's a manmade body of saltwater. It was done in Australia, taken from a reef one of our divers discovered. But regardless, it was all wrong from the word go."

"Okay, so you're claiming you didn't give the green light to this water that my uncle said was good? Am I getting that right?"

"Sort of."

"Okay, so what does 'sort of' mean?"

Tucker rasped a sigh, but he was finally forthcoming. "What I've been accused of is simple. They claim I gave the green light to the water, knowing it was bad, and sent it into production anyway because it meant millions of dollars lost if we didn't and the risk factor was low. In fact, they have an email from me to production, stating I gave it the thumbs-up and passed off the poor results from Gomez as minimal collateral damage compared to the bigger picture. Also, there's over a million dollars missing from H2O-Yo, and it all points to me skimming and hiding it in offshore accounts in the Caymans. But as I stand here before you, Esther, I'm telling you—*I'm telling you all*—I would never have endangered lives had I ever sensed even a hint of an issue. The only test results I saw said everything was a go. The water was good. And those were the tests from your uncle that I received in an email—which have mysteriously disappeared into thin air."

His face was so sincere, his eyes boring holes into her. If he was lying, he was either the best actor ever or a total sociopath.

On impulse, Esther reached out and grabbed his

wrist. She couldn't explain why, but she believed him. "So, you think you've been set up?"

"That's exactly what I think. I don't know by whom or even why, but someone wanted me out of the company, and they did a fine job of getting me gone."

"You got fired from your own family's company?" she asked in disbelief.

"I didn't just get fired from the company. I got booted out of my pod."

There was that crazy word again. Pod, pod, pod.

Nina narrowed her gaze at him and sucked her teeth. "What you're saying is, her uncle probably knew the water was bad and he said as much, but some greedy fuck got ahold of those tests and changed them to look like everything was okay, so you'd sign off—which you did. Shit went into production as planned, and then when that guy died and people got sick from the water, this greedy fuck showed up with the email from you and the real test results, which said the water was shit? So, like a whistleblower kind of thing?"

Tucker's face went hard, the lines around his mouth deepening. "In a roundabout way. When my father—who's not Poseidon, by the way, but a distant relative—and his team researched the trail of paperwork leading up to production, he found the alleged test results from Gomez, and someone anonymously sent him the email I supposedly sent to production, telling them the risks weren't worth halting production. My father, being the man he is, honorable if not stubborn as hell, banned me from the company and the pod until further notice."

She'd gone from outraged on his behalf to frightened in the matter of just a few minutes. "You think my uncle found out someone changed his tests, and he was going to tell you or your father, and got himself murdered because he knew the truth?"

"I absolutely do," he said, his words tight.

Now she had to lean against the wall, bracing her body from the trembling. "That's horrible." Even though she hardly knew her uncle, to find he quite possibly had been killed scared the hell out of her.

Nina slapped Tucker on the back, her face full of sympathy. "Fuck, dude. That sucks. Does this mean you're banned from the mermaid Slip 'N Slide, too? Like, do you live in this community where all you guys hang out?"

Tucker grimaced. "Fortunately, I don't. I live closer to the office complex for obvious reasons. The gated community mostly houses married mers and families."

Her ears perked up. So did that mean the hot fish wasn't married?

Oh, bad, Esther. Bad! What do you care if he's not married? Hysterical bonding is real, Esther Sanchez. You'd do well to remember that.

Still, she couldn't help but wonder if he had a girlfriend.

But she didn't have to ask. Nina took care of that for her. "So, no kids? No girlfriend? Wife?"

"No."

"Good thing, seein' as you were porking Esther

with your scales at a funeral because you thought she was hot, huh?" Then Nina laughed at her joke.

But Esther wasn't laughing. If someone had killed her uncle, if for nothing else other than the memory of her grandfather, she wanted justice. It would have killed Salvador Sanchez to think his son had been so unhappy he'd killed himself—even if the alleged suicide was over a mistake.

Someone needed to get to the bottom of this. Now.

But then she remembered Jessica. She didn't seem upset with her brother at all. So he wasn't totally alone. "Your sister seems supportive, though."

Tucker gave her a glimmer of a smile then. "She is. She's tried reasoning with my father, but if you knew Getty Pearson, you'd know once he's made a decision, especially if it involves the company he worked day and night to grow himself, you'd know there's no changing his mind.

Esther blew out a breath of pent-up air. "Any thoughts on a suspect? Someone who was holding a grudge? A jealous colleague who thought he should have your position?"

"I can't think of a single person who'd want my job, or who's openly made it clear they'd want my job. Whoever it is, they're good at staying hidden. Of course, I've been locked out of all my accounts at the office, so I couldn't dig around even if I wanted to."

Pushing herself off the wall, she approached Tucker with a look of determination. "So, what do we have to do in order to prove my uncle was killed to cover this up and clear your name? Never mind. Let's just *do it*. Let's find out who set you up and killed my uncle."

~

Tucker watched as the women—who refused to leave Esther alone with him, or alone at all, for that matter—sat together in the dining room while a very British, very proper man named Archibald, whizzed about Esther's kitchen, preparing a meal for everyone.

They'd invited him to stay, which was more than he deserved after not coming clean about his intentions where Esther was concerned. But that they were willing to help him because of her, brought him a strange peace.

They were an eclectic brood, this lot, but as he observed their camaraderie, he had to admire the way they worked together to help a complete stranger.

They were loud while they did it, but they were determined to figure out how to help Esther not only get her mermaid tail in order, but find out who had murdered her uncle.

And he was damned sure someone had murdered Gomez Sanchez to keep his mouth shut. He had a call logged from Gomez just before he'd supposedly killed himself. No voice mail left, just a call from him. It only strengthened Tucker's belief that he was being set up. That had to be what happened. He refused to believe otherwise, not just because Gomez had been a trusted subcontractor for H2O for over twenty years, but because his life had gone to total shit as a result, and he wanted it back.

He wanted to get up every morning with a purpose, rather than just watch his life go down the shitter while he skimmed Netflix for the next series he could devour. There was nothing worse than empty days filled with nothingness.

If he could just get into his computer at work…but then he thought, whoever had done this surely would have covered their tracks. But he held on to the hope that maybe there was some kind of residual tech imprint, a trail he could follow that would lead to an answer.

And his father?

Damn that stubborn, difficult man and his unshakeable ethics. The moment he'd discovered Tuck had allegedly signed off on this whole mess, a mess he'd wanted nothing to do with from the start because of the risk the divers were taking to get the water, he'd gone after Tuck, balls to the wall.

There'd been no talking, no coercing, no amount of swearing to the gods he'd had nothing to do with it that could convince his father otherwise. Even his mother, Serafina, had begged his father to at least listen, but Getty dismissed them both because there was proof. Hardcore proof.

And there *was* proof. It was *his* handwriting on that production order—or someone who was really good at forging his handwriting.

But the worst was the email where it claimed he'd considered the bacterial risks in the water minimal to the profit they could make. That his father believed he'd ever allow people to consume tainted water and become collateral damage, even water that was a little tainted, blew his mind. But it also infuriated him.

He'd worked his ass off to get where he was in the company. There'd been no slack for Tuck Pearson, or his sister, for that matter. Their father demanded perfection, and he demanded they start from the bottom up.

Fresh out of college with an MBA and he'd found himself in, of all places, the mailroom. But he'd gritted his teeth, swallowed his pride, shut his yap and, in less than eight years, proven himself worthy enough to take on the role of VP of Production.

Now, at thirty-five, it had all gone to shit. But with the same kind of determination he'd used to get to where he was in the company, he'd also figure out who the fuck was framing him.

Lost in thought, he didn't hear the doorbell ring as he sat on the couch, covered in Mooky and Marsha, who'd taken a liking to him. "At least someone still thinks I'm a good guy, eh, Mook?"

The odd combination of Doberman and wire-haired terrier looked up at him and rubbed his jaw against Tuck's hand with affection, making him smile.

"Are you Esther Sanchez?" someone with impressive articulation asked.

He sat up straight, sliding to the end of the couch,

and just as he was about to get up to see who was at the door, he heard her say, "I am. Who are you?"

"I'm Rory Shevchenko from Action News, Channel 8. Care to comment on the collusion between your uncle and the Vice President of Production at H2O-Yo, Tucker Pearson, to sell tainted water and embezzle a million dollars?"

And everything went off the rails from there.

CHAPTER 9

Lightbulbs flashed and popped, and a roar of chatter erupted from a small crowd of reporters gathered at the edge of her tiny front porch. Tucker was the first one out the door, setting Esther behind him. “Get out of here *now*!” he roared into the howling wind.

But another reporter, with slicked-back blond hair, jammed a microphone in Tucker’s face and asked, “Don’t you think it’s suspicious that you’re here at the home of Gomez Sanchez’s niece? The man responsible for killing one man and making countless others sick? Reports allege—”

“Hey!” a hulking figure bellowed from the shadows, stepping into the light from the front porch, making everyone turn around. “Y’all might wanna move along here, now! You’re on private property—which means you better skedaddle ’fore I call the po-po.”

As the enormous figure approached, pushing his

way through the lot of vultures, Esther didn't need an introduction. Nina had mentioned her demon friend Darnell was coming in case there was any trouble. He, according to her, was big and loveable and could help in Wanda's stead. Wanda, who was hard to keep awake and not supposed to be on her feet.

Yet, to see him for the first time was undoubtedly intimidating. He was bulky and crazy tall, his round face hard and angry, and he didn't look at all loveable right now.

As he made it past the small throng of people, he turned and held up his phone. "I'ma tell y'all one last time—get! Ain't nobody here got nothin' to say to you. Go on now," he demanded, waving an arm in their faces, making everyone duck and gasp before he crossed his arms over his brick wall of a chest and waited for everyone to leave.

As the crowd dispersed, frightened by a man as imposing as Darnell, he turned to Tucker and held out his granite slab of a hand. "I'm Darnell. Good to meet ya, man."

Tucker grabbed his hand and shook it hard. "Pleasure's all mine."

And then, with a smile that transformed his entire face, making his eyes gleam, he spotted Esther, who was still in shock. "You," he said, pointing a finger at her and wiggling it, "must be Esther. C'mon and give ol' Darnell a hug." He held out his bulky arms, his NY Giants shirt shifting to reveal his soft center.

Yet, she was a little afraid. He was a demon and she

was a good Catholic girl. And that was some crazy mixed-up dichotomy of religion.

But Nina gave her a light shove from behind. "Don't be a chicken-shit, Little Fish. He's not that kind of demon, nitwit. Long story short, he escaped hell. He's on the good side."

Oh, well then, you could never get enough hugs from a guy who looked like a big brown teddy bear with a wide smile and more chains around his neck than a set of tires in the winter who was on good's side, could you?

Esther went willingly into his embrace, finding it warm and reassuring, and it didn't hurt that he smelled good, too. "I'm Esther. It's nice to meet you."

He patted her shoulder with his thick hand and set her from him. "Look at you. A mermaid. Sweet! And you ain't got nuthin' to worry about anymore. I'm here now. I'll keep you safe. Welcome to the family."

Suddenly shy, because there were so many of these people welcoming her into their fold with almost no questions asked, she choked up a little. "Thank you, Darnell. Please come in."

And as he did, and the ladies greeted him with hugs and kisses, and Carl, his smile beaming like a fluorescent bulb, thumped him on the back, Esther and Tucker stood and watched.

"They're like this bizarre family of misfits, huh? Wait, maybe the word isn't bizarre. Maybe it's more eclectic, but they all move in tandem, even if they yell a lot and Nina snarls. There's real love there."

Tucker nodded, his eyes hinting at sadness as he put his hands in the pockets of his jeans. "She is good at snarling, isn't she?"

"She's also good at pretending, and lifting, and a plethora of things I've heard about but haven't witnessed. Except for those fangs. Jesus, those fangs."

Tucker leaned into her, her shoulder just touching the top of his muscled pecs. "Yeah… I hate to admit it, but I had no idea vampires were real, by the way. Or werewolves, or any of this, for that matter."

"Thought you guys had the market on the paranormal, didja? Kind of presumptuous, wouldn't you say?" she teased, taking a step away from him because he was just too dang close and he looked and smelled too dang good.

He scrubbed his jaw and shook his head in wonder. "I think I did. I mean, it's not like we don't communicate with the outside world, or surface people, as we call them, but this? This is really something else."

Esther nodded and smiled, but she felt a little empty inside, and maybe even a little jealous. Sure, she had friends—good friends—but they weren't ride or die like these people were. Maybe their dire circumstances had called for such loyalty, but if what Marty said was true, they'd been together for almost ten years now when they didn't have to be together.

They chose to be together—which was pretty awesome.

And watching them, seeing this interaction with Darnell, made her miss her parents and her grandparents more than ever. But when she looked up at Tucker, she realized how self-indulgent she was being. He'd been booted out of his family, for heaven's sake.

Reaching out, she touched his arm and willed her fingers not to test the bump of muscles by tracing them. "I'm sorry about what's happening with your family right now."

He stared off into the kitchen, where Archibald hugged Darnell before giving him a plate full of pasta. "I am, too. I'm also sorry the press is hassling you. I don't know who tipped them off or even how they'd link you to this mess, but—"

Wanda, who was finally awake, though still quite sleepy-eyed, waddled toward them and held up her phone in Tucker's face. "This is how they've managed to link Esther to you. The disgusting vultures."

Esther and Tucker read the headline from some site on the Internet.

Ex-VP of H2O-Yo Woos Niece of Dead Scientist Responsible for Tainted Water Debacle.

Attached to the article was a picture of she and Tucker sitting on the beach today, his arm around her. Thankfully it was after she'd gotten her legs back, but that someone was skulking around, taking pictures of her without her knowledge, scared the shit out of her.

"I will kill whoever did this," Tucker spat, pulling his phone from his pocket. "Wring their bloody necks!"

Esther gulped, swallowing hard as she looked to Wanda, dread filling her stomach. "So now my uncle's name is out there as the person responsible for the death of that man. Perfect."

"Jessica!" Tucker shouted into his phone. "We've got a goddamn leak, and I want to know who the hell it is! The sonofabitch leaked her uncle's name to the press and took pictures of us today while we were on the damn beach, for Christ's sake! We need to find out who's doing this, Jess. I won't have another person hurt in this mess—especially not Esther, who's totally innocent."

As he stomped off toward the bathroom, away from the noise in the kitchen, Wanda gave her a sympathetic smile and wrapped an arm around her shoulders. "Come eat, honey. Let's sit down and have some of Arch's amazing Bolognese and figure out what we're going to do next. Yes?"

Esther let Wanda lead her away toward the kitchen, but a bowl of pasta wasn't going to make this better. This kind of exposure looked bad—so bad. Not only for her. She wasn't anyone of note, with some big job where she was thrust into the spotlight. She mediated divorces far messier than this. It would pass for her, but for Tucker? It was the worst.

He didn't just look like the scum of the earth for producing tainted water, or scummier for embezzling money. Now he looked like he couldn't care less, because he was off courting the niece of the man who'd killed himself after discovering he'd fucked up some water tests and killed an old man.

Shit.

~

Okay, so maybe a bowl of Bolognese did solve some things, she pondered as she used her thick slice of lightly toasted garlic bread to wipe up the last drop of sauce. Wiping her mouth on a napkin, she reached over her table and impulsively grabbed Arch's hand.

"Thank you, Archibald. I haven't had a meal like that since my grandfather died. It was amazing, and so are you."

He bowed and lifted his head, his eyes twinkling. "Oh, Mistress Esther, you shame me with your praise," he teased, patting her hand and grinning as though it were nothing.

But to her it was something. It had been quite some time since she'd felt nurtured and cared for, and even if these people disappeared when they figured this out, she'd remember this time with them, and remember it with gratitude.

Tears welled at the corners of her eyes, but she kept them at bay. The changes in her body and life were wreaking havoc on her emotions. "Thank you for dropping everything and coming here to help babysit me while we investigate this. I don't know if I'll ever be able to thank you enough."

He threw one of her tea towels over his shoulder and dismissed her with a wave of his hand and a kind smile. "It's nothing. If I didn't come and feed this lot while they chased after the bad guys, they'd eat potato chips dipped in pig slop and wash it down with some sugary carbonated swill or another. It's my duty as a member of the family to keep them in fighting shape."

Marty laughed, the first time today, which meant she had to be feeling better. Pulling her gleaming hair up into a bun at the back of her head, she stuck a pencil though it to secure the bulk of strands in place and grabbed empty plates. "I, sir, take offense to that comment. I most assuredly would not eat potato chips dipped in pig slop, funny man. It's Doritos in pig slop for the win, thank you very much!"

Wanda pulled Archibald to her and kissed his cheek. "You're so fresh, mister. You'd better quit talkin' smack about me or I'm going to take away your favorite kitchen tool," she teased.

Archibald mimicked an arrow through his heart. "Oh no, Mistress Wanda. I beg of you, not the Fry Daddy! Whatever shall I do if I can't slave over hot oil, making chicken wings on football Sunday for the men in your lives? Woe is me!"

Everyone burst into laughter as they made quick work of clearing the table and loading the dishwasher, refusing to allow her to help.

Finding herself with nothing to do, and Tucker having excused himself to make more phone calls, Esther scooped up Mook and went into the living room to sit by the fire and consider what they'd do next.

Carl sat cross-legged on the floor by the fire, flipping through one of her books from the built-in shelves. She touched him on the shoulder before curling up on the chair under a blanket, with Mook in her lap. "*Where the Wild Things Are*. One of my very favorites," she commented. "My grandpa used to read it to me often when I was a kid. Do you like to read, Carl?"

He turned to her, his pale green skin glowing by the firelight, his lopsided smile warm and genuine as he reached out and scratched under Mook's chin. "Yesss," he whispered, using his duct-taped finger to point proudly to the pages. "So much."

She smiled back. "That's so wonderful, Carl. I read all the time when I was a kid and in college. I should do more of it nowadays instead of watching so much TV. Some of my happiest memories are from the nights my grandfather and I read together."

He paused and looked at her for a moment, his deep eyes swirling. Then he asked with his limited words—words Darnell had assured her he was working on, "Sad?"

Leaning forward, Esther paused, too. Nina had explained Carl's existence, and his place in their family, to which she'd done some more open-mouthed gaping. But he was the kindest soul, and had the most endearing qualities as he played with Mook and Marsha. When he ate broccoli, of all things, and mostly when he was surrounded by the people he loved so much, he was at his most precious.

"What do you mean by sad, Carl?"

He reached out his hand and touched her cheek with the gentlest of gestures. "You. Sad?"

She had to think about that for a minute. That this sweet soul had picked up on her emotions touched her. "I don't know if sad is the word I'd use. But being with all of you reminded me of my family. So maybe I'm happy-sad?"

He grinned and held the book up. "I read…to…you? Like Grampa?"

She snuggled Mook close to her and had another private moment of gratitude before she nodded and smiled warmly at this new friend she'd made. "I'd love that, Carl. I'd really love that."

As Carl began to read, showing her pictures, and they shared small moments smiling and laughing, right this second, the world was a peaceful, beautiful place, and everything else faded away.

~

The next morning, after a breakfast of fruit, scrambled eggs, and fluffy blueberry scones courtesy of Arch, Nina, Darnell, Tuck, and Esther piled into the SUV Marty had parked two streets over behind a deserted snack stand to avoid the possibility of press and headed toward the city to her uncle's apartment.

After Darnell had spent the night doing some pre-investigation, they'd found her uncle had actually lived in a very nice area of Brooklyn with a doorman to his apartment building.

They were going to somehow talk their way into that building and sift through his belongings. He'd only been dead for five days, his things couldn't have gone far yet, and if they got lucky, maybe they could find some of his research or his computer or anything that would prove he'd never approved that water.

The ride was mostly quiet on the way, with Nina at the wheel and Darnell riding shotgun, while she and Tucker sat lost in their thoughts in the back.

As they sped along the highway in the early morning light with the sun just poking its head out, her thoughts turned to what they could come across on this hunt to clear Tucker's and her uncle's names. She didn't want to believe someone had hurt her uncle to keep him quiet, but she didn't cherish the idea he'd killed himself, either.

Was he unstable enough to take his own life? Had she failed to be there for him when he needed someone most? Should she have put herself in her car and driven here to Brooklyn and demanded he see her? Guilt ate at her.

Though, if he'd been anything even remotely like her father and grandfather, he was a tough cookie and he'd have never stood for someone besmirching his name if he wasn't responsible.

Knowing so little about him was frustrating, but she was also going to go through some of her grandfather's boxes she'd remembered tucking away in her guest bedroom. Maybe she'd come across a clue of some kind that would help.

As they pulled up to the apartment building, a brick structure with shiny glass doors framed in brass and a cheerful elderly gentleman for a doorman, Esther's stomach revolted.

She wasn't very good at subterfuge. She'd pulled yesterday off on a wing and a prayer, because keeping herself and all these other mermaids she kept hearing about safe had been paramount. She'd never be able to live with herself if someone was hurt due to her negligence.

Tucker reached over and grabbed her hand, leaving her with that funny tingle again. His hands were rougher than she'd expected. He did work in an office, after all, but his lightly calloused hand enveloping her softer, smaller one sent a thrill of awareness up her spine.

"It's going to be fine, Esther. I promise I won't let anything happen to you. But if you want to bail, I don't blame you. This isn't your problem."

But she shook her head firmly and squeezed his hand before pulling it away and putting it in her lap. "Nope. Teamwork makes the dream work. I'm your in. If nothing else, I can tell the doorman I'm a mourning relative. We need all the ammunition we can get to get inside."

Nina parallel parked and turned around in her seat, her sunglasses and sunscreen in place. "Okay, so let's go over this shit one more time. You're his grieving niece and because you missed his funeral, you'd just like to be in his space to have time to say goodbye, right?"

"Yes." Her stomach jolted again, twisting and diving until she thought she'd vomit. It wasn't a big deal. It wasn't like she was lying about being his niece, but the intent was to rifle through his things, and that made her feel dirty—even though she knew they had no choice.

Nina nodded, turning the ignition off. "And if you could fucking summon a tear, that'd be icing on the cake."

Tucking her chin into her favorite blue and purple scarf, Esther nodded. "Got it. Tears."

Darnell swung around and eyed Tucker with his friendly smile. "You got this, man?"

Tucker also nodded his dark head. "I'm her boyfriend here for emotional support."

Darnell winked, pulling his Giants cap down over his eyes. "If you got any trouble at all, y'all text me. I'll come runnin'."

Nina twisted around and held her fist out to them. "Knuck it up for luck, guppies."

They each reached forward and bumped the vampire's fist before Tucker turned to her, brushed a strand of hair out of her face and said, "Let's do this."

Hopping out of the SUV, Tucker came around and offered his arm to her, pulling her tightly to his rigid side as they crossed the street and approached the doorman.

The sun was bright, glinting off the falling leaves,

just now changing to the bright oranges and yellows of autumn. Trees lined the quiet street, railroad-tie planters filled with mums and marigolds at the base of each trunk.

The surroundings surprised her. This seemed more like a setting you'd find families in, where they'd raise their children and play in the small park across the street with its slide and swing set.

She'd always pictured her uncle living somewhere less family oriented—less beautiful to look at and more practical or maybe industrial, like a warehouse.

Upon seeing them, the doorman smiled, and before he could even wish them a good morning, Esther almost forgot everything but what she was here to do—get inside.

But Tucker slowed her roll and bid the cheerful man in a dark blue uniform, hat, and white gloves a, "G'day, mate. Pleasant day, wouldn't you agree?"

The man instantly smiled, the bright sun highlighting the wrinkles by his eyes. "Australia?"

Tucker grinned, his hand tight against her waist, making her feel safe and secure. "Yes, sir."

"How can I help you two on this lovely fall morning?" he asked, his white-gloved hand on the brass handle of the glass door.

Esther gave a dramatically sorrowful sigh and leaned toward the doorman, her eyes wide and sad. "I'm Esther Sanchez. My uncle, Gomez Sanchez, lived here for many years. I was out of the country when I found out he..." She stopped and bit her lip hard, hoping the sting would inspire tears. "Well, I'm sure you know by now what happened. Anyway, this may seem a little out of the blue, but do you think I could just see his apartment? Maybe spend some time with his things? I know it sounds stupid, but somehow, it brings me comfort. You see, I missed his funeral due to a flight delay in Brussels. Oh, and I forgot to get my allergy medicine, right, honey?"

She looked to Tucker, who nodded and smiled indulgently.

"It's just hell on earth for me if I fly without them—and my gel cold pack. Absolutely have to have the gel pack or I slam shut like a trap door. Sinuses, you know? And then, of all things, there was this huge rainstorm on the way to the airport, hail and thunder and...and we got caught in it and we were already late. Honestly, I thought I'd have a heart attack because of the stress. But then we got to the airport, only to find out our flight was delayed. And after that harrowing ride in such poor weather! So we tried to book another, because I desperately wanted to attend my uncle's funeral and pay my last respects. It had been so long since I'd seen him. I think it was back in 2002 at a polka festival. Bet you didn't know he loved to polka, did you? Neither here nor there—"

Tucker stopped her incessant babble when he poked her in the ribs. "Lover?" He hitched his jaw to indicate the doorman had opened the door for them.

"Oooo, thank you!" she chirped, taking a deep breath and squeezing the doorman's arm.

He tipped his hat at her, his light brown eyes sympathetic. "It's my pleasure. Mr. Sanchez was always pleasant to me. I knew who you were the moment I saw you. He'd shown me your pictures throughout the years. He thought the world of you… As you know, he'd been here for years and years, so I felt a little like I knew you. Anyway, I'm so sorry to hear about his…your loss."

Immediately, she went contrite, letting her eyes get watery even though she was confused as hell about her uncle showing someone her pictures. She shook off the oddity and said, "I appreciate that. Has anyone else been here? A friend, maybe? Girlfriend? We'd been out of touch for a few months, so I haven't kept up."

"Oh, no. Mr. Sanchez…" He looked off into the distance, as if he didn't know how to tell her something. "He didn't have many visitors."

"No one's come to clear his apartment out?" Tucker inquired.

The doorman shook his head. "No, sir. But I just got word from the board today a cleaning crew is coming tomorrow. So, it looks like you're just in time."

"And his apartment number? I can't seem to recall what it was," Esther responded.

"34B," the doorman provided, sweeping his arm inward to motion they should enter.

"Thank you. You've been very kind. We'll just be on our way," Tucker said, steering her over the threshold of the building and toward the shiny black elevators.

He pushed the button, keeping her close to his side until they were behind the elevator doors.

Once inside, he glanced down at her and chuckled. "You were on quite a roll, young lady. Hail? Allergies? Polka?"

As she stared at their reflection standing side by side in the elevator doors, trying to keep her mind off the idea of them as a couple, she snickered. "Too much, right? When I get nervous, I get a little yappy. Mostly when I have to lie, I get *really* yappy and things just fall out of my face before I can put the brakes on."

"But you *weren't* lying, Esther. He is your uncle."

"Yeah, but that's about the only thing I didn't lie about. I've never even considered going to Brussels and I don't have a single allergy to anything."

Tucker barked a laugh, motioning for her to exit in front of him. "Good to know."

"And how strange that he said he knew me from my pictures? I had no idea my uncle knew anything about me, other than I exist."

"I've had a thought or two about your uncle. In all the communications I'd had with him over the years, it was clear he was a genius, and certainly introverted. We'd invited him to every Christmas party and company barbecue we'd ever had, and he never once attended. Surely, that speaks to an introvert's nature—or maybe he just wasn't a party animal? But I wonder, due to his high IQ and factual, rather than chatty emails, if maybe it was more than introversion? Maybe we're talking somewhere on the autism spectrum? I don't know what you know about his health history, but I'm just throwing it out there as something to consider."

A light bulb went off in her head. That made complete sense. It would explain so much. She didn't know a lot about autism, but she knew enough to know, in part, it fit the conversations her grandparents had had about her uncle over the years.

"That's a good point. I guess I never gave it a lot of thought, but it's certainly something to think about. Maybe we'll find some answers at his place."

"Fair enough," he said.

Thinking about the possibilities Tucker had mentioned, she wandered down the long hallway with only four apartment doors, all in the same color red, until she stood in front of her uncle's. And then she realized something.

"We don't have a key." Damn. That was something she hadn't even considered. She'd been more focused on getting into the building than getting into the apartment.

"No worries," Tucker assured her, pulling a pen from his pocket and holding it up with a gleam in his eye. "I did my fair share of mucking about before I got serious about life."

Her gaze went wide and she grinned at him. "Reeeally? I'd have never thought a VP of Production at a Fortune 500 company—who's a mere thirty-five, mind you—would be one for mucking about. Seems to me you'd have to be pretty focused to get where you are."

He knelt down and drove the pen's tip into the doorknob. "How do you think I got to be VP? And how did you know I was thirty-five?"

"It said so in that article about us. It also said I was thirty-four. Which I am not, thank you very much. I'm thirty-two."

He jiggled the pen. "Well, there was plenty of incorrect information in that article. So let's just pretend the damn thing ever happened."

She leaned against the beige plaster wall and wondered something out loud. "Any thoughts on who gave us up to the press yet?"

He shook his dark head, a lock of hair falling over his forehead as the lock clicked and he stood up. "I have Jess on it. I'm hoping she can find something out, because I can tell you, I have no idea who it could be. But if and when I find out, I'll make sure they pay. I don't care what the press says about *me,* but it was unfair to bring you into this. It never even occurred to me there was a risk, due to the fact that no one had any names concerning the water. I'm sorry for that, Esther."

But she waved a hand at him and moved away from the heat of his body, remembering her hysterical-bonding theory. "I don't blame you at all, Tucker. I hope you know that. *Really know that*. It was an accident. This is all an accident. Let's just get inside and see what we can find."

"Done deal," he agreed, putting his hand on the doorknob. "You ready?"

"As I'll ever be."

When Tucker pushed the door open and they took their first look of the interior, they both gasped.

CHAPTER 10

Tucker put his hand on Esther's waist as she attempted to wade her way into the living room around stacks upon stacks of papers. All manner of papers. Newspapers, sale circulars, wrapping paper, tissue paper, and ream after ream of computer paper. The piles were everywhere, covering walls, in some cases almost hitting the top of the windows that overlooked the beautiful park across the street.

"What the hell?" Tucker murmured, craning his neck to scan the entire room.

"He was a hoarder," she breathed, covering her mouth in shock. "Oh my God. I had no idea... Maybe this was why he never invited anyone over?" Could this be the reason her grandfather often came back so upset after a visit with her uncle?

Flashes of conversations came back to her in bits and pieces. Phrases like "It's not safe" and "You can't even move" floated to the surface of her brain.

Tucker ran a hand through his hair and looked around once more. "But you said your grandfather visited him frequently."

"He did, but he never said a word about something like this," she said, looking around in wonder. "Though, it sure explains why he was always so sad when he came back from a visit."

She could vividly remember her grandmother whispering in soothing tones to her grandfather on several occasions after he came home from a visit with Gomez.

Her grandmother had stopped making even the occasional trip when she began showing symptoms of Alzheimer's. In fact, her grandfather had refused to bring her after that, promising Gomez would come see her in the nursing home she eventually retired to when she couldn't be cared for at home any longer.

Esther didn't know if he ever did visit her grandmother, but hindsight had her wondering about all those hushed conversations her grandparents had, and if they were about this.

Tucker tipped her chin upward and peered into her eyes, his gaze concerned. "Are you okay? This is a lot to take in."

Sucking in a shuddering breath, she had to agree. She almost couldn't even see the kitchen from the living room for the stacks of paper. "I'm just shocked. I had no idea…"

"Did I hear you say your grandparents raised you?" he asked, pulling his leather jacket off and throwing it over his arm, because really, there was nowhere else to put it.

"They did. From the age of nine." Inevitably, he'd ask what had happened to her mom and dad, so she decided not to give him the opportunity. "My parents died in a boating accident."

He didn't bat a sexy eyelash, but he did give her a look of total sympathy. "I'm sorry, Esther. I wouldn't have pried had I known."

She shook her head and dismissed the notion as she waded her way through the first pile of newspapers. She managed to end up in the middle of the living room, if she stuck to the path that her uncle had created to make your way through the maze of paper.

"It's fine. It was a long time ago." That was all she could handle saying at this point.

But she remembered them so clearly—even now. Dark and tall, Eduardo and Anita Sanchez were both slender and athletic and moved like two graceful cats. Ironically, her father had met her mother at her best friend's pool party and they'd hit it off. She vaguely remembered her mother telling her she knew the minute she met her father that he was going to ask her to marry him, and she was going to say yes.

And he did ask her, and she did say yes, and as a young couple they'd moved to Staten Island, where her father took over running the shoe store Salvador had built from the ground up, and where her mother worked as the store's bookkeeper.

There weren't many times she could remember

being happier than when she'd have the day to loll away in her grandfather's store. There were always hugs and laughter, good food, amazing holidays, and frequent trips to the beach.

Until there weren't.

Her phone beeped then, pulling her away from the memories she so cherished and forcing her to focus on the task at hand. Which seemed insurmountable.

As she read Nina's text, and replied, Tucker looked to her with a tentative expression from behind a stack of Christmas wrapping paper. His hand hovered over the pile. "May I? I don't want to move anything if you're not comfortable."

But she looked away from his scrutiny and brushed off how overwhelmed she felt right now. "That's what we're here for, Tucker. Let's not pussyfoot around because this could take all night. I don't even know where to begin."

But he stepped around the pile and came to stand next to her, gripping her chin with his wide hand. "This is upsetting you, Esther. The last thing I want to do is bring up bad memories for you. You have enough to deal with."

Pulling her ponytail tighter, she rolled up the sleeves of her bulky cable-knit sweater and moved backward again, away from the heat of his hand. "Know what upsets me more? My uncle being accused of killing someone because he screwed up some important test. Worse? A suicide that wasn't a suicide at all, but a murder. My grandfather was probably rolling around in his grave. So it's on, as far as I'm concerned. The sooner we start, the sooner we'll know what we're dealing with."

He gazed down at her for a long minute, searching her eyes with his, deep furrows in his forehead. "You're a good egg, Esther Sanchez. Thank you for helping me." He reached out and took her hand in his for a brief moment before he turned and began to chip away at a pile.

~

"Jesus," Nina muttered, looking around and squeezing Esther's shoulder. "You okay, kiddo?"

She reached up and patted Nina's hand and nodded. "I'm fine. Grab a pile and start looking. I'm going to start digging through each room for a computer or laptop or whatever," she said, never missing a beat.

Tucker looked up from his pile of computer paper and watched as Esther directed Nina and Darnell to other stacks of paper so they could sift through them, but he wasn't hopeful.

He was overwhelmed, as overwhelmed as Esther herself—even though she was putting on a good show of pretending she wasn't at all feeling the insurmountable pressure of digging through this mess.

Her determination did something funny to his chest...tightened it...shifted his heart around in a way he wasn't entirely comfortable with. In fact, he wasn't comfortable with the way he was feeling about her, period.

Undeniably, he'd been attracted to her from the start. That's what had brought them to where they were now. But that his attraction had grown, that he wanted to reach out and touch her at every opportunity, was where his discomfort stemmed from.

She was already in this mess deep enough. He wouldn't drag her into it any further. But he'd date the hell out of her under any other circumstances.

Deciding to see what he could find aside from what was visibly obvious, he followed the path that led to Gomez Sanchez's kitchen and began opening cupboard doors. Despite the fact that he seemed to have an affliction for collecting paper, he was quite clean.

There wasn't much to speak of. A set of plates, and matching cups and bowls, some pots and pans that didn't look like they'd had much use. A coffee maker buried behind yet more papers, some potholders, but nothing really of note.

Surprisingly, the counters, the interior of the refrigerator, and the appliances were free of dirt and grease, suggesting Gomez kept health issues in mind, and he supposed, being a scientist, that would be a primary concern.

How odd that he collected nothing but paper. It was clear he was a hoarder, but would this also be considered obsessive-compulsive?

Sighing, he followed the path back into the living

room, where Nina and Darnell had made space on the floor and sat, digging through the endless collection.

"Dude," she whispered to him when he sat on his haunches beside her. "We need reinforcements. We'll never get through all this shit if we don't get some help."

Tucker grimaced. He had to agree, so he nodded at this pale, frighteningly confrontational woman he hardly knew but rather liked, despite her constant state of agitation, and said, "I don't think we're going to find much, to be honest. Maybe the better place to start would have been his lab at Tecton."

"Tecton?" Darnell asked, tilting his head as he looked up from some pink tissue paper. "You mean that place over by H2O-Yo? That ol' building, all steel and glass?"

"That's the one. That's the lab where Gomez worked. I get the feeling he didn't do much living in this space. Maybe he slept here, but his kitchen, despite the papers everywhere, is pretty clean. I don't know how you could live here or where you'd sleep, but I feel like we've touched on something I don't understand."

Esther poked her head out of the bedroom. "I don't think he slept here either, and if he did, he slept with a bunch of these piles next to him. Yet, the bed is made. I don't get it."

Tucker rose and attempted to make his way toward her, once more following the clear path Gomez had laid. "The kitchen's the same way. It's clean as a whistle except for the paper."

"Kiddo?" Nina called out. "You want me to call Marty and Wanda and have them come help? We'll never get through this shit alone."

Esther held up a finger as he approached. "Hold that thought for just a minute, Nina. I think Tucker might be right, in that we're wasting our time here. I don't think my uncle did much living here at all. Either way, let me just give another quick skim of the bedroom and bath, and then maybe we should rethink this rifling through all those piles."

Nina gave her a thumbs-up and went back to sorting though another pile as Esther carefully made her way into the bedroom with Tucker behind her.

She looked to him and pointed to the bed. "Can we move some of these piles so I can at least look under the bed? I've already scoured the nightstands and the dresser."

As he began to pick away at the paper, setting smaller piles on top of another batch of bigger ones, he watched Esther kneel down and push her way to the side of the bed. As she lay flat on her belly, he caught himself staring at her ass in her tight-fitting jeans and forced himself to look away.

"Boxes," she muttered. "There's a bunch of boxes under here." As she began to pull them out, she set them aside until she had them all. "Hey, you know, I was wondering about something while I was in here. Do you have any idea where they found my uncle? Was it here in his apartment or at his lab? I can't believe I never thought to ask, but none of the articles I read about it say anything other than he committed suicide and, after last night, that he's responsible for giving the go-ahead on the tainted water. In fact, they're more focused on what *you* had to do with it than anything else."

"We fought hard to keep his name from the press, Esther, called in favors. You name it, we did it, because he was a valued friend to our company."

"It's okay, Tucker. I believe you. I really do. Whoever leaked this sucks, but that's neither here nor there now. So where was he when they found him?"

"I believe he was found here in the bathroom, if I recall correctly."

He watched her swallow, watched the gamut of emotions play over her face. "By whom? Do you know?" she squeaked, her voice husky.

Squatting on his haunches, he looked at her, her wide eyes brimming with tears, her thick hair falling in wisps about her pretty face. "I don't know who found him. I only know the police told my father it was very clearly an overdose of sleeping pills."

She worried her lower lip before she said, "And no one asked the police or the medical examiner who'd found him?"

Tucker scratched his head. He remembered the conversation with his father vividly. He remembered being called into his office. He remembered a feeling of dread, but couldn't account for where it was coming from. And then his father had told him Gomez Sanchez had taken his life over this business with the tainted water.

The police had asked him a few questions about Gomez's state of mind due to their emails back and forth, but they hadn't divulged anything pertinent to his suicide.

It was the beginning of the end for him that day. After hearing that news, everything was a blur.

"I don't know. I just know he was found in the bathroom and that was because my father told me. After that, I was considered a part of this, and they locked me out of all conversation."

"Have the police contacted you about your connection to Gomez? Do they suspect you at all? I mean, when Detective Johns came by, I honestly thought he was coming for *you*. If I were a cop, after finding out all the information—and I'm not at all accusing you here, so don't get bent out of shape. But with the money missing and my uncle dead, if I were a cop, I'd be thinking what you're thinking—someone murdered him. But I'd think that someone was you."

Yeah. He'd thought that, too. He knew his days were numbered at this point, especially after that leak to the press. "No, the only contact I had with the police was about Gomez's state of mind, but as this unfolds, I'm betting my days are numbered, for some questioning at the very least."

His words had her up and pushing her way past more piles to get into the bathroom, where she stopped in the doorway.

"He was found in the bathroom? Are you sure?"

He rose, fighting his way through the debris to get to her. "That's what my father told me, just before he fired me and booted me out of the pod."

Her shoulders sagged, but then she straightened. "I think we need to speak to the person who found him. I also think we need to hit the coroner's office and find out what led them to rule this a suicide. I want to know what kind of drugs they found in his system, if he ever had a history of taking drugs. I want to talk to his doctor, if he had one. I want to know who this man was, because the more I think about this, and because I believe your story, the more I think someone hurt him. But I need to know the truth. Yet, I'm afraid to stir up any trouble because it'll shine attention on you—which we don't want."

He smiled at that. At least she believed him. For some crazy reason, that meant almost more than his father believing him.

"Don't think about me, Esther. Think about your uncle. If he was killed because he knew something, I want that person caught. Hell, I'll go with you."

She winced. "Are you sure, Tuck? It'll only draw attention to you."

But he nodded to confirm. He couldn't ask her to hold off on finding out what happened for his own selfish reasons. Then he remembered something. He'd been so distracted by the press showing up at her house, he'd forgotten to tell her about Gomez's phone call. Shit.

"Have I mentioned your uncle called me the night he supposedly took his life?"

"What?" she said in disbelief. "He called you? Why didn't you tell me?"

"He didn't get through, and he didn't leave a voice mail, but I have the log on my phone right here." He pulled out his phone to show her.

"Did you tell that to the police?"

"I did, when they asked me whether I knew if he was depressed or not. They thought maybe he was reaching out to me. I think that, too. I think he was reaching out because he knew something. Because he didn't sign off on those tests, Esther. I feel it in my damn gut. I think that's what that phone call was about."

"Damn," she muttered, her eyes welling with tears.

Putting a hand to her shoulder, knowing he shouldn't but doing it anyway, he asked, "What? Talk to me."

She shook her head and swiped a finger under her eye. "I just wish I'd known him better so I could gauge whether he was the kind of person who'd take his own life. I mean, it's obvious he had some issues from the stacks of paper. I'm not sure why he only collected paper, but I feel incredibly guilty about taking this all at face value and not looking deeper. But you can bet your ass, I'm not only going to Tecton, but to the police. I want some answers."

Again, knowing he shouldn't, he did it anyway—pulled her into his arms as she buried her face in his shirt. He let his chin rest on the top of her head, inhaling the scent of her fruity shampoo. "Please don't feel guilty. Your uncle was just a story to you as a kid. I know there isn't much I can say to make you feel any better, but we've all got that one relative who's a little left of center, Esther."

She snorted against his chest and shook her head. "Do you have a crazy mermaid in your pod?"

"Someday, when we have more time, I'm going to tell you all about my crazy aunt Nita and her collection of seashells."

She tweaked his chest playfully. "Shut up. You're just saying that to make me feel better."

He chuckled, liking how she fit against him. "I'm not even a little saying that to make you feel better. She has a two-thousand-square-foot house with three bedrooms, all of which are dedicated to her seashells. Every imaginable type of seashell in every imaginable art form. Wind chimes, picture frames, the list goes on. In fact—"

Esther silenced him with her lips. She didn't give him any warning, she didn't change positions, she just reached up, grabbed his face, and laid one on him.

CHAPTER 11

She didn't know what had come over her. She wasn't known to be terribly impulsive, but hearing his words, knowing he could relate, had made her very sore heart come alive.

And it didn't hurt that he had the best lips ever. Like, bar none, the best lips she'd ever locked with.

They were firm in all the right places, soft, gentle, forceful. They were everything, and as he dipped his tongue into her mouth, she saw stars. Literally saw stars; they made her heart crash against her ribs

And as her hands crept upward and around his strong neck and her fingers threaded through his soft, thick hair, as his thick arms encompassed her, she almost stopped breathing. Her stomach plunged to her toes, her knees went soft and buttery, her eyes nearly rolled to the back of her head.

Until she heard, "Excuse me, but can you please put Big Fish's tonsils back where they belong and fucking join us in the living room?" Nina stuck her face between theirs and planted a hand on each of their cheeks, pulling their lips apart.

Esther hopped back like she'd been burned, her cheeks going bright red when she realized what she'd done. But he'd been so sweet and understanding, and he'd related to her, and she'd lost her fool mind.

Taking another step backward, she almost stumbled on a pile of papers, but Tucker grabbed her. Her head was reeling from that kiss—that luscious, hot, mind-melding kiss—but she managed to find some focus with Nina leering down at her. "Did you find something?"

She grinned then shook her head, her charcoal eyes peering into Esther's. "No. Not a GD thing so far, but Whiny and Cranky are here and they want to know where you want them to start. So quit looking for each other's lungs by way of your tongues and get your asses out there." With those words, she cackled and turned, weaving her way back out of the bedroom.

She looked up at Tuck, his eyes darker, his lips still flushed from her kiss, and she wanted to do it again. But she had to remember she was only hysterical bonding. "I'm sorry."

He used his thumb to rub the outer corner of her lips and smiled his delectable smile. "I'm not."

"You should be."

"Why would I be sorry a beautiful woman kissed me?"

He thought she was beautiful?

Stop that right now, Esther!

"Because it was wrong of me to kiss you. The circumstances are all wrong."

He grabbed her fingers in a loose hold and kissed each tip. "Well, I admit, it's not exactly ambiance central here, but I'm okay if you're okay."

She frowned at the shivers he evoked along her skin. "I'm not okay. What I just did was called hysterical bonding."

He paused, but only momentarily before he resumed kissing her fingertips as he looked at her over her hand with a facetious smile. "Say again?"

She sighed, hoping it didn't sound breathy, but to note, she wasn't pulling her fingers from his lips like he was Satan eating her flesh off, either. "It's called hysterical bonding. When a couple is in a stressful situation, they sometimes turn to one another for comfort."

"I don't feel hysterical," he assured her with confidence.

She pulled her hand away from his lips, due to the distraction, and inhaled. "You are, you just don't know it," she insisted.

"Nope. I'm quite un-hysterical, actually."

She twisted a strand of stray hair around her finger. "Is that even a word?"

He shrugged and smiled. "I have no idea, I just know I don't feel at all hysterical. Good, yes. I feel quite good, actually. But not at all hysterical."

"Well, here's something to chew on while you're not hysterical. Sometimes you don't recognize hysterical bonding when it's happening. It's usually reserved for married couples—and a spouse who cheats. But what I just did was definitely a branch off the tree of hysterical bonding."

Tucker moved in a bit closer, making her cheeks flush hot again. "Do *you* feel hysterical?"

"I feel stupid."

"Because?"

"Because I just face planted you with my lips, Tucker. I don't do things like that."

He mocked a serious face. "And why did you do that? Face plant me with your lips."

"Because you were being so nice and..." *And you're super sexy. Duh, Fish-man!*

Tucker made a big to-do about giving her words thought before he said, "So, do you kiss everyone who's nice to you the way you kissed me? I mean, there was tongue and everything, Esther. That's almost like we're engaged or something. Now, I'd like to think you reserve that for a really good kiss, but how would I know? We hardly know each other."

She giggled, fighting a snort. "What kind of question is that?"

"I'd say an honest one, considering your alleged hysteria."

Esther waved a finger at him. "I'm telling you, Tucker Pearson, that's what this was. In the meantime, look up hysterical bonding. You'll see it applies. And now, I'm going to take myself and my out-of-control lips back into the living room and pretend we weren't just caught making out in my uncle's bathroom."

"Okay, but I'm telling you. I don't feel at all hysterical." And then he dropped a quick kiss on her lips before she could turn and fight her way out of the bedroom before she did something stupider, like ask him to marry her.

As she made her way back to the voices in the living room, she found Wanda and Marty had joined them and they were all still sifting.

Putting her hands on her hips, she looked at the sprawling mess and said, "I think this is a waste of time, guys. I don't think the answer lies here. I think it lies with Tecton and/or the coroner. Maybe the people my uncle worked with. I guess I was so caught up in my own life, I didn't think to dig deeper and wonder how this all went down. My uncle's attorney called and said he'd taken his life, and I… I don't know what I thought, but I was careless, and I feel like an ass that I didn't consider looking into this. But now I want to know what the hell's going on, and they'll have to tell me because I'm my uncle's only living relative."

Marty smiled up at her from her place on the floor, her eyes less hazy since last night, her hair up in a messy bun, her leggings and boots as fashionable as the woman herself. "I'd lean toward you're right, honey, but I'm afraid to abandon this and find out later we missed something. So, grab a seat, Little Mermaid." She patted the space next to her.

And that's what they did, for almost ten hours

straight—sifted through useless paper after useless, empty paper while Wanda intermittently napped on the crisp burgundy leather armchair they'd found pushed against the wall under a stack of more papers, and Darnell went and grabbed sandwiches for their lunch.

"Okay," Esther said, rising to stretch out her legs, cramped and tired. "I'm calling this. There's nothing here. You're tired. I'm tired. We're all tired, and we've been cooped up in this veritable paper factory all day long. I can't thank you all enough for the help you've given me, but you guys need to go home and sleep…see your families…do whatever paranormal people do." Then something occurred to her. "Wait. Nina, how are you awake when it's well before midnight? How were you even awake last night? Oh my God! Am I keeping you from vampire sleep, or whatever you need? How rude and selfish of me—"

Nina popped up from the floor, stopping her tangent. "First, I sleep normal hours just like you, Tina The Tuna. I've learned to tolerate daylight because of these two fucking nuts. They leave for the discount mall at eight sharp in the morning, and they drag my ass with them. There is no sleep with these two. Second, no one goes anywhere until we find out the truth about your uncle and someone teaches you how to be a mermaid. I like Big Fish, don't get me wrong. He's nice enough. Cute accent, blah, blah, blah. But I gotta tell ya, I'm not a fan of his fucking family right now. I mean, fuck—his own father thinks he had some shit to do with this? Uncool. If that's the kind of welcome you're going to get from them, I'll bite you myself so you can join *my* clan just to keep you from that bunch of misguided morons."

Esther threw her head back and laughed, throwing her arms around Nina's neck. "You're the best thing that's happened to me in forever, you know that?"

As Nina pried herself loose from Esther's grip, Wanda woke up, rubbing her eyes. "I'm dreaming, right? Did someone just say Nina was the best thing that ever happened to them? That has to be a dream," she said groggily, covering her mouth to hide a yawn.

"Nay!" Nina crowed, holding her hand out to Wanda to help her up. "In fact, this is not a dream, Sleeping Beauty. Esther just has the good damn sense to know I'm the nicest one out of all of you. I'm honest and I get to the fucking point. Some people still value that shit. Now, c'mon, Drooler. Let's get you back to the cottage so Arch can fill your endlessly empty fucking tank."

As everyone began to work their way to the front door, Esther held back, taking one last look at her uncle's apartment, knowing someone was coming to empty this all out tomorrow, and closed her eyes.

I'm sorry, Grandpa. I'm sorry I didn't force my way in here. I'm sorry I didn't think to look closer at the circumstances surrounding his death. I'm sorry.

She scoured every last inch of his apartment with her eyes, memorizing the plain beige walls, the tiny kitchen with its brown Formica countertops barely visible, the towering piles papers, and inhaled, wiping her tears.

Tucker leaned down near her ear. "You ready now?" he asked, taking her hand.

And she let him, her nod one of determination. "Let's go catch a killer."

~

"Esther, it's so amazing to see you again," Jessica, Tucker's beautiful sister, said with a warm hug. "Are you ready to be a mermaid?"

Esther peered around, still unable to tell Tucker she didn't know how to swim. But in for a penny, in for a pound, right? That's what she kept telling herself as she, Marty, Nina, and Tucker gathered around the lake these mermaids owned, shivering.

They'd decided nothing else could be done until the morning, so what better time to teach Esther how to be a mermaid than tonight?

It was a chilly midnight, filled with a light mist of fog rolling in across the manmade lake, constructed just for this purpose. And even with the fog, it was like something right out of a Disney movie. Nothing deterred from the magnificence of the scene before her. Not even her terror.

Mermaids, their sparkling tails in all colors of the rainbow, appeared before her eyes, surfacing to slap the water, only to dive back under again and disappear into the glittering depths. Enormous rocks, grouped together and fashioned to resemble cliffs, housed women of all shapes and sizes, soaking up the moon's rays as they sprawled out along the craggy surfaces, their hair flowing out in satiny ribbons behind them. Men, too, their chests bare, their signature wristbands glowing in the dark, sat with them, resting and enjoying the evening.

The moon, full and high, glowed bright in the sky, giving their skin an almost ethereal tint. The water swished in hushed pools, dipping in small circles as another mermaid surfaced and dove back under. Seeing their graceful glides, watching them frolic with such ease, Esther couldn't help but smile.

The lights from the houses, set farther away from the lake on a hilltop, cast dots of light on the horizon, making her wonder what these people in Tucker's pod were like.

And Esther?

Well, she was terrified, as Marty held her hand and Jessica peered at her with gentle eyes. "Please don't be frightened, Esther. I'll teach you everything I know. You'll be glorious. I promise you. I just need you to trust that I'll be close, and so will Tucker, and if you become afraid, we'll help you."

Chester popped up behind Jessica, his wide chest and boyish good looks even better looking under the moonlight. "I'll help, too," he said with a wide smile.

Marty tucked Esther's hair behind her ear. "This is just a trial run, sweetie. We can bail anytime you want. You don't have to learn everything in one night, right, girls? It took me a long time to learn to be a werewolf. Ask Nina."

Nina nodded, her eyes glittering in the dark. "Holy fuck, if that ain't the truth. There was more whine than a damn vineyard while she learned how to be a werewolf. But I think I got your number, Esther, and I'm pretty sure you're a badass bitch. Now, go do mermaid things like a good girl, so Auntie Nina can go back to the cottage and watch *Stranger Things* and poke holes in their bullshit theories about the paranormal."

Nina shooed her with a hand, but Esther gripped Marty's hand tighter, digging her heels into the sand.

Tucker came to stand in front of her, his warm hands cupping her face as he looked down at her, his eyes soft. "I'll be there the whole way, Esther. I won't let you out of my sight. But you need to know how to do this. The urge will call you, and when it does, you'll need to know how to handle your tail and fins. I can teach you. *We* can teach you. Most importantly, Jessica can teach you. Our tails are designed differently as males and females; she can teach you how to navigate."

She let go of Marty's hand and gripped Tucker's wrists, her next question filled with worry. "Won't you get into trouble for being here? Maybe we should leave and you can teach me another time? You've already been kicked out of your pod. I don't want you to get in more trouble because of me."

Sure, sure, she was stalling about getting in the water. But she wasn't lying about her worry he'd get caught. It was enough that he'd likely be questioned in her uncle's death once she started poking around.

Jessica shed her coat and her shoes as she said, "Don't worry, Esther. I'll make sure no one says anything to him. He's here with me, and they'll just have to like it. Besides, his evacuation from the pod has to be run past a council. My father's not the be all and end all of merpeople." Her face looked cross under the moonlight, convincing Esther if nothing else, she was loyal to Tucker.

Shaking off her sheer terror, she tried so hard to suck it up—she didn't have a choice but to do this. If this urge was going to call to her, she had to know how to handle it correctly.

"Okay," she murmured, giving Tucker's wrists one last squeeze before she, too, shed her jacket and kicked off her sneakers.

Nina drove a playful knuckle into her ribs and smiled at her. "That's my girl. Swim, fishy, swim!"

"But wait. What about..." She circled her breasts with her hands. "The last time I turned into a mermaid, I was sort of naked. Those women out there don't look naked."

Jessica nodded her head and chuckled. "Those are scales covering their breasts. They're soft, almost like satin, though. Once you're in the water long enough, you'll acquire them, too. But I brought you a bikini top, just in case." She grabbed what looked like a beach bag from the sand and dug around until she pulled a hot-pink top out. "We're about the same size, I think."

Yeah. In what fantasy?

Esther nearly laughed out loud. They absolutely were not even close to the same size. Jessica had full, round stripper boobs and Esther had training-bra boobs, but whatever. It was nice of her to compare her so generously. She liked her now even more than she had the first time she'd met her.

Marty held up a colorful beach towel with a whale on it and winked. "Let's get you changed, young lady."

As she stripped down to her bikini undies and shrugged into the bikini top, she shivered, her skin withering beneath the cold night air. "If I get frostbite, Pearson, you pay the hospital bill. Go that?"

Tucker laughed, his deep chuckle husky and sexy in her ears. "Consider that a deal, Sanchez. You ready?" He'd shrugged off his jeans and shirt as though he took his clothes off in front of women everyday.

And if she were honest, he should. If her body looked like his, she'd wander everywhere naked. She'd food shop naked.

God, he was sexy. He had more ridges and ripples on his body than ten bags of Ruffles potato chips. From his wide shoulders and his heavily muscled chest with a sprinkling of hair between his pecs, to his thick thighs and tapered waist, as he stood in front of her in nothing but his red boxer-briefs, she had a harder time not staring at his perfection than she did being in a bikini.

Yes, she jogged. Sure, she tried to watch what she

ate, but in the end, she didn't look like Tucker, who looked like he belonged in *Perfect Body Monthly*.

As Marty stood in front of her, holding up the towel, Esther leaned in and whispered, "I don't want to say I'm intimidated here, but hello. Is it fair I should be undressing in front of Body Beautiful?"

Marty's laughter tinkled in the chilly air and she made a face. "You have an incredible body, Esther. I'd kill to have an ass like yours. You have nothing to be intimidated about. Now, go be a mermaid. We'll be right here when you surface."

Said the beautiful blonde with perfect makeup and sexy curves like a mountain road. But okay. There was nothing she could do about her cellulite now.

Jessica held out her hand to Esther and gave her another reassuring smile, and as she led her to the edge of the water, and Esther violently shivered, all she could do was pray somehow her newfound mermaid-ness would negate her inability to swim.

Or she was gonna swim with the fishes, all right.

Face down.

CHAPTER 12

Nina and Marty sat cross-legged on the beach towel, fist pumping and wolf whistling as Esther began to wade into the water, but she halted when the water hit her waist and froze on the spot as the soft sand beneath her feet squished between her toes.

Tucker turned to her, his lean hips now covered in the water. "Esther?"

And when he looked at her with that question on his face, she became a blubbering idiot.

"Okay, so look. Here's the thing. I can't swim. That's how this all started. Well, no. I stand corrected. It didn't start there. It started at a funeral. I just mean, that's when I found out I was a mermaid. Anyway, when my tail finally decided to show its face…er, fin…I was at a Mommy and Me class taking swimming lessons with babies because I'm a thirty-two-year-old sissy who's afraid of the water. I don't know the first thing about swimming but the little I learned at my first class with Maurizio, which was blowing bubbles. So I'm going to sink like the proverbial rock right in front of you and there's nothing I can do to stop—"

Tucker stopped her by pulling her close to him, their skin meeting for the first time, leaving her fighting a gasp as every nerve in her body caught fire. "I figured as much."

She snorted against his chest. "Really? Was it the masterful way I floundered like the *Titanic* was going down at the beach the other day that gave me away?"

Now *he* snorted, his arm curving around her waist, warming her from head to toe. "Just a hunch," he teased, tilting her chin up so he could see her eyes. "Listen, Esther, I won't let anything happen to you. I promise on my very life, you'll be okay. If anything at all goes wrong, I'll be there."

Jessica, now gloriously slick with water, the beads clinging to her supple skin, nodded her head. "I'll be there, too, Esther. Promise."

Chester, who'd remained quiet and patient, gave her a thumbs-up sign and winked.

She knew she could trust them. It wasn't that at all. It was herself and her reactions to the water since…

But she nodded and smiled at Tucker. "Okay then, let's do this. What do I do first?"

He grinned at her and pointed to the water. "You take my hand and we go under. It's as simple as that. But one thing—don't fight the water. Hold your breath until I tap you on the shoulder, and when I do, I promise you, you'll be able to breathe. Your gills will allow you to breathe. Getting you to accept that is going to take an enormous amount of trust in your part, and I know that. But I need you to believe me. Just believe, Esther.

Yeah, yeah. *Just believe,* she told herself as they waded deeper into the water and she blindly held his hand, feeling like a lamb going to slaughter. Unlike a Disney movie, where the heroine gives the handsome prince her unwavering trust just because he says she should, she felt the exact opposite.

This was bananapants. Like, who in their right mind would believe any of this was real?

But, she reasoned, the girls were here, and they wouldn't let her drown. She knew that without a shadow of a doubt. And they were real. She'd seen they were real. She'd seen her tail was real, for crap's sake. Still, she wished she'd worked out some kind of SOS with them as a just in case.

A million thoughts ran through her mind at that point, but before she knew it, the lights of the houses above the lake were fading and she was under the water, forcing herself to think of nothing but the task at hand.

Be a mermaid.

And then stark panic set in and she did exactly what Tucker said not to do. She fought the notion that she would eventually breathe through her gills and she began to struggle, her limbs twisting, her chest so tight she thought it would burst.

But then Tucker was there, pulling her toward him with a strong hand as Jessica's voice vibrated in her head, soothing and clear as a bell.

"Open your eyes, Esther. Look and see what's around you. It's beautiful. Open your eyes."

When Tucker tapped her on the shoulder, she forced her eyes open—and all at once, the panic fled, seeping from her body as she stood on the bottom of this lake that had been turned into a watery paradise.

It was incredible, breathtaking, utterly magnificent, and as she looked around, clinging to Tucker's hand, she took it all in.

The water was crystal clear, turquoise and green, just like the beaches she'd seen so many times on television. Small castles, almost like the ones you'd see in a fish tank, sprang up in the distance, their candy-colored peaks and arched windows serving as portals for the mermaids to swim in and out of, frolicking with one another as though they were at some sort of mermaid version of an ice cream social.

Seashells and conchs the size of living room furniture sat along the bottom, scattered about like one would chairs arranged in the lobby of a hotel. Coral reefs crafted in bright pink, green, orange and blue cropped up in the corner of her eye as Tucker pulled her to him and swirled her around. There was even a small sunken ship in all its wooden glory, where merchildren chased each other from one end to the other, the tattered sails wafting with the water's movement.

Fish in every color of the rainbow and every variety swam by in schools, their fins gracefully swatting the water, propelling themselves forward, and this time she heard Tucker in her head.

"Look, Esther. Look down," he said, pointing to the sandy bottom of the lake with a grin.

Esther did as she was told and, without any warning, and no tingle to suggest otherwise, her limbs were gone and her yellow and aqua tail was suddenly there, resplendent as the water washed over them. It glimmered against the backdrop of the water, fascinating her.

Instantly, her hands went to her breasts to cover them, but as promised by Jessica, her bikini top had been replaced by scales, and just like Jessica said, when she skimmed her hands over them, they were as soft as silk.

And then she realized something else—her chest was no longer tight. Her lungs didn't feel as though they were going to explode.

She was breathing through her gills, just like Tucker said.

She experienced a moment of pride—a deep sense of satisfaction that she wasn't freaking out, but listening and following directions, trusting her body.

"You're beautiful!" Jessica whispered. *"Now, listen to me. Your tail can be used for many things, Esther. Not just for swimming. But let's learn the basics for now. At first, this*

will feel cumbersome, heavy, but once you learn how to maneuver, you'll be magnificent and you'll swim faster than any dolphin. Watch me and do what I do."

Jessica's tail and fins were as beautiful as she was, in gold and deep hues of pink and crimson, and as she shot out in front of them, her hair making an auburn cloud around her gorgeous face, there was still a surreal feel to all of this.

So, Esther blinked. This was really happening.

She was really underwater, in a lake, with a hot merdude from Australia and his sister, learning how to be a mermaid.

But she didn't have time to ponder for long, as Jessica, with Chester by her side, summoned her, holding her hands out and beckoning Esther to take them. But she didn't know how to get lift off. Using her fins to propel her upward wasn't like using her feet.

A small thread of panic threatened to wend its way through her, but Tucker swam under her and gave her a nudge with his head, propelling her upward and forward until she was in front of Jessica. Reaching out, she grabbed Jessica's hand, clinging to it for all she was worth.

Chester swam past her, his stunning tail in green and gold swishing, his muscles bulging and flexing.

"Roll, Esther. Follow Chester, and roll your torso like me."

As Jessica dragged her forward, Esther watched, attempting to mimic the grace with which Tuck's sister glided through the water, her body rocking with the flow of the waves, but she rather felt like one of those memes on Facebook.

This is what you think you look like when you're trying to be a mermaid—sexy, seductive, capable. But this is what you *really* look like—awkward, lumbering, half woman, half fish, plodding through the water with a ton o' hair in your eyes like some big clumsy manatee.

Tucker grabbed her tail and began to move it up and down, almost like the heavy rope she used at the gym for strengthening her arms.

And suddenly, it clicked.

She got it...she felt it...she was living it.

With a shot forward, she lost hold of Jessica's hand as she forced herself to adopt the motion Tucker had used. The harder she rocked her tail, the faster she went, until everything became a blur of motion she didn't know how to stop.

Where were the brakes on this damn tail?

"Hey, mermaid! Wait for me!" Tucker shouted in her head, followed by a hearty laugh.

He swam up beside her, grabbing her hand to slow her until they were side by side—and that was the moment she got a true look at him in merman form.

She hadn't even imagined what a merman looked like, but she should have known, even Tucker could make some shiny scales and a tail look rugged and edgy.

His scales were sapphire blue and faded to iridescent silver, his tail long, wide, and gleaming under the water like a beacon of light. The scales around his wrists matched his tail, but the most amazing sight of all were his fins. They were enormous, deep purple blending into black, gracefully swatting at the water as he swam next to her.

And okay, his chest, covered in muscles, wasn't exactly a blight on the entire package either, but whatever. Now, her focus had to be on swimming like a mermaid, not a sexy merman.

That's when it hit her.

She was swimming—for the first time since she was a child, she was swimming. And in a silent, mindful moment, she hoped her dad and her grandfather could somehow see she was giving this her all.

Esther let Tucker lead her, the water zooming past them, making bubbles with their speed. He pulled up short near what looked like a series of caves that left her wondering exactly how deep this manmade lake went.

Diving down toward the mouth of the cave, he pulled her with him until they were inside the craggy walls, the dull sounds of the water clearing as he pulled her to what, as she looked upward, looked like a sparkling-wet ledge made of rock. He surfaced and hoisted himself up, his muscles gleaming and slick with the beads of water, then put his hands back in the water at her waist and pulled her up to sit next to him.

The moment she rose above the surface, she gasped for breath. It happened automatically, making her frown. She gave him a confused look as she took in the small, almost cove-like setting, where warm water bubbled in a small turquoise pool to their left and the air was temperate enough that she didn't feel cold.

She spread her arms wide. "How is this possible?"

"The cave's like an air pocket. I figured you're not quite ready to graduate to learning our ways of underwater communication, and I wanted to check and be sure you're faring well."

She almost didn't know what to say. The experience had left her almost speechless. "I... I'm not...sure... I don't know if I can articulate it. It's amazing. I can't believe I'm actually swimming in a big fish tank for adults. It's..."

He drove his hands through his hair, slicking it back, revealing his rugged features. "Crazy, right? I know this all seems unreal, but you're taking it like a champ, Esther. I'm really impressed."

She shouldn't be so giddy that he was impressed, and she did all she could to tamp down her excitement, but she *was* giddy—stupidly so. Looking down at her fins, swishing with the movement of the water, she muttered, "Thank you. It hasn't caught up with me yet, I think. It's like I'm wandering around in some fairytale. How can this have existed without anyone ever knowing?"

He chuckled. "We're very careful, that's how. We have to be. To everyone on the outside, it looks like we're a highly sought-after gated community that no one can get into without homeowner-association approval. We've cultivated that notion since the beginning."

She cocked her head, wiping residual water from her eyes. "But you chose not to live here. Why?"

"Because I don't have a family that can fill a four-bedroom house. I don't need that kind of room. I have two cats and me. An apartment suits me just fine."

It was interesting to learn something private about him. "You have cats?"

He chucked her playfully under the chin. "You make it sound as though a monster like me couldn't possibly have pets," he teased on a chuckle, his chest rising with the effort.

She poked him in the ribs with a light nudge. "I said no such thing. I'm just surprised a big, rough merman like you has pets."

"Aye. I do. I told you that already. Freckle and Fran have me wrapped around their paws—both rescues, and the *real* monsters in this story."

Twisting her body toward him, she gave him a thoughtful glance. "So, no girlfriend, no wife, just you and a couple of cats?"

"So, no boyfriend, no husband, just you and a cat and a dog?"

Esther laughed out loud, the sound pinging the walls of the cave. "Yep. And a cottage I love. Some good friends I see a couple of times a week if my schedule's not too packed, and that's pretty much all there is to Esther Williams Sanchez."

"I think there's a lot more. For instance, you're a

divorce mediator? Any reason you chose a profession that has two people duking it out over linen napkins?"

Esther grinned at him. "To be honest, I used to mediate all sorts of things. But divorces are where the money's at because there are so many of them. Far more than corporate mediations."

He patted the place on his chest where his heart beat and mocked a frown. "That's so damn depressing. I'd think you'd agree, coming from a family as close as yours."

"Ah, well, my parents—my grandparents were rarities in a sea of overwhelming stats in favor of divorce. Marriage doesn't mean what it used to anymore. There are all manner of loopholes nowadays."

His eyebrow rose. "Loopholes? Meaning?"

"Meaning, the 'I wasn't cheating on you. I was just having an *emotional* affair online with some woman in Tucson. Never touched her,' theory. Or the ever popular, 'We're just friends, and friends share dick pics all the time, don't they?' Then there's 'We've just grown apart. We have nothing to talk about anymore.' Yet, somehow, the cheater is always able to find plenty to talk about with his sexy secretary. And don't think I'm gender biased. Women do it, too. Also, it's too damned easy to get a divorce these days. It's the answer to anyone who doesn't want to do the work, see a therapist, find a solution. I see it everyday, and it's so ugly that by the time they get to me, by the time they need an intervention with someone like me, they hate the sight of one another, and they're willing to pay good money to just find a resolution so it can all be over."

She shook her head, unclenching her fists and stopped her rant, giving him a sheepish glance. "Sorry. I get a little preachy when it comes to something I've never even done, don't I?"

His laughter was light and soft. "No. I agree with everything you said. Total commitment. I don't always love the way my father handles things, but he and my mother are devoted to one another. They're as crazy in love as they always were, and he dotes on her. Believe me, my parents have been married for centuries—"

"*Centuries?*" she almost shrieked, startling a school of puffy fish weaving in and out of the cave.

He wrinkled his nose. "Right. I forgot to mention. We're immortal," he responded, as if living forever were the new normal.

Esther held up her hands in shock. "Whoa. Gimme a sec to absorb. You mean, I'll never die? That's what that means, right? Like *forever*-forever?"

He winced, his handsome face going apprehensive. "Yes?"

"And how old are you?"

"Old?"

Esther couldn't help but giggle and give him a playful shove. "But I thought you were in your thirties?"

"Well, with the age of the Internet, that's what we put out there. Immortality aside, I feel the same way you do. There are too many distractions these days. No one makes a promise and keeps it—which is why I've never married. But when I do, when I fall in love, it'll literally be for an eternity."

His words hummed in her ears, followed by a Celine Dion song about falling in love forever. She shook her head, jamming a finger in her ear to rid herself of the earworm. "Interesting."

His face went all disbelief and shock. "That's all you have to say to a guy with old-fashioned values?"

She patted him on the back, gulping at the warmth of his skin stretched tightly over all that muscle. "That's nice."

And it was. Very nice. But likely as empty as all the promises people made to one another before it all goes sideways. Finding out she was going to live forever could make "I'm never getting married" a real-life challenge. Yet, she found herself wanting to believe Tucker. Wanting to believe that there were still men out there like her father and her grandfather.

Maybe it was just because he was so good-looking, and he could have any woman he wanted at any time, that she struggled to believe he'd live for eternity with just one woman. Especially seeing as he apparently didn't age.

Which meant she didn't either. Gah! This portion of being a mermaid was all too much right now. Too much information to process. It would have to wait until she sorted everything else out.

Grabbing her hand, Tucker stared into her eyes,

concern riddling his. "Hey, let's talk about something more serious."

"More serious than living for an eternity and a centuries-old marriage? What else ya got up your tail, Pearson? Oh my God—can I fly? Do I have X-ray vision? Will I see dead people?"

Tucker laughed and shook his head, but then his eyes grew somber. "When will you be ready to tell me about your fear of water?"

Pushing the hair from her eyes, Esther looked down at the water, blue as a cloudless summer day, and bit her lip. "I'm not—"

"Tucker!"

Someone roared his name so loud, it bounced off the cave's walls and echoed throughout the cavern.

"Father, no! Let him be!" Esther heard Jessica plead from a muffled distance.

The water in the cave swelled then, rushing up over her tail and splashing her in the face as the single most intimidating hulk of a man blew into the small space, his flowing white hair streaming behind his bulky body.

"*Who is this?*" the man shouted as he rose up out of the water and filled the cave like some whirling dervish to confront Tucker, his broad chest expanding as he huffed the question.

But Tucker, who looked suspiciously like the new merman, didn't back down at all. In fact, he sat taller and puffed his chest out, too. And then he grinned wide, purposefully, almost in direct opposition to this man's ire.

"Father. As always, I'm as giddy as Great-Aunt Gilda to see you."

Ooo, shit. Tucker's father—that meant they were in trouble. And she'd like to avoid trouble with this guy because he wasn't just big, he was scary. Maybe scarier than Nina, with his handsomely lined face, light blue eyes, long white beard, and daunting expression.

"*Who. Is. This?*" he bellowed again, his breath so strong, so fierce, he almost blew Esther's hair dry.

Tucker, totally unaffected but for the clench of his jaw, very calmly said, "This is Esther, Father. I turned her into a mermaid. Quite by accident, of course, but nonetheless, she's a mermaid."

She didn't like the tone Tucker used when he spoke. It sounded a lot like a neener, neener, neener. Sort of like, "Hey, Dad. This is my meth-head friend, Esther, and we're going to make crack together. Cool, right?"

Esther's finger shot up before anyone could say anything else, the mediator in her instantly aware and standing at attention. "Mr. Pearson!" she shouted without meaning to, then lowered her voice. "My name is Esther Williams Sanchez, and this was all an accident I can explain, if you'll be kind enough to let me."

But Tucker's father clearly wasn't in the mood for pleasantries. In fact, he scowled with such ferocity, Esther literally fought a violent shiver.

"*Sanchez?*" he repeated none too quietly.

Oh, damn, damn, damn. She'd forgotten all about the H2O-Yo business. But Daddy Dearest had not.

Jessica rushed in then, her face a mask of worry as she looked at Tucker and Esther, an apology in her eyes. Putting a hand on her father's arm, she tugged, her face angry. "Father! Please! Stop bellowing. You're disturbing everyone and frightening Esther!"

Mr. Pearson saw red at his daughter's warning, his light blue eyes swimming with outrage. "Don't you tell me what to do, young lady! Did you allow this? Did you let him bring this woman here? To our pod?"

Tucker slipped off the ledge, cool as a cucumber, taking Esther's hand as he did and pulling her back into the water. "Jessica had no idea I was coming here tonight, Father, and now, it's late and we have to go. Good night," he said, before he dove into the water, dragging her with him and propelling them out of the cave.

As he held her hand in a tight grip, a swell of water pushed at her tail, forcing her body to jerk, making her lose Tucker's hand.

In that moment, when she should have relied on her tail to help, she floundered, and then the water turned murky as something stirred the sand up from the bottom of the lake. Esther twisted around helplessly, trying to remember to roll her upper body, but her control was gone, and her tail began to feel like it had before—less like a part of her, more like an anchor.

And suddenly, she was sinking as fast as if she had concrete blocks on her feet. She couldn't breathe and she couldn't get liftoff. All she could hear was the muted sound of someone howling, the thunderous roar sending her into a frantic panic. She couldn't see Tucker anymore for the haze of swirling sand, and her fight to keep from sinking to the floor of the lake was lost.

While she sank, she remembered she'd sunk like this once before. Frozen as surely as if someone had tied her hands and legs and dropped her to the bottom of the ocean like a sack of rocks.

Fear gripped her so tight, so hard, she flailed, angry with herself. Yet, those visions of when she was just a child, alone, afraid, assaulted her mind's eye, playing in her head like a movie in repeat.

"Esther!" someone yelled with urgency, but she couldn't move for the weight of her tail. No matter how hard she tried, her big ass wouldn't get off the damned floor of the lake.

And that was when a pair of hands reached around her throat and gripped—gripped hard.

Her heart crashed as she struggled, her hair swirling around her face, preventing her from seeing anything. And just as she was about to reach up and pull the hands away, they were gone.

But then more hands grabbed at her, different hands, bigger hands, reassuring hands, and, without pause, she was thrust upward and rushing to the surface. Just when she thought her lungs would burst, she felt cold air on her face, the chilly sting of a fall night clashed with her wet body.

There was splashing and commotion, and then she heard Nina yell, "Little Fish!" as she was scooped up by the strong vampire and carried to the shore, where she placed her on a blanket, pushing the longs strands of Esther's hair from her face. Cupping her cheeks with both cold hands, Nina stared down at her, coal eyes frantic. "What the fuck, kiddo?"

As she fought for breath, Marty lunged at them, throwing a towel around Esther as her teeth chattered and she shivered violently. "Sweetie!" Marty cried, hauling her upward to smack her back. "Cough, Esther, cough it up!"

Esther sputtered and coughed as she was told, water flying from her mouth while she wheezed for air, clinging to Nina's wrists.

While she was trying to catch her breath, there was more commotion coming from the water in the way of more loud splashes and voices, rising up in the air, frenzied and frightened.

"Back the fuck up, you vultures!" Nina shouted angrily, her eyes and fangs flashing in sync when a crowd of surprised people began to gather around Esther. "Tucker? Where the fuck are you?"

"And *who* are you?" Tucker's father asked, staring down at them, his barrel chest rising and falling as someone handed him a towel to wrap around his waist.

Nina unceremoniously handed her off to Marty and was up on her feet in a shot. "I'm the bitch who's gonna fuck you up, that's who I am! So how do ya like your shit fucked up? Over easy or scrambled?" she shouted in his face, actually making him pause as they eyeballed each other, their nostrils flaring.

Well, that is, until Tucker's father snapped his fingers and a wall of sparkling water rose up from the lake in slow motion, and just as slowly smashed down over their heads.

CHAPTER 13

"Father!" she heard Tucker bellow. *"Knock it off!"*

Esther, who still had her tail and fins, slammed down against the hard ground when the water hit her full force, knocking the breath from her lungs. She wheezed as she tried to get ahold of anything to give her leverage to sit up, but failed miserably.

"Esther!" She vaguely saw Tucker scramble toward her, his arms reaching out to scoop her up and sit her upright. But from the corner of her eye, she realized she didn't need his help as much as Nina would.

"Get the vampire," she wheezed to him, as she watched helplessly while Nina stormed toward Tucker's father and shook her head, her long hair spewing droplets of water everywhere, her eyes seething with rage.

"Is that the best you got?" Nina hollered, scaring everyone who'd gathered as she rushed Tucker's father and jammed her face up toward his. "C'mon, you fishy fuck! Let's go!"

Giving her over to Marty, Tucker ran to prevent an argument that she supposed would be epic if it got out of hand.

"Nina!" he yelled, putting himself between the vampire and his irate father. "Stop! Both of you stop!"

But Tucker's father wasn't of a mind to listen. As displayed when he howled, "How dare you bring these people here and expose us, Tucker! Have you lost your bloody mind? How dare you come here after I've banished you! Get off my land—take these miscreant ground people, and *get off my land*!"

"Getty Pearson!" a female voice shouted from the lake. "What are you doing out here, carrying on like some unleashed animal? I won't have this in my home, you beast!"

Everyone's eyes turned to the lake, where a beautiful woman, her long golden hair spilling around her shoulders and down into the water, trudged forward as someone ran to her with a towel and wrapped it around her. Moonlight shone down on her perfectly sculpted face, her cheekbones high, her lips full, her alabaster skin unlined.

Tucker was the first to react as he turned around and nodded curtly. "Mother," he acknowledged.

So, this was Tucker's mother? God. Why was everyone so pretty? She didn't look like she could be anyone's mother, let alone someone as old as Jessica or Tucker.

As she strode to stand where Nina, Getty and Tucker faced off, she did so regally, ignoring the stares and gaping open mouths of the other merpeople until she approached her husband.

Delicate hands on slender hips, she gazed up at her husband with angry eyes. "What are you out here screeching about, Getty? Honestly, why must you communicate as though you were raised by Neanderthals?"

Getty—strong, proud, very, very loud—blustered then waffled, his wide chest deflating when his wife cocked an eyebrow at him and waited for an answer. "You know why, Serafina," he offered quietly. "Yet, I'll say it again for posterity. Money is missing from our company. Some of it accounted for and found in *Tucker's* accounts, some of it not accounted for and still missing. And not some small amount, wife. Over a million dollars. I want to know where the money is. The money that feeds our pod, the money that belongs in pod members' 401Ks—not in Tucker's pocket. Until such time, he's banished from the pod. And again, I'll say, you *know* this. You know why I had no choice but to take such swift action."

Wait. There was *more* money missing? Beyond what they'd found in Tucker's accounts? Had she heard that right? Oh, hell on wheels, this just kept getting worse.

But Serafina wasn't to be thwarted, her freakishly deep purple eyes flashing. "I most certainly do not! All of this—all of it is foolishness, Getty, and *you* know it. There's no one more trustworthy than your own son!

But if you must be such a dolt, I won't have you out here screaming like some animal in pain and frightening everyone who wishes to enjoy the light of the moon because of your stupidity! Do you understand me? I will not allow you to tear my family apart because you won't trust his word!"

As Getty attempted to gather his manhood, Tucker stepped in and wrapped an arm around his mother's slender shoulders, his face pleading and soft. "Mum, please don't fight on my behalf. Father chose this path. It is what it is. Let it be for now. Don't interfere. *Please.*"

She stood on tiptoe and kissed Tucker's cheek, inhaling deeply. "Who are your friends, son? Why have you brought them here? Are you all right?"

Tucker gave his mother a quick hug and set her from him. "I'm sorry we came and disrupted you and your nightly swim. My friends are here because they're helping me, and it's a long story. For now, I'm asking you to let this be, and we'll go. I'll call you in the morning, okay?"

Her beautiful face fell—until she caught sight of Esther, lying cold and wet on the ground, watching all this play out but afraid to move. "Is this...?"

Jessica appeared from behind the crowd, Chester's hand in hers, pushing her way through the people until she reached Tucker, her eyes full of guilt. "She knows, Tuck. I told her about Esther because she was so worried. She hadn't heard from you, and..."

But Serafina wasn't paying attention to anyone, her eyes zeroed in on Esther. "Oh, you're beautiful!" she declared, crouching and holding out her hand for Esther to take. "I know the circumstances are outlandish, but I'm so pleased to meet you, Esther. I hope we'll be able to have coffee and get to know one another soon? Please say yes."

"You will do no such thing!" Getty thundered.

But Serafina patted her on the shoulder then rose, her eyes wild, her hands on her slim hips. "I will do exactly that and more, you big ape! I might even have them over for dinner. What do you think about that, loud mouth?" she yelled, rounding on her husband. "And another thing—if you don't end this foolishness soon, you'll be sleeping *alone* for eternity!" With those words, she turned apologetic eyes to Esther before glaring at her husband and pointing a finger to the lake with a stern face. "Go home, Getty. *Now*!"

Nina smirked at Getty, crossing her arms over her chest, but thankfully she didn't rub it in his face with words.

As Tucker's father stomped back to the lake and dove in, making a loud splash, Serafina gripped Tucker's hand and held it against her cheek. "I'm sorry, Tucker. My apologies to all of you for his atrocious behavior," she whispered to the group before she followed her husband, her shoulders slumped.

Silence fell over the crowd, despite their curious eyes, but Jessica intervened by shooing them away. "Nothing to see here, folks. Go back to your swim, please," she ordered, pointing to the water before she turned to Tucker. "I don't know how he found out,

Tuck. He never swims at night anymore. He's been such a bear since this whole thing went down…"

Grabbing his towel, Tucker gave his sister a quick hug. "It's okay. We'll get through it. We have some ideas. But for now, we have to go. I need to get Esther home. I think she's had enough mermaiding for one night, don't you?"

Jessica squatted down next to Esther and sighed sadly. "I'm sorry you met my family this way. I swear, we're not all heathens. Just my father, and usually he pretends to be nice enough around strangers, if not gruff. Can you forgive me for outing you? I had to tell my mother. She was so upset as it was. I'm sorry."

Esther reached out and squeezed her hand, still shivering so much her teeth were chattering, and she wasn't sure if it was from the fear of Tucker's father or the cold. "It's fine. Family drama happens. Thanks for your help tonight. It was awesome while it lasted."

Jessica rose, blowing Tucker a kiss before she headed back into the water without another word, diving into the dark depths and disappearing.

Looking up at Nina, who stood beside her like a guard dog, she said, "Vampire? At ease, huh? It's over. No harm, no foul."

"I shoulda kicked his scaly, loud, overbearing ass," she muttered, her eyes narrowing as she rolled her shoulders and cracked her knuckles, still posturing.

But Esther tugged at her wet pant leg. "There, there, Dark One. Let it go. We have bigger fish to fry," she said, then laughed at her own joke. "Get it? Bigger fish to fry?"

Nina knelt down and covered her with another towel, scowling while Marty rubbed her tail. "I get it, Lucille Ball Fish. Now shut it."

Esther tweaked the vampire's cheek and giggled, then she looked to Tucker, who'd begun to help Marty dry her tail, too. "Hey, merman. You okay?"

"He's a loud son of a bitch, isn't he?"

Esther nodded, trying to relax enough to make her tail disappear and her legs return. "My ears are still ringing. But it's okay. He's under a lot of stress right now. Some people display that stress by yelling…and in your father's case, creating a tidal wave. Oh my God, he made a tidal wave! Can I do that, too? No, forget it. This isn't about me. We're talking about you. Anyway, it's just water, right?"

Tucker grimaced, unconvinced, the lines above his eyes deepening. "I'm sorry, Esther. He behaved so poorly. I'd have at least expected him to have some decorum around strangers."

She cleared her throat before she reminded him of something. "Well, let's be fair here, Pearson. You did introduce me in an in-your-face fashion."

Tucker smirked, but he didn't stop rubbing her tail, continuing to warm her. "I did not. I was simply stating a fact. It's true. I did turn you into a mermaid, didn't I?"

Esther snorted, her sarcasm clear. "Oh, sure, you were simply stating a fact, Tucker. 'Hey, Daddy-O. Are you good and angry yet? Because I've got some icing for your cake made of ire. Meet the chick I turned into a mermaid. Neener, neener, neener.' You all but waved my tail under his nose, Tucker. And don't get me wrong, I understand the need to strike out. You're angry and hurt that your father didn't take your side in this mess—despite irrefutable proof on *his* side—because that's what father's do, and that makes your rebellious streak get flaunty. Like I said, we all handle stress in different ways."

"Flaunty, eh?" he asked on a chuckle, still rubbing vigorously.

Leaning back on her elbows, Esther nodded, her head not quite as heavy as her hair began to dry. "Yes, flaunty. Either way. I get it. But you can't blame him for all of it. You have to own some of your part in this. One doesn't make things better when they get mouthy and showboaty."

Stopping, Tucker looked up at her from where he sat at her feet and smiled in the dark. "I can see why you're a mediator by profession. Now, look at your feet and behold the magic of relaxing."

Never, for as long as she lived—and apparently that was forever—would she ever get over how her feet disappeared and reappeared with no warning at all. Wiggling her toes, Esther grinned back at him. "Perfect. Now, let's go back to the cottage and plot ways to get you back into this pod where you belong."

As Tucker helped her up, their chests met and connected, and all those lovely things he'd said back in the cave before his father had shot in there like a torpedo came back to her, while her girlie bits burned lava-like flames of lust and longing.

But Marty nipped that in the bud when she put a hand on each of their shoulders, her hair soaked, her clothes, too, and said, "How about we save the mating dance for a time when Marty doesn't have a big fat headache?"

Esther hissed her disapproval of yet another headache, and she said as much. "Another Spanx headache? Maybe you should just let your freak flag fly and quit wearing them altogether?"

But Marty shook a finger at her. "Nuh-uh-uh. Don't you try to mediate me out of my Spanx. That'll never happen," she said on a chuckle. "Now move it. To the car, fishes! We have a big day tomorrow if we hope to crack this case of the tainted water."

Yes. Tomorrow they'd go to Tecton and speak to her uncle's co-workers, or maybe even a friend or two. At least, she hoped he had a friend or two.

Either way, it was time to find some answers.

Because who wouldn't want the chance to rejoin this pod with a man who yelled at the top of his lungs and had the ability to create a hurricane?

~

Esther looked up at the big glass and steel building with large block letters spelling Tecton Inc. and sighed when she looked to Tucker, cupping her hand over her eyes to block out the sun.

Last night, she'd gone home and literally passed out from exhaustion. Being a mermaid was work. Being around Tucker's father was no small task, either.

He'd made it clear she was unwanted, but she wasn't sure what that meant. Did it mean she was forever doomed to swim the endless depths of the ocean alone with no pod of her own? Which sounded ridiculously dramatic, but could be the case if Getty decided she had no business being a part of his group. But did she *need* a group? Did she need other mermaids to survive?

Not technically, but it might be nice to have someone to relate to. Sort of like when you went to an AA meeting for support or a critical disease support group. Everyone in the group could relate to the way you had to live your life.

And had that been Tucker's hands grabbing at her neck last night in an effort to save her? They'd felt different, but it had all been so chaotic that, now, in the clear light of day, she couldn't be sure.

But those questions hadn't haunted her until this morning as she'd grabbed a quick shower—where she thankfully did not sprout a tail and fins—threw on some makeup, pulled her hair into a neat bun, covered it with a scarf, and put on her most professional work suit.

All while she'd applied her makeup and dried her hair, she'd pondered what last night had meant for her. If they figured out someone had killed Gomez, and Tucker was exonerated of any wrongdoing, where did that leave her?

And then she chastised herself for being so selfish. This was about Tucker and her uncle, and the possibility Gomez hadn't left this world of his own volition.

Yet, now that they stood in front of the imposing headquarters of Tecton, her stomach empty save for a cup of coffee, dark glasses and scarf on to hide her identity, she became nervous. What if they were talking murder here?

As the cool morning air swished his hair around his ruggedly handsome face, Tucker gazed down at her as he tipped his dark sunglasses forward, his hazel eyes almost green today because of the color of his crewneck sweater. "Esther? You okay? If you're not ready to do this, we can forget it. I'll find another way to get information. I don't want you involved in anything you're uncomfortable with."

Smoothing her scarf around her face, she almost laughed. "You're a real noble guy, aren't you?" she teased.

He rocked back on his heels and clucked his tongue. "The noblest."

"So, how long do you suppose we can last in there before people realize who you are?" They'd both put on dark glasses and attempted to at least cover their faces, but it might not be enough.

"Or you, for that matter," he reminded, pushing his glasses back on his nose. "You were in the article, too. Which is why I'm against this, Esther. I'm worried for your safety."

"Are you saying you don't think I can handle myself

with a bunch of science nerds? You suppose they've brushed up on their ninja skills between studying quantum physics and the theory of relativity?"

"I don't mean I think they're going to beat you up. That would never happen as long as I'm here. I'm worried that if someone in there hurt Gomez, and you're fishing around for some answers beyond suicide, they'll hurt you, too."

Clucking her tongue, she shook her head. "We don't have a lot of choices. I'm his niece. His only living relative. If they're handing out information like Halloween candy, I'm pretty sure I'm the one they'll give the Snickers bar to."

His sigh rasped from his lips—lips she couldn't stop thinking about since she'd kissed him. "You have a point."

"Wait," she said, gripping his arm briefly. "I've been meaning to ask you about this money that's missing, according to your father. I remember you saying some of it showed up in your accounts, but what about the rest of it?"

Tucker's eyes narrowed. "You mean the one-point-five-million dollars that someone stole and no one can find?"

"Yeah, that," she said, her tone dry.

"Someone stole it, Esther," he said, deadpan, shifting his glasses to glare down at her.

She rolled her eyes and nudged his arm. "I know that, but why didn't you mention it before—or at all? You just said money turned up in your account."

Rolling his head on his neck, he grimaced. "I didn't really matter at that point. Money gone is money gone, no matter the amount. I'm still being accused of doing something greedy and detestable."

She peered up at him and narrowed one eye against the sun penetrating her sunglasses. "You know, if I didn't believe you, I'd wonder why you didn't tell me."

He ran a finger down her nose and smiled. "Then it's good you believe me."

"Here's something to chew on. Does your father think you'd have the balls to show up at the lake after allegedly doing something so horrible? That's audacity, and as far as I'm concerned, maybe even preposterous. Why wouldn't you just take off with the money and go join another, less troublesome pod?"

Tucker ran his hand over his jaw and stared off down the quiet sidewalk. "You know, in a way, I almost understand what my father is doing. All the evidence points to me. He's letting everyone in the pod know even his own son can't steal from us."

She thought about that for a minute and decided, sure. That was fair. But why spend years proving yourself if you can't at least expect a modicum of trust in return when things go awry?

"Okay, fair enough. Your father's in a shitty position, but in this instance, I'm on your side. Yes, the evidence points to you, but he's known you for however many ridiculous years you've been alive. He ought to know you better."

He shook his head in disbelief. "I can't believe I'm

saying this, but things got very ugly at H2O-Yo, very fast. Word spread like wildfire after the police showed up. Many in the pod were waiting for my father to take action, and he did, and while it makes me as angry as I've ever been that I was someone's scapegoat, he did me a favor, because all those hushed whispers and angry faces looking at me around the H2O-Yo cooler weren't a pleasant way to spend my workday."

She reached out a hand and grazed his arm. "I'm sorry, Tucker. But that's why we have to do this. Redemption and all, and I'd like to do it before the police start asking you questions. I keep looking over my shoulder, thinking they're going to pop out at us around every corner and take you into custody. Especially after the news broke that it was supposed to have been *you* who approved those tests."

His face went hard under the morning sun and his fist clenched. "I could kill whoever the leak is."

Esther pointed to the big revolving glass door. "Well, we're not going to get any answers killing anyone or standing out here. So, let's get 'er done. Are you ready?"

Tucker put a hand to her waist and nodded. "As I'll ever be, I suppose."

With yet another excuse to touch him, she patted him on the arm. "This is the easy part. My uncle was a respected member of this company. There's no reason why his co-workers shouldn't want to talk to me."

"And if they don't?"

Esther made a face at him as though the answer

were obvious. "Duh. I'll cry, of course. Big, ugly, snotty tears. Obviously, you've borne witness to my acting skills when we tried to get into my uncle's apartment. How can you doubt I'll get us in there?"

Tucker's shoulders shook as he chuckled. "Ah, yes. Your thespian efforts surpass even that of an Academy Award winner. How could I have doubted?"

She held her fist up to him, knuckles facing forward, and smiled. "Wonder Twin powers, activate."

He withheld his fist and frowned. "Who twins?"

"Forget it. How's teamwork makes the dream work?"

He bumped her knuckles with his, lifting his glasses to wink a sexy eye. "*That* I get. Now, scoot. We need to find Armand first, and maybe he can help us to find other people Gomez connected with."

Without another word, she strode through the shiny revolving glass doors of Tecton and crossed the equally shiny marble floor to approach the blonde behind the sleek white and black desk.

She sat prettily in front of the Tecton logo, a computer before her, Bluetooth in her ear, her red dress formfitting, accentuating her teeny-tiny waist.

Esther immediately smiled at her with as much warmth as she could muster, despite the fact that Tecton gave her a cold, sterile vibe, and tucked her scarf tighter around her nape. "Hello, I'm Esther Sanchez," she said, emphasizing her last name. "I'd like to see Armand Mendes. He was my uncle Gomez Sanchez's lab assistant."

The pretty blonde with the high ponytail and even higher cheekbones pursed her raspberry-colored lips and frowned. "You can't see him."

She had to remind herself to stay calm and not start demanding things. All good mediation began with compromise. "Any particular reason why?"

The receptionist tapped a nail on the marble counter in front of her, pressing her other hand to the Bluetooth earpiece. "You can't see him because he no longer works here."

CHAPTER 14

"Say again?" Tucker responded, leaning his arms on the shiny marble counter, taking off his glasses to stare into the receptionist's eyes.

Her green, thickly fringed eyes went sultry as she smiled coyly at Tucker. "I said, Armand Mendes no longer works here. He quit last week. Oh, and I looove your accent. Very sexy."

Esther and Tucker looked at each other for a moment, their silence awkward and confused. Why would her uncle's assistant quit a perfectly good job? "Are you sure he quit?"

"I watched him leave right through that door with a box of his things from his office, and the word around here was he quit. Said he couldn't work for anyone but Gomez," she assured them while she kept a close eye on Tucker.

Esther was flabbergasted, but she rebounded quickly, tucking her purse under her arm. "Did he leave a forwarding address? Some way to get in touch with him?"

She held up a finger as she took a call, stretching her sleek arms, indicating they should wait.

Tucker looked at Esther in confusion. "I think a man leaving his livelihood because his boss died is a little much, don't you?"

"Well, judging from what I've learned about my uncle and his social skills, I'd say it was an extreme reaction. I mean, there's loyal and then there's loyal, and my uncle didn't seem like the kind of man who inspired attachment or sentiment. But what do I know? Maybe he was different with his colleagues."

But Tucker didn't say anything, instead, she watched the wheels in his head turn as he processed Armand's departure.

Then she leaned into him, and whispered, "Hey, do you think they'd let us see my uncle's office?"

"I'm afraid that's not possible, Miss Sanchez," someone from behind them said.

Both she and Tucker looked at one another as they were approached by a smart-looking forty-something-year-old man in a Brooks Brothers suit and horn-rimmed glasses.

Aha. She knew what was going on here. "Receptionist Barbie snitched!" Esther whispered to Tucker, hitching her thumb over her shoulder at the pretty woman. "You lay low behind a palm tree over there by the window, and I'll handle this." Sticking out her hand, she directed it at the man as Tucker escaped behind a potted plant to avoid being recognized. "And you are?"

He took her hand and smiled tightly, his penetrating eyes never leaving her face. "Campbell Richter, Director of Human Resources."

"And why can't I see my uncle's office?"

He continued to smile, the light coming from the long glass windows highlighting his hair, graying at the temples. "Because it's been cleaned out and is currently in use by another. I'm sorry, Miss Sanchez, we had no idea you existed. After contact from Gomez's attorney, and instructions to donate his tools and remaining monies with the company to a worthy cause, we did just that."

Esther nodded, as though she thought his statement was perfectly reasonable. "Wow. Talk about out with the old, in with the new, huh?" She tried to lighten his clearly sour mood, but he just looked at her as though she'd grown another head. She decided it was best to forget any attempt at charm. "Can I ask you something, Mr. Richter?"

His smile remained fixed as he brushed imaginary lint from his suit. "Of course. Gomez was a valued member of our team."

"You mean, until he killed someone and made a bunch of people sick?" she asked, purposely being facetious.

Sucking in his cheeks, Campbell gave a sharp nod of his head, probably hoping to brush that statement under the carpet along with her uncle. "That was indeed unfortunate. All of this has been quite unfortunate."

She blew out a breath, pulled off her glasses and gave him her sad eyes. "It sure was. Anyway, is there anyone here who might be able to tell me a little about my uncle? Some friends? Co-workers?"

By which, he was not moved. "You didn't know him?" Campbell asked, cocking his head as though the notion was preposterous.

Keeping her eyes locked with his, she didn't blink. "Not well, no."

"I'm afraid I still can't help you, Miss Sanchez."

"Okay, then how about Armand, his assistant? He quit, I'm told. Did he leave a forwarding address? A reason why he quit?"

Campbell's lips thinned. "I'm still unable to help. Armand's information is confidential and can't be released to anyone."

She leaned into him as though they were conspiring. "But he *did* leave a forwarding address. Of course he did. I mean, you have to send him his last paycheck, right?"

But Campbell took a step backward, his stiff shoes creaking. "I'm afraid it's as I said, I can't offer you any help. Now, if you'll excuse me, I have work to do. I'm terribly sorry for your loss." He didn't mince any more words. Rather, he pivoted on his heel and left, leaving Esther boring holes into his back.

She turned to find Tucker striding back across the

floor, his thick thighs bulging against his jeans. "No go?"

Her shoulders slumped as she hoisted her purse to the crook of her arm and put her glasses back on. "No go. It was like pulling teeth to get anything out of him. C'mon, let's get out of here and figure out a plan B."

As they turned to leave, Esther slapped the marble countertop where the receptionist sat. "Snitch!" she called out, before she turned to stomp toward the doors and pushed her way out into the cool fall day.

Clouds had begun to form, making the day darker, much like her mood. What now? Lifting her eyes skyward, she asked just that. "What now? Where do we go from here?"

"Miss Sanchez!" a male voice cried out, making both her and Tucker turn to find a man in a lab coat running toward them, waving a piece of paper.

When he stood in front of them huffing for breath, his round cheeks red, the lone swirl of hair atop his head waving at them from the force of the wind, he held up his hand. "Wait. Please. Wait," he gasped with a thin wheeze, bending forward at the waist.

Tucker looked down at the man with concern, placing a hand on his shoulder. "Are you okay?"

He tugged out the pocket of his lab coat and pointed to an orange nebulizer. "Asthma," he managed to rasp.

Esther pulled the nebulizer from his pocket and wrapped her arm around the man's shoulders, pulling him upright slightly. "Open your mouth. Tucker, hold his chin," she ordered, bringing the apparatus to his mouth, preparing to give it a good pump. "Breathe deeply. Just breathe." She patted him on the back as he wheezed upon inhaling, breathing in slow increments until he was finally able to stand fully.

"Better?" Tucker asked, taking a step back, but keeping a grip on the gentleman's shoulders.

He sighed and nodded, straightening and smoothing his really ugly tie. "Yes. Thank you. Running… I shouldn't have run. But I had to catch you!"

"Why?" Esther asked, moving to the side of the building to avoid the people passing by them on the sidewalk.

"Because of Gomez," he said in his soft Piglet voice, as though she should understand his reasoning.

"I don't understand. You knew my uncle?"

He nodded, smiling at her quite amicably. "Yes. Oh! Introductions. I forgot," he said, shaking his head. "I'm Dr. Joffre. We…er, Gomez and I worked together. Well, not together, but in the same general vicinity."

"And?" she asked, hoping he'd offer something, anything to the conversation.

He wrinkled his brow in a frown, driving his hands into his lab coat, clearly unsure what to say. "And?"

"*You* stopped *us*, Dr. Joffre. You obviously had something to tell Esther?" Tucker encouraged, leaning his shoulder against the wall of the building.

Dr. Joffre smacked him palm against the side of his

head. "Of course! Yes! Here," he said, holding up a piece of paper. "This is Armand's address."

Esther's eyes widened as she took the paper from him and smiled. "Oh, thank you, Dr. Joffre. You have no idea how much this might help us. How did you know I was looking for Armand?"

He smiled perceptively, his sweet face beaming. "The walls of Tecton have ears, Miss Sanchez."

"Did you know my uncle well?"

His open, gentle face fell, his eyes avoiding Esther's. "We worked in the same place for thirty years, and we hardly ever spoke, I'm sad to say. My granddaughter, Persimmon, says I should have tried harder."

Tucker gave the doctor a sympathetic look, but she knew he didn't understand any more than she did. "Tried harder to what?"

Dr. Joffre sighed, the sad sound swirling in her ears. "To connect. To make friends, of course. People like me, Miss Sanchez, people in my profession, so consumed with research and finding answers to the universe, well..." He shrugged his slumped shoulders. "We tend to become quite self-absorbed, and I have no excuse at all for not at least trying to make polite conversation with Dr. Sanchez, and I regret it deeply. I wish I would have asked him why he thought living was far worse than dying."

Esther put a hand on the doctor's shoulder. "You believe he killed himself, Dr. Joffre? Did you see any signs of it? Erratic behavior? Anything at all that would lead you to believe he wanted to die?"

Now the doctor blustered, obviously uncomfortable. "I don't know because I didn't know him, and I didn't stop to look. That's what I'm saying, Miss Sanchez—that's my whole point here. I don't know what his state of mind was, nor did I ever think to ask. But that's all changed now. From this moment on, in honor of Gomez, I'm going to ask everyone I work with how they are. I'm going try very hard to remember there's more to life than my work."

Esther's smile was sad. "Here's something that might make you feel better. I didn't know him either, Dr. Joffre. Not even a little. He was quite distant from my family, and even though I tried to reach out to him when my grandparents died, I didn't try hard enough. And now...well, now, I wish I had forced myself on him instead of letting him ignore me."

Dr. Joffre thumped her on the back with an age-spotted hand. "I'm sorry, Miss Sanchez. Sorry for your loss, sorry for the science world's loss. Gomez was brilliant. His enormous talents were wasted here. This wasn't the place for someone like him. But it paid the bills, and that I do understand."

"There's something else you'd rather be doing? Forgive my naïveté, but I don't know a lot about science and the corporate ladder." She thought a scientist was never happier than when buried in beakers and data.

He barked a laugh but followed it with a smile. "We'd all rather be studying string theory. But alas, we do what we must when grants are few and far between. Like water testing."

"Speaking of water tests," Tucker said. "I'm sure you know the mess surrounding the tragedy at H2O-Yo, and maybe you even know who I am?"

He bobbed his head. "I do, of course. I'm sorry for your suffering, and for the trouble it's brought you and your family personally."

Tucker grimaced. "Armand was the one who sent me the results of the water tests Gomez did for us. The tests that said everything was fine. The tests I signed off on and approved. Until, I believe, someone swapped them. And now we hear he's gone. Did Tecton find something awry they're keeping from the public?"

Dr. Joffre scratched his head and pondered. "I don't know, but we all had to admit, it was awfully suspicious that Armand quit. Which was why I made sure I asked for his address before he left. In my quest to better connect, I didn't want him to leave without knowing how much I appreciated his efficiency. Armand assisted me on occasion, too, and now to find he was actually dismissed without a word saddens me. He was an incredibly efficient assistant, and quite loyal to Dr. Sanchez. He didn't deserve the send-off he got."

"So, you know for sure he didn't quit, but was instead fired?" Esther asked. How curious. What did he know that Tecton didn't want anyone else to know?

He clucked his tongue and sputtered. "I don't know anything for sure, Miss Sanchez. So please don't quote me. I only know what I hear in the cafeteria, and that was that Tecton asked Armand to leave. They gave him a fine compensation package, from what I understand."

"You say you got this address from him; did you ask him why he was leaving?"

"I did, and he said he couldn't work without Gomez, but I'm not sure I believe that, now that I've overheard some conversations from a group of young secretaries in the halls. Most people don't notice me, the chubby, old scientist who has his nose buried in a book. But I know what I heard!"

"What did you hear?" Tucker asked, his dark brows smashing together in concern.

Now his soft, pudgy face went cross, his cheerful, innocent eyes flashing. "I heard them say Armand and that human resources man, Mr. Richter, had an awful argument just the day before Armand was to supposed to have quit. They said Armand told Mr. Richter he was going to tell everyone. I don't know what he meant by that, and the women were interrupted by none other than Mr. Richter himself before I could hear anything else. Thus, the conversation ended abruptly. But it surely made me rethink the notion Armand quit."

Esther blew out a breath, and then she held it again. What if someone was watching them talk to Dr. Joffre right now? What if simply talking to her would bring him trouble?

She couldn't stand the idea he'd be hurt because she was snooping around, so she took his hand and smiled at him. "Dr. Joffre, you've been incredibly helpful. I can't thank you enough. But I wouldn't want you to risk your good favor with Tecton by talking to me. Please, I implore you, don't tell anyone we spoke, and if someone brings it up, simply tell them you were offering your condolences."

Now he frowned, pulling a pair of glasses from his pocket and setting them on his nose, peering closely at her. "Do you think it could be dangerous to talk to you? But why?"

"I can't really explain it right now, or go into detail, but you'll do what I ask? No one has to know you gave me Armand's address, or that we talked about anything other than your condolences, all right?"

"Of course. I can keep a secret with the best of them," he said on a wink.

She smiled warmly at him, pulling a pen from her purse and ripping the piece of paper with Armand's address in half. "Good to know, and here, take my number. If you need anything at all, or anyone approaches you, hassles you, whatever. Please call me."

"Will do, Miss Sanchez. It was a pleasure to meet you, and again, I'm sorry for your loss."

Esther was inspired to give him a quick hug for giving them their first break, which he reciprocated in his own awkward way before taking his leave.

She looked to Tucker, whose face went hard when he asked, "Do you suppose Armand knew something Tecton was afraid of—or are they just covering their butts, seeing as he was the one who sent me the email with the green light?"

"I don't know. I just find it really suspicious that Armand was asked to leave a job he'd had as long as my uncle. So, you know what we need to do next, right?"

Tucker rubbed his nonexistent belly and grinned. "Get lunch? I'm starving."

She reached into her purse and pulled out a protein bar. "Eat that. It should tide you over until we're done talking to Armand."

"Aw, c'mon," he whined with a chuckle. "Who eats this and calls it lunch? Can't we just stop and grab a sandwich or something?"

"People who don't want to be accused of murder, that's who," she said, already halfway down the sidewalk.

He ran and caught up with her, grabbing her hand. "So, I guess there's no tempting you with a juicy cheeseburger?"

Her stomach growled. Fueled by nothing but coffee this morning, despite Arch's insistence she needed to eat something, she fought the visual of a cheeseburger, fought the thrill of the touch of her hand in his, and plodded forward.

"Cheeseburgers clog your arteries, merman. If you clog your arteries, how will we catch a killer and clear your good name?"

He stopped her by tugging on her hand, pulling her into a darkened corner of an alleyway. "Do we think it's a good idea to go talk to Armand? What if doing that puts him in danger, too? You did hear what the doctor said he heard from those secretaries, didn't you?"

Deflated, she nodded. "He said he was going to tell everyone. Yes, you're probably right. We'll have to be very careful. I say we call in the vampire and send her in first, to make sure the coast is clear."

He'd positioned himself in front of her, their bodies inches apart, and he looked down at her and asked, "Nina? Aw, c'mon, Esther. She's mean and surly. Especially during the daytime. Also, she nearly created all-out war with my father last night. Does Armand need that in his life? If he's as timid as Dr. Joffre, she'll give the poor bloke a heart attack."

But Esther giggled at him because, despite Nina's scary front, she really liked her. She had balls. She had grit. Yeah, she was loud and bold, but who didn't want to say some of the things Nina said out loud?

"What if I make you a deal?" she asked him, her cheeks growing hotter by the second as he put his hands on the brick wall on either side of her head and his minty breath wafted over her face.

"I'm listening," he offered in his silken tone, the one that never failed to slither along her spine in waves of warmth.

"Cheeseburger for a vampire."

"What?"

"You let me call Nina to help us, and I'll buy you a cheeseburger."

"That's so unfair. It's like asking me to choose

which I'd experience I'd like to have. World War One or Two."

"Speaking of, were you around for those?"

He grinned and dropped a kiss on her nose, making her giddy once more. "I'll never tell. Now stop trying to find out how old I am and feed me. I know a great place not far from here."

Chuckling, she tamped down this feeling of pending doom and trailed behind him to find a cheeseburger.

CHAPTER 15

"You sure this is the place?" Nina asked, looking up at the graffiti-covered brick building.

"That's what the paper Dr. Joffre gave me says. Look for yourself," Esther offered, handing the paper over to Nina from the backseat of the SUV.

Esther had texted Nina, and while she and Tucker ate juicy cheeseburgers for lunch, with chocolate milk-shakes for extra artery clogging, Nina and Wanda came to their rescue to help vet Armand.

But Esther was worried about Wanda and her pregnancy. She was desperately tired, and fought admitting as much the entire way. Still, Esther was afraid to say anything because Wanda was also hormonal and easily riled. Mermaid versus halfsie wasn't something she wanted to experience. So, she tread lightly.

"Wanda? Are you sure you're okay out here alone,

keeping watch? I feel like I'm keeping you from something," Esther said, putting her hand on Wanda's arm.

Wanda patted her hand and smiled her flawless smile. "Do you mean can the big fat whale keep her eyes open long enough to keep watch for the bad guys?"

"Fucking leave her alone, Wanda," Nina groused, giving her friend a light shove. "She's just lookin' out for your mean ass. Jesus. Would you rather have Heath breathing down the kid's neck if something happens to you? He can be a real asshole when his Mama Bear's unhappy."

Wanda pursed her lips and made a face. "He'll do no such thing. I'll box his ears if he puts any blame on Esther. I do as I wish."

Nina snorted as she applied sunscreen to her nose in a thick slather. "Oh yeah? Well, I'm gonna box yours if you don't quit taking offense to every fucking thing we say. You is strong. You is good. You is smart. I don't know how many times we can tell your needy ass that. But you is also the biggest mess of fucking hormonal-pain-in-the-ass pregnant. Nobody doubts your abilities, Wanda, or your usefulness. You're the reason we have OOPS at all. But we also never thought you could get preggers. That Heath even knocked your ass up is a fucking miracle. Don't take that miracle for granted, and shut the fuck up before I shave your head while you're sleeping, Mouth Breather. Feel me?"

Out of nowhere, Wanda laughed until tears came to her eyes, leaving Tucker and Esther fighting a snicker for fear of retribution. Reaching over, she pulled Nina to her and planted a smacking-wet kiss on her cheek. "You're horrible. Go talk to Armand. I'll keep watch for any bad guys."

Nina squirmed out of her embrace and flipped her the bird. "Whatever. Now, let's talk about this before we make a move. This guy's probably pretty freaked out, if what the nerdy scientist told you about what he heard at Tecton is true. We don't want to freak him out any more."

"And somehow *you* come to mind when calm subtlety is a necessity?" Tucker asked on a laugh.

Nina stared him down with her piercing coal eyes, quieting him instantly. "Shut the fuck up, Sharknado. I'm not gonna say it again. I'll show you subtlety when I pop your head off your shoulders."

"Yeah. What Nina said. Knock it off, you monster, and put your disguise on," Esther teased, driving a finger into his chest.

Tucker held up his curly black wig and glasses and made a face, but he put them on, just as Esther put on her long blonde wig and a beanie. The fear the press were lurking somewhere around a corner was very real, now that the news had broken that Tucker was accused of stealing the money and selling tainted water.

But after their conversation with Dr. Joffre, it became realer. So, Nina suggested wigs and glasses to further amp up concealing themselves.

"Ready?" Nina asked, not waiting for an answer as

she popped the car door open and pulled her hoodie over her head.

"Let's go see what we can see," Esther said, opening the door and sliding out to join Nina and Tucker.

As they headed across the street, Esther couldn't help but notice how dismal and depressing this neighborhood appeared. There was an empty lot directly across from the building, weeds and garbage lining the chain-link fence surrounding it. It almost looked deserted, but when someone came out of the building, she felt a little better knowing there was at least one inhabitant.

Yanking the dirty black door open, Nina shoved them ahead of her. Steps leading to the second floor, where Armand apparently lived, sprawled out in front of them, rickety and crooked. The inside of the building was freezing cold and as dismal, if not more so, than the outside. The scent of bacon and sweat assaulted her nostrils, making her wrinkle her nose.

As they climbed the steps, her heart pounding in her chest, she hoped against hope Armand had some answers. Funnily enough, this wasn't just about her uncle anymore. This was about a nice guy who'd gotten a shitty rap. She truly wanted to help clear Tucker's name.

His father's anger last night had upset her a great deal, and knowing what it's like to lose your parents made her more determined than ever to figure out what was going on. He was a good guy, and she believed that one hundred percent. Someone was railroading him, she knew it in her gut.

As they reached the second-floor landing, three doors, all rather crowded together in a small L shape, defined each apartment—one just as shabby as the next, with chipped paint and rust peeking through.

Nina pointed to the middle one and cocked her head in question.

Without saying a word, Esther nodded, adjusting her blonde wig. Nina's hand rose to knock on the battered kelly-green door—just as they heard a loud crash.

"Helllp meee!" someone screamed from behind Armand's door, making Nina react without hesitation.

She rammed her shoulder against the door, pushing it open as though it wasn't made of steel but flimsy cardboard, and flew inside with Tucker and Esther hot on her heels.

A tiny man, with a thick head of snow-white hair and reed-thin arms stuffed into an overly large plaid bathrobe, lay on the floor, sprawled at an awkward angle.

Esther only caught a small glimpse of someone pushing their way out of the tall window and landing on the fire escape before she rushed to the man, and Nina and Tucker took action.

Nina, in a blur of motion, ran after the attacker, flying through the window with so much speed and efficiency, Esther had to blink her eyes before she could focus on the man whimpering on the floor. A man she assumed was Armand.

Tucker went right behind Nina, hurling his big body through the window with ease and clomping onto the fire escape—and then she heard Nina scream, before there was a series of screeching crashes against the metal of the fire escape.

"Nina!" Tucker hollered from what sounded like somewhere far away.

"Hold on! Don't move, please!" she ordered the man on the floor, running to the window to see Tucker running behind Nina.

Seeing that everyone was still in working order, she went back to attend the man on the floor. Esther knelt beside him and brushed a lock of hair from his fore-head as she kept an eye on the window. "Can you move?"

He nodded his head weakly and attempted to sit up, but Esther stopped him. He looked so fragile. "Maybe I should call an ambulance? Tell me what hurts."

"Everything damn well hurts, but I don't need an ambulance," he grumbled, managing to sit up, using the edge of a torn blue sofa to do it. "Who are you?"

As she put her arm under the man's back and helped him to his feet, he wobbled and stiffened, moving with reluctance. "I'm Esther Sanchez. I promise you, I'm here to help. And you must be Armand, correct?"

He flopped down on the couch and inhaled a

rattling breath. "You're Gomez's niece?" he asked in a frazzled tone.

She straightened her blonde wig and her shoulders, feeling quite unsure of herself. "I am."

He sat on the couch and stared at her, his hair mussed, his bathrobe wrinkled, and huffed a shuddering breath.

In return, she eyed him closely for any injuries, afraid to touch him for fear of scaring him further. "Are you sure you don't want me to call an ambulance?"

"No!" he all but shouted, then lowered his voice. "Don't call anyone. *Please.* Don't call anyone."

Esther instantly became concerned. "You *are* Armand Mendes, aren't you?"

He shrank his frail body back into the couch "Why do you want to know?"

Looking down at him, so small, his skin so papery thin, she shot him a sympathetic glance. "Because I want to help you, Armand. I promise, I'm here to try to make things better, not hurt you. I want to clear my uncle's name, and I think you can help."

His faded brown eyes went fearful as he folded his gnarled hands together. "How…how do you think I can help?"

Esther pointed to the chair opposite him, an old cracked-leather armchair. "May I?"

"My manners. Forgive me. Please do."

As she slid into the chair, she asked, "Before we discuss anything else, who was that who just ran out of here like they were on fire?"

"I don't know," he murmured, his eyes now gone terrified.

She reached over and patted his hand to console him. "Did you see him? Can you describe him?"

Armand shook his head in a rapid motion, his thin chest pumping with his effort to breathe. "No. He had on a black mask. He didn't say a word, but he meant business. I know he meant business. He had his hands around my neck just as you burst down the door."

Had his hands around his neck. Hmmm.

"Do you think he was here because of what happened with my uncle?"

For the first time since she'd found him on the floor, Armand became animated, lifting his bony finger to stab it in the air. "I know Gomez didn't kill himself! I knew him as well as I know myself, and he was too selfish and cantankerous to take his own life!"

She had to smile at that. At least it was some kind of confirmation they weren't chasing rainbows. "*How* do you know that? You don't think he killed himself because of those water tests for H2O-Yo?"

Armand fisted his hand and banged it on the arm of the couch. "I *know* he didn't kill himself because of those tests! Those weren't *his* tests!"

"How do you know, Armand? Where did he go the night he died?"

"He left work early. Left me to close up shop. Said he had to go to his apartment."

"Did he say for what?" she asked.

"Gomez went there at least twice a week. So it

didn't seem strange at all to me. But when he didn't come home, and I called and called with no answer, I began to worry, and then the police called and told me he was gone…"

Her heart clenched tight for the misery emanating from Armand. "Who found him?"

"The night doorman, Lester. He'd seen Gomez go up and had forgotten to give him a piece of mail. He brought it to him, and when he didn't answer, Lester grew worried. So he called the police."

Maybe they should be talking to this Lester?

Armand's eyes shone with tears as he collapsed back against the sofa. "It's my fault, you know. It's all my fault. The only man I ever loved is dead, and it's all because of me."

Esther's mouth fell open just as Nina hopped back in the window, with Tucker behind her. "The fucker got away. Man, he was slick AF. I fell two damn stories and it slowed me down. Got Wanda lookin' out for him, but I'm not holdin' out much hope."

"Esther?" Tucker said, coming to stand next to her, his wig crooked. "Is everything all right?"

But she hadn't gotten past Armand's admission. She held up a finger. "Are you telling me, you and my uncle…?"

His chin fell to his chest as tears fell from his eyes. "Yes. We were lovers. For many years now, and if I had remembered to lock the office—our office—whoever it was who sent that damn email to H2O-Yo with those test results never would have gotten away with murder. I'm telling you, someone murdered my Gomez!"

"Whoa," Nina muttered as she came to stand in front of Armand and looked at Esther. "Any idea who the dude was that attacked him?"

Esther gulped in some air as she processed. "No. He had on a mask, but he definitely wasn't here for a beer, according to Armand. He tried to strangle him."

Nina knelt down in front of Armand and gripped his hand, her eyes meeting his. "You a tea drinker?"

Armand swallowed hard and nodded with a shaky answer as Tucker put a blanket from the couch over his lap. "Yes."

The vampire patted him on the hand. "I'll go make you some, okay? You relax. Everything's gonna be fine from now on."

As she rose, Tucker stuck his hand out to Armand, using the other hand to pull off his wig and set it on the shabby end table. "I'm Tucker Pearson, sir. Pleasure to meet you."

Armand smiled wide, his perfect white dentures flashing at them. "Oh, Tucker. It's such a pleasure to finally meet you after all these years, too!"

Tucker sat on his haunches in front of Armand and smiled a gentle smile. "Same here. Are you okay? Are you hurt?"

He shook his head. "No. No, I'm fine. Forget about me, and tell me about you. Tell me why you're here."

"Do you mind explaining what you mean about locking your office and the emails you sent?"

Armand deflated right before their eyes, his slender shoulders sagging. "Those tests, Tucker. I'm sick over those horrible tests. Those tests weren't the tests we sent you. We sent you tests proving the water was bad. I know we did. Gomez frowned for days over the results of those tests. He knew the water could cause harm. He tested and retested and logged everything. We never, *ever* sent you anything that said the water was good, but someone must have gotten into my email and written one up, because there it was, plain as day when the police came and seized my computer! Everything, all his work, was gone. Of course, Gomez blamed me. The old coot had the audacity to say I didn't lock the door to the office, but I know I did, Tucker. *I know it.*"

"So, you think someone swapped the tests? Because I can tell you, as sure as I stand here, Armand, I would not have approved something that was even a little fishy—not if there was the slightest chance it could cause even a small problem."

Armand reached out and grabbed Tucker's hand, leaning forward on the couch. "I know that, Tucker! Of course I do. We've worked together for years. I also know you didn't send out some memo, telling production the water was a go. What you've got is a hacker, that's what ya got. It's all just a bunch of fiddle-faddle, that's what it is. And Gomez was almost to the bottom of it, too. I know he was. He told me as much the day he—" Armand choked up then, his throat working to swallow his grief.

"Armand," Esther said, tempering her words. "How do you know Gomez was on to something? What proof can you provide that proves he was on to something?"

He gave her a sad look. "Therein lies the problem, my dear. I can't. I don't know the first thing about computers and hacking, but he was convinced he was close to figuring out who'd swapped those tests and sent that email from my address. He was sure we could find the records of his logs. So, I ask you, if he thought he was on to something, why would he kill himself—in that mess of an apartment of his, to boot? Gomez almost never went there. He stayed here with me most nights."

Nina handed him a cup of tea and asked, "You know about his apartment?"

"Are you asking if I knew the man I loved for over thirty years was a hoarder? Yes. I certainly did, and he wouldn't let that terrible apartment go for all the tea in China, no matter how I begged. So, we came to an understanding, and he moved in here with the promise he could keep his old place."

"Did he have an official diagnosis for Obsessive Compulsive Disorder?" Esther asked.

But Armand shook his head. "He didn't need one. Gomez knew all the things he was without some doctor's diagnosis. OCD, with a healthy dose of high-functioning autism. He knew, and he always said he didn't need some doctor to tell him. But here, with me, he was different. So different... I wouldn't have allowed his hoarding here, but I was the only one who could get through to him, explain things to him," he said, his voice sad again. "Oh, don't think for a moment I didn't know how kooky my Gomez was, or that he was a selfish son of a bitch. But he loved me in his own way, and he would never take his own life. He was too ornery. But to take his own life with sleeping pills, no less? Preposterous!"

Esther's eyes grew misty. This life of her uncle's, this life he'd shared with Armand, left her feeling so sad for not pushing her way into it and making him engage with her.

"Oh, Esther," Armand croaked. "I've upset you. I never wanted to upset you."

She bit the inside of her cheek and shook her head. "No. No, no. There's just so much I didn't know. So much I should have known, had I pestered him to let me in. But I didn't, and even if he was cranky and selfish, at least he would have known me. I would have known *him*."

Armand waved a dismissive hand and frowned. "Bah! Gomez was difficult on a good day, Esther. Your grandfather knew it, so did your father. Small children made him nervous, and he wasn't much for barbecues or parties. You can't be blamed because Gomez didn't want to engage, dear. That was just Gomez."

"So, my grandfather knew about you? My father, too?" She felt like this whole secret life had existed around her and, aside from the occasional hushed, overheard conversation between her grandparents, she'd been oblivious.

Armand bobbed his head and his eyes twinkled. "They did, and they trusted I'd take care of him, and I tried, Esther. I really tried. Except for that day. That damn, damn day."

Tucker rose from his haunches and sat on the arm of Esther's chair. "Armand, were you forced out of Tecton? We were there today, and one, it's awfully suspicious that someone broke in here and tried to strangle you. Two, they said you quit. Which I find incredibly hard to believe, considering the length of time you were there."

Armand puckered his lips in displeasure. "Oh, you bet your bunions I was forced out. The minute they got wind of the fact that I supposedly sent that email, they moved in for the kill. It was over before I knew what hit me, those bastards. Thirty years of my life, gone like I never existed."

Tucker clucked his tongue. "So basically, they were worried you'd sent the email stating the water was good and they were avoiding collateral damage?"

"You bet they were, and they want nothin' to do with that kind of press. That slick fella, Richter from HR, told me as much. Said my memory must not be so good, and if I wanted my retirement package doubled, I'd shut my pie hole and go peacefully. But I told 'em I was gonna tell everybody. I didn't want their blood money. I just wasn't sure who to tell without some kind of proof."

"Then they must think you have something here, something that can prove someone hacked into your emails, right?" Esther asked, hoping against hope he did.

"But I don't have anything, Esther. Other than my heart, which tells me Gomez would never leave this planet willingly."

"And his suicide email? He sent one to you, didn't he?" she asked.

"Bunk!" he crowed, wagging a finger. "All bunk. Yes, it says it came from his email, but those weren't Gomez's words."

Esther's heart pumped a little harder. "Can you tell me what it said? Do you mind? I don't want to intrude…"

"You can't intrude on something that isn't real. I'd let you read it, but whoever sent it, sent it to my work email, and as I said, they confiscated my work computer. All it said was, 'I can't live knowing I killed someone,' with Gomez's pretentious signature with a list of his awards and degrees at the bottom, and that was it."

Her stomach turned. She didn't know Gomez, but seeing as he wasn't terribly personable or communicative, it didn't sound outrageously unlike his personality. Which made her ask, "How do you know it wasn't him that wrote it?"

Armand actually chuckled, sipping his tea, appearing to relax a little. "Because if you knew Gomez the way I knew your uncle, you'd know he'd prattle on and on about how much the world was going to miss him before he ever got around to telling anyone his reasons for offing himself in an email. Gomez loved to hear himself talk. I know that probably sounds strange to your ears, because he was so antisocial, but if we were talking about him, he was quite the Chatty Cathy. A suicide email from Gomez would have been far more complex. And sleeping pills? It's ludicrous. First off, where did he get them? He lived with me, if you'll remember. He didn't even like to take a damn aspirin for a headache. Secondly, he'd no sooner take sleeping pills than he would arsenic."

Closing her eyes, Esther inhaled and pulled off her silly wig, defeated. How were they going to prove someone had hacked into her uncle's email, and Tucker's for that matter? Jesus, what a mess. Not to mention, how were they going to protect Armand?

God, she didn't want to do this, because it put Tucker at risk, but they had to call the police. She wasn't going to let someone accost an old man to keep him quiet.

"We have to call the police," she murmured. "Armand was attacked, and it's probably because whoever's made this mess wants to start cleaning it up and they're afraid Armand knows something."

Tucker nodded, but his face was stoic. "That was my next suggestion. I agree. I wholeheartedly agree. I don't want to see you hurt, Armand."

"Bananas!" he shouted, setting his tea on the end table with a frown. "The police didn't listen to me, why would they protect me? They don't think anything happened to Gomez to begin with, and Tecton's not going to help. They're going to cover up whatever they can to keep their stinkin' noses clean!"

Tucker sighed, crossing his arms over his chest. "Well, that was before the embezzlement business about me got out. I'm not sure if you've heard, but someone leaked it to the press. The entire story of how I gave the green light to the production of the new line of water. The missing money. There's even a memo I allegedly sent to production, downplaying the severity of Gomez's results. Which, as a by the way, I checked the timestamp on, and discovered I was indeed in my office when it was sent. Hacker? Probably. But who? Who wants me gone? Or who needed the money enough to blame me?

"I'm feeling pretty sure the police are going to think I killed Gomez to keep him quiet, now that they have that particular piece of information. Esther and I were just talking about how strange it is that they haven't at least brought me in for questioning after that report."

Armand slapped his hand on the arm of his ratty couch. "Well, I'm sure not going to help you do it. I'm not letting you ruin your life by going to the police, Tucker. I know you didn't kill Gomez. I know it deep down. But they'll pin it on you, with so much evidence against you. And if you call them and put the spotlight on you, I'll lie and tell them nothing happened to me. I'll tell them you're both nuts."

"But we can't just leave you to your own devices, Armand," Esther insisted, even though his loyalty touched her heart. "Not without risking you getting hurt. Someone thinks you know something."

But Armand looked miserable, the lines in his aging face deepening, and he clenched his fists. "Please don't do this, Tucker. *Please*. Gomez was so fond of you. He'd hate this."

Nina, who'd been silent this entire conversation, finally spoke. "How about this: It's probably not gonna be long before the cops come lookin' for you anyway, but what if we bring Armand to Heath? If that's okay with Armand, seeing as he doesn't know us from Adam. We'll send Darnell to keep watch and he'll be safe until we can figure this out. Then I'm going to call my brother-in-law, Sam, and see what I can find out about this hacking biz. He's ex-FBI."

"I feel like this is a ticking time bomb, Nina. It's just a matter of time," Tucker said with a grim tone, rubbing his hand over his jaw.

But Armand smiled wide. "I don't care if you're a bunch of Satan worshippers. I'll go with you if it gives you more time to figure this out and stick it to Tecton and whoever else is involved, the bastards! Thirty damn years of my life, all to be treated like some doddering fool!"

Nina and Esther smirked at each other. If only Armand knew how close he was to the truth about who was going to babysit him.

Nina shot him one of her beautiful smiles. "You're sure you're comfortable, Armand? I don't want you to do something against your will."

Armand began to rise from his place on the sofa, slipping to the edge and smiling up at Nina. "I'm just fine, and you're dang pretty. If I played for the other team, you'd have to beat me off with a stick."

Nina threw her head back and laughed, giving Armand her hand. "Let's get you some clothes packed, Player."

As she led him off to the bedroom, their feet padding over the worn shag carpet, Esther shivered. Finally, a break. Maybe a small one, but a break.

As they waited for Armand and Nina, who were laughing and joking, Esther took a look around at thirty years' worth of two lives spent together.

The apartment was sparse, save for some very old furniture and a couple of paintings, but there was one wall—a wall filled with degrees and pictures. Tons of pictures of her uncle Gomez, who looked so much like her father, at work in his lab, his face serious, his expression determined. Several of him and Armand together were tucked into ornate frames. Armand's arm around the shoulders of a reluctant Gomez, who stared at the camera as though it were a flying purple people eater.

And then, a surprise. Pictures of her grandparents, locked in an embrace in their old kitchen, playing pinochle in the summer under the big tree in her front yard. Pictures of her parents, waving from the shore of the beach at her cottage, sitting in the small motorboat they'd owned. Swinging Esther between them, during a walk on the beach.

And stranger still, a picture of Gomez holding her as a baby, right alongside her high school graduation picture.

Armand, now dressed in some black trousers and a periwinkle-blue sweater, put a light hand on her back. "He loved your family, Esther. He might not have shown it, no one other than those closest to him could detect it, but he loved your father, his parents, and even you, in his odd way. No, he didn't know you—or even try to get to know you—but he'd smile at your accomplishments when he'd get mail from your grandfather. I know you tried to reach out to him, and I know he ignored you. We had many disagreements over the years about his family. He just couldn't accept that *they* accepted him."

Tears stung her eyes. "I wish I had known. I didn't know anything about you or your relationship."

He winked at her. "But you know me now, and I hope when this is all over, you'll keep in touch. Also, I found this on Gomez's nightstand. Forgot all about it till that cutie in there made me pack up my clean underwear." He handed her a scrap of yellow lined paper.

As she read the scribbled words, she frowned. It was clearly someone's email, but there were only two letters before the gmail.com, and due to the way they were spaced apart, she wasn't even sure if the letters were meant to be together or if there were more letters in between. So, who the hell was PF?

"Is this what he found while he was looking for the hacker?"

Armand cupped his chin and shook his head. "I can't say for sure, Esther. I can only tell you, he emptied his pockets every night before he went to bed. It's been there since he…"

"Hey, you guys ready?" Nina asked, holding up Armand's overnight bag, handing it to him. "Darnell's outside."

"When you are," Esther whispered, and then she put her hand on Armand's arm. "Can I ask a very personal, possibly intrusive, maybe even offensive question?"

He tucked his overnight bag over his arm and smiled. "Of course, dear."

"Why here? Why this apartment? It's so… The neighborhood doesn't look very safe."

"It wasn't always like this, Esther. Twenty-five years ago, this area was what you young kids call hip. Over the years, life has taken its toll. But the primary reason? Rent control, dear. Gomez wasn't willing to split a rent any higher than this because he just couldn't give up his apartment full of all those crazy papers—that I will never, so long as I live, understand. In essence, your uncle was a cheap bastard. The cheap bastard I loved."

A penny saved was a penny wise. Her grandfather had always said that. Esther threw her head back and had a good laugh as they made their way out of the depressing apartment and back to the street, to tuck Armand safely in the car with Darnell.

CHAPTER 16

"Right here in the ocean? I mean, loud and proud?" Esther asked Tucker as the chilly wind blew. "Is that safe?"

They'd decided to take time out from worrying about the email address and anything else involving the H2O-Yo mess and practice Esther's mermaiding. But as she looked at the ocean, so rough compared to the manmade lake, she wasn't sure this was a good idea.

Tucker chuckled, shedding his pants and shoes, because Body Beautiful wasn't afraid of anyone seeing him in just his britches. "It's where all good mermaids began, Esther. We didn't always have manmade lakes. I'll be right here next to you, but we have to practice. You have to learn how to mermaid, pretty lady."

She gripped his arm as she stared out into the vast ocean in front of her cottage, now dark and rippling with frothy waves. "Speaking of being a mermaid, when you saved my clunky butt from drowning last night, did you grab my neck?"

He gave her an odd stare, his chiseled face twisting under the moonlight. "No. Not that I recall. I recall grabbing for you around your shoulders, or maybe it was your waist, I think. Definitely not around your neck. Why would you ask that?"

She shivered at the memory of last night. "Because Armand said someone tried to strangle him, and I know this sounds dramatic, maybe even crazy, but when I was sinking and couldn't get myself to propel upward, not only couldn't I see because of my bountiful mermaid hair, but someone gripped my neck. It was quick, and then I was being swept upward." She shrugged. "I dunno. I think I'm just connecting dots that maybe don't necessarily connect."

Now Tucker gripped her arm and swung her to face him. "Esther! How could you forget to tell me something like that? If someone from the pod tried to harm you, it needs investigating."

"It was all so chaotic! One minute your father's yelling at us, the next we're shooting off in a fit of anger, and then it was like an underwater tidal wave exploded."

His eyes narrowed. "Yes. The tidal wave. You can do that, you know. It doesn't make it any better that my father did it out of anger, because it's dangerous when your emotions are so out of control. But if you're ever in jeopardy, it's useful. Water hitting at that speed can crush all the bones in someone's body, Esther. It's not much different than folks jumping to their deaths. On impact, it will crush you. You're immortal, but not infallible."

She shivered, tucking her sweatshirt under her neck. "Okay, forgetting for a moment the hands around my neck, why would I ever be in jeopardy?"

"Oh, you know, sharks, whales, interlopers."

"Sharks?" she squeaked. Sweet Jesus. She'd never even thought about the rest of the ocean's inhabitants.

"It happens so rarely, it's like hen's teeth, Esther. I promise. We mean no harm to our sea-dwelling brethren, but there's been a time or two when a shark's come just a little too close for comfort. A tidal wave helps deflect and disorient, and it gives you time to get away."

She stared up at him, unable to voice how crazy this all sounded. But she had to keep reminding herself, so did have a tail and fins.

He chucked her under the chin and grinned. "There's more..." he teased, pulling her to him, letting his bare chest press against hers. The heat of him seeped into her, warm and soothing, hot and exciting all in one embrace.

She plucked at his skin with a light pinch, loving the feel of it beneath her fingers. "More? I knew it! It's X-ray vision, isn't it? Oh, what will I do when I can see all the other little mermaids with their perfect bodies naked?"

Laughing, he shook his head. "Hardly. First, we can communicate underwater, as I'm sure you heard the other night. You'll learn that in time. But also, bubbles. You can turn bubbles into bullets. All ya gotta do is blow."

Now her mouth fell open before she forced herself to snap it shut. "And you found this out *how*?"

"How do you think mers kept all those invasive sailors away? Also, something else to give thought to. Underwater, your strength increases by leaps and bounds."

"Meaning?"

"Meaning, you could probably manage to grab on to a whale and swing him like a baseball bat."

She continued to stare at him in wonder. "I'm going to collapse under the weight of all my superpowers if you don't cut it out."

With a chuckle and a grin, he flashed his hand at the water. "Then how about we get started?"

"Are you afraid we'll get caught?" she asked, looking around at the deserted landscape of the beach. As the day dimmed and went dark, she fought the fear of discovery.

"Well, it's almost seven o' clock in the evening, and there hasn't been a soul out here almost all day, according to Marty. Also, it's pretty cold, which doesn't inspire folks to take walks, and all the summer people have gone home. Plus, we have this," he pointed to her faded dock. "We can hide under it if we need to. I've done it before."

Nodding, she decided there was something else to address. She'd thought about this all day as they'd gotten Armand settled, eaten dinner with everyone, and pondered their next move. It was time for some honesty, so that nothing held her back from immersing herself.

As she pulled reluctantly from his embrace and stepped out of her yoga pants, she dropped them on the towels on the sand. "Time for some full disclosure, in case I freak out on you again under there."

He stopped what he was doing and cocked an ear. "Esther, you don't have to if you're uncomfortable or not ready. I understand. I know there's something wrong...something tragic...but I don't want you to feel forced to talk about whatever it is."

Sighing, she looked out at the purple and blue horizon as the day ended and took several deep breaths before she said, "My parents drowned. I was with them when it happened. I guess you could have looked it up online, if you'd wanted to. I'm sure somehow there's probably an article up about it by now, though, there was no Internet when it happened. Anyway, I was with them. There was a sudden thunderstorm, and we were out in our tiny motorboat—an early fall picnic. One of the last one's we'd be able to have until spring, my dad said. I don't remember much of it other than how loud and scary the thunder was, and all the rain. So much rain and wind, and my mother, checking my life preserver before we tipped over. I don't even remember how anyone found me, or even *who* found me. My grandfather said is was another boater, caught up in the storm, too. The only thing I do remember is how cold and wet I was for what seemed like a hundred years…and alone. I felt very alone."

Tucker pulled her into his strong arms and rested his chin on the top of her head. "Christ, Esther, I'm sorry. Sorrier than I'll ever be able to express in words. But I have to give it to you for being so brave last night. It took incredible strength for you to get in the water. You're so strong."

She shook her head, letting her cheek rest against his bare chest. "It took me over twenty years to take a Mommy and Me swim class. I'm not sure that's brave."

"I disagree," he said, threading his fingers through her hair. "But what say you and this vast body of water make some peace with one another? It can be an amazingly beautiful place. Especially when it's shared."

Tears stung her eyes, but she nodded. He was right. She had to figure out how to do this without so much residual fear. "I'm all yours."

"You aren't yet, but you will be," he teased cryptically, letting her go to run into the small waves crashing against the shoreline, the water splashing against his muscular silhouette. "C'mon, mermaid! Let's take a swim!"

She wished she had the guts to ask him what that meant, but her spine literally collapsed at the mere thought.

Instead, she watched him enter the water by her private dock…and that was when she felt an invisible tug. A strange, deep-seated need to touch the water, feel it slice across her skin, let it work its chilly fingers through her hair. And as she pulled the rest of her clothes off, she didn't hesitate to run directly into the water and join Tucker.

Winking at her, he ran ahead until he was deep enough out to dive into the frothy waves.

You'd think at this time of year, it would be enough to give her hypothermia, but she didn't feel the cold at all. Instead, she felt invigorated as the salty water stung her eyes and danced on her lips. Following Tucker, she ran farther into the water, until the tide lifted her and pulled her toward him.

And then she dove deep, like she'd seen her father and grandfather do so many times, like they'd once taught her so long ago—before she was afraid, and when everything in her life had been perfect.

Just like it had last night, her tail sprouted, shedding her limbs with the ease of melting butter. She felt the width of her fins catch the underwater current and move in sync with her arms, her hair floating about her shoulders as she pushed through the water. There was no panic this time, she didn't even think about breathing, she just did, and it was incredible, freeing, perfect.

Tucker popped up in front of her, his smile wide as he gave her the thumbs-up and pointed forward, indicating she should follow.

The ocean wasn't at all like the lake, so clear and blue. It was murkier here, but still just as exciting, with seaweed swirling about her. As they passed through seaweed and groups of fish, Tucker spoke.

"Let's give this a try, Esther. All you need to do is blow

like this," he instructed, pursing his lips and spitting out a bubble that zoomed past her face, growing as it went. *"The harder you blow, the faster they hit. Try it."*

It seemed so simple, but it was a lot harder than it looked, as per the bubble she blew that nearly took off Tucker's head.

Her eyes went wide, but he just laughed. *"Aim your sphere of death that way."* He came through loud and clear in her head and pointed forward, moving to hover near her.

Pursing her lips, she tried it again, only to find she was a little erratic and her aim kinda sucked in a slightly crooked, zigzag way.

Tucker swam under her and grabbed her waist, pulling her deeper until they were on the ocean floor.

Holy shitballs, they were on the ocean floor.

"I think a little practice is in order. But let's try something else," he suggested with a grin, swimming away from her.

Without even a moment to consider, Esther spoke without ever opening her mouth and without realizing it. *"Not tidal waves? Seriously? Do you mean tidal waves?"* A small fissure of excitement skittered along her spine. How many people could say they could make tidal waves?

Tuck nodded as a fish swam around him, and he dodged its nosy presence. *"Remember to steady yourself and roll with it, Esther. Just roll right into it. Let it carry you, don't try to carry* it."

Pulling his fingers together in a ball, he swiped

right, spreading his hand open wide, and as he did, the water exploded in front of her, creating that wave that had panicked her so last night.

But this time she was ready and held her ground, flapping her arms and riding the wave just as Tucker instructed. When it hit her, she rolled, bending at the waist and tumbling head over tail directly into the eye of the wave. She almost lost her way when the force of the water shoved her with such power she nearly toppled, but then Tucker was there, grabbing her hand and pulling her back down to the ocean's floor again.

"You try," he encouraged, closing her fist with his hand and guiding her arm as though she were going to throw a baseball. *"Take it slow, don't bowl for dollars, rather hit it like you're playing badminton."*

As he pulled her arm out straight, he whispered, *"Let 'er rip, Esther!"*

Giving her arm a huge push, she let her fingers open wide—and the water just exploded.

Okay, it didn't just explode, it whooshed, making a muffled rumble so loud, it hurt her ears, but beyond that rumble, she heard Tucker's hearty laugh. When the water cleared, and he was right in front of her, he grinned and hauled her close, dropping a kiss on her lips.

"Well done! You're a natural, Esther. We just need to fine-tune it."

In hindsight, she couldn't say what made her wrap her arms around Tucker's neck as they hovered deep in the vast ocean while seaweed and kelp fluttered past them. Maybe it was her excitement at finally getting the hang of something, or maybe it was because he was so regal as a merman, but she did exactly that.

She threw her arms around his neck and pressed her mouth to his, and when she did, all sound completely stopped. Nothing moved but the two of them, floating together as their mouths fused and their merforms wrapped around one another. He drove his tongue between her lips, demanding she meet its silken glide, making her dizzy with the impact and force of his kiss.

Her body responded in kind, heating up until she thought she'd pass out, her fins swishing at full tilt, and all of the magic she'd read about a first kiss in fairytales came true for her.

Tucker wrapped his arms around her, strong and sure, his moan deep and husky in her head. He drove a hand into her hair, twisting it around his hand and pulling her even closer, leaving her melty and needy.

But somewhere, far off in the distance, she heard barking. And Tucker must have heard it, too, because he pulled away from her, giving her a confused look before pointing up, meaning maybe they should surface.

Taking her by the hand, he shot upward like a torpedo with Esther by his side, and they surfaced just under the dock.

Her head whipped around as the water cleared from her eyes. "Is that Mook?"

"Hey, Surf and Turf!" Nina's husky voice rang out

against the wind. "We got something. Quit playing hide the fish and get the fuck up here!"

~

"Let me watch it again," Tucker said, hitting play on the video Nina's brother-in-law, Sam, had sent to them. Ex-FBI, now a vampire and married to her half-sister, Phoebe, he'd somehow gotten his hands on Tecton's video surveillance of not just the night Gomez took his life, but two weeks prior to his death, as well. Yet, that was as far back as the videos went, which was, according to Sam, very common, to erase them after they'd been viewed.

Just as Armand said, it showed him locking the door to his and Gomez's office

After each of them had reviewed hours of tape, including Wanda, everyone was shaking their heads, having found nothing.

But then Tucker shouted, "Hold on! Look." He pointed to someone in a suit entering Gomez's office. "Those sneakers on this guy here. Look at them. Damn it! Why do I know those sneakers?"

Esther leaned in and peered closer at the video as she sat beside Tucker at her small dining room table, while Carl played with Mook and Marsha, and the women all scoured their laptops, re-watching the video over and over.

"Isn't he the IT guy? He's dressed just like the rest of them we've identified so far." She looked at the list of names Sam had sent with each employee from each department, trying to compare faces with the sometimes-fuzzy images of IT employees wandering up and down the halls.

This particular man's head was turned away from the camera, almost as though he knew it would capture his image. He was dressed in a suit much like many of the Tecton IT employees wore. And according to emails between the IT guys, this man was just doing routine maintenance.

"But why is he wearing sneakers? They all have dressier shoes on. See? Watch *this* guy's feet, coming from the IT department just the day before Gomez was killed."

Everyone gathered around Tucker's computer to watch, but Nina made a face. "Maybe dude hates stuffy shoes? I fucking hate heels. I can identify. These two hens wear 'em every day, but I'd rather shit acid."

Esther snorted at Nina's joke. "But he has a point. If there's a dress code at Tecton, this guy shouldn't be wearing sneakers."

Tucker slapped his hand against the table in frustration, making her bowl of fake red apples jump. "But I'll be damned if I know why I recognize them. They're pretty average except for the shape of the heel. It's pronounced..." He shook his head as though to clear the cobwebs. "I don't know what it is. Maybe it's absolutely nothing at all. Maybe I'm simply making something out of nothing."

Archibald dropped a plate of delicate cookies in

front of Tucker. "Make something out of *this*, mate," he said in a cheesy Aussie accent, his grin wide.

"Aw, Arch, I think you're starting to like me," Tucker teased, reaching up to tweak his cheek.

"I do no such thing," he protested with a grin. "I made them because they had to be made, cheeky man. Now, eat. Rest. Catch your breath. Food always helps swish away the cobwebs."

"Or make a bigger cobweb," Wanda moaned from her chair, putting her hand to her belly and rubbing. "You absolutely have to stop making scones with clotted cream for breakfast or I'm going to need someone to stick a pin in me."

Marty smoothed Wanda's belly with a gentle hand and laughed. "But think of this little miracle you're growing, eating all those scones."

Wanda nodded her head, her eyes watery. "It is a miracle. A miracle indeed."

Nina had told Esther about Wanda's journey, about her baby zombie, about how she'd become a halfsie to begin with, and hearing her story made Esther mist up.

Now, in moments like this, when the women and their cohorts were all together, were when Esther missed her family more than ever. It had been small, but mighty—which made her that much more determined to figure out who'd done this. Because her uncle's stellar reputation was at stake, and she couldn't rest until it was rescued.

She liked these people. She liked how they rallied behind, supported, even taunted one another, and she'd miss the activity in her house when they vacated her guest bedrooms and Arch took his cooking skills back to Wanda's.

Rising to stretch and maybe clear her thoughts, she meandered into the living room, where the lights were dim and she could look out at the inky expanse of the ocean. Sighing, she listened to the sounds of everyone laughing, eating, talking about everyday things, and her throat tightened.

"Little Fish?"

"Mean Vampire?"

"You okay? You do know we'll fucking figure this out, don't you? I don't want you pouting over here, thinkin' we won't get this shit together. Because we will."

Esther turned to look up at Nina and smile. She liked all the women, but Nina was her favorite—even as cantankerous as she was. "It's not that. I was just enjoying the sounds of life in my cottage. It's nice, don't you think?"

Nina stared down at her. "If you don't have vampire ears, it's peachy. When you have vampire ears, it's GD fucking annoying."

"You stop," Esther teased. "You don't mean that, and you know it. You like the noise. It means you're part of something. Don't take that for granted."

Crossing her arms over her chest, Nina cocked her head, her gloriously wavy hair falling down around her shoulders. "Is that what this shit's about?"

"What shit?"

"Why you're so quiet. Because you don't feel like you're a part of something?"

Sighing, she cast her eyes down at her tennis shoes. "Maybe a little. I miss my family today, I guess."

Nina chucked her under the chin with a long finger. "Well, here's some shit to think about. Now that you've met us, you're a part of this group forever. Whether you like that crap of not. Believe me, I can't stress that enough. *Whether you like it or not.*" Then she chuckled.

"You're friends with everyone you guys help?"

"We're framily," Marty chirped from behind her, wrapping an arm around her shoulder to give it a brief squeeze. "Nina made that up, but it fits. Everyone we've helped is now a part of our group. The entire lot. I think it's thirteen cases strong now, not counting our own, of course, with all manner of the paranormal, too. I'm sure Nina told you about the dragons, and demons, and cougars. But each one is special. Each one a bond that just seems to happen. Maybe because it's so chaotic and we all become each other's safe place to fall, but it's a bond nonetheless."

"Hysterical bonding. It's sort of a branch of hysterical bonding."

Nina shrugged her shoulders under her dark hoodie. "You know, I used to think that shit. Yeah, this whole 'turned into something paranormal' is full of adrenaline, lots of noise and some seriously fucked-up shit sometimes. But we don't have to see each other when this shit is done. All the crazy might have forged our friendships, but it ain't the glue that holds 'em together ten years later. So if you're worried we're gonna dump your ass when this is all said and done, gird your fucking loins. Because you've got no choice in this anymore. Dinners and shopping, fucking trips to the stupid outlet mall, holidays, birthdays, Groundhog Day, whatthefluffever, these nuts find a way to celebrate it, and you're in—*always*. Period."

Esther gulped, her chest so tight, it felt like someone had put a thick rubber band around it. But she didn't say anything. She couldn't say anything for the gratitude blooming in her heart.

Instead, she took Nina's and Marty's hands and squeezed them.

And they squeezed hers back.

CHAPTER 17

Long after everyone had gone to bed, Tucker stared at the computer screen, replaying the fucking video until his eyes burned, but he'd be damned if he could figure out where he'd seen those sneakers.

Taking care not to make noise, he slid his chair back and stood up, noting Esther had fallen asleep on the couch with Carl's head in her lap. They'd decided he should stay here, for his own safety, in case the police went looking for him at his place, but he was uncomfortable as hell putting everyone in jeopardy. The press already knew about this place and Esther, why wouldn't the police?

Looking down at his phone, he reread the texts from his mother, Chester, Jessica, all wondering the same thing. *"Where are you?"* and *"The police were here, asking questions, looking for you."*

And the worst: *"Someone from the family of the man*

who died called the police and wants to know why you haven't been arrested. Please call me."

But long before he'd gotten the texts, he'd already decided—tomorrow, he'd go to the police. Whoever had done this, whoever had killed Gomez, would come looking for him, and he didn't want these decent people in their path. But he also knew, realistically, the police were going to at least want to question him. Christ knew they had plenty to build a case on. He couldn't keep ducking them anymore. Especially with Esther involved.

Though, when he figured this out—and he would if it was the last thing he did—he was going to kill the motherfucker. Not just because this person had wreaked havoc in his life, but because he'd killed someone—*two* someones—and for that alone, whoever this was would beg for their death when he was done.

Stretching his arms, he padded out into the living room and smiled at Esther, her arm around Carl's shoulder, her head flung back, exposing her long, creamy neck.

Tucker Pearson was hot for Esther Williams Sanchez, and he wasn't afraid to admit it, and the only reason he hadn't taken things further tonight was because his future was so uncertain.

But he'd like to have been afforded the time to show her not all relationships had to end up in mediation. She was skeptical due to her job and in spite of her family's successes in the marriage arena, and he got that. But what he was feeling for her, beyond his desire, was real…and if he could prove they weren't hysterically bonding, he'd show her there was true chemistry there.

He a little more than liked everything about her, from her sense of humor, to her thoughtful words, to her curvy hips and her super-hot tail. As a mermaid, she was incredible—stunning. But he also liked her kind heart, and how easily she'd rolled with the punches in terms of turning into a mermaid.

Now, as he stood watching her sleep, he wished he'd already told her as much. So whatever happened afterward, she'd at least know his intentions were very real.

Running a hand through his hair, he fought a yawn and paced to the front door. So far, since Darnell had cast some kind of demonic spell to keep the press at bay beyond the edge of Esther's property, they hadn't run into them anywhere else, but that, too, wouldn't be far down the pike, if someone was asking why he hadn't been questioned.

Leaning his head against the wall, he closed his eyes and took a deep breath, letting the few moments of freedom he'd likely have left for a very long time sink into his soul.

That was when everything clicked.

When he opened his eyes and looked down at the shoes by the door, all neatly lined up in a row on a blue throw rug with splashes of red. In particular, Carl's sneakers.

And the letters of that email…

And one by one, he put the pieces together before he went back to the table and grabbed his phone, texting his father and ordering an Uber, before he grabbed his jacket, threw it on and headed outside to wait for his ride—to wait for the end of this nightmare.

~

Esther slipped from beneath Carl's gentle grasp, rubbing the crick in her neck. Somehow, she'd fallen asleep on the couch after they'd read together. Tucking the blanket under Carl's chin, she brushed a lock of his hair from his forehead and dropped a kiss on his cheek.

Scooping up Mook, she clucked her tongue softly at Marsha so she'd follow her into her bedroom and padded down the small hall, noting everyone was fast asleep. Even Nina, who'd chosen to share a room with Archibald, snoozed peacefully.

Thinking about how much she loved having her house so full as she pulled down the cream and white comforter on her bed and threw the throw pillows in red and turquoise to the floor, she paused and looked around.

Where was Tucker?

"Tucker?" she hissed, returning to the kitchen, dark but for the small light under the microwave. "Tucker!"

Spinning around, she scanned the living room again, even though she'd just left it, her heart beginning to throb in her chest. "Tucker!"

"What the fuck, Little Fish?" Nina asked, scaring Esther and making her jump.

"Where's Tucker? He didn't go home, did he? I thought the plan was for him to stay here tonight, just in case the police have begun asking questions. I fell asleep on the couch. I haven't seen him since I went to read with Carl."

Nina's eyes narrowed, the charcoal depths glimmering. "That was the plan," she answered, stomping to the front door and throwing her work boots on. "I'm gonna kill him if he's off doin' somethin' stupid."

She flung open the door, with Esther hot on her heels. "Maybe he just went for a swim? Do merman need to swim like you need blood or Marty needs to shift?" She'd never thought to ask, but maybe that were true. She had experienced that strange call to the water tonight. Maybe he had, too?

Nina shook her mussed head and clenched her fist in anger. "How the fuck should I know?" she asked, flying out to Esther's small front porch and peering into the darkness.

Esther tucked her sweater closer under her chin and shivered. Damn, it had gotten even colder since they'd been out earlier practicing. "Tucker!" she called into the wind, now fully panicked.

Nina stopped all motion then, lifting her nose to the night air, her nostrils flaring. She spun back around and narrowed her eyes as she made her way back to the front door. "He was out here—definitely recently. I can smell it."

"Where could he have gone?"

"Goddammit. Why doesn't anyone ever fucking listen? If he went to the police, I'll rip his face off!" Nina yelled, stalking back into the house.

Esther followed, her heart pumping at an alarming rate as she shut the door to find everyone awake.

"What's going on?" Marty asked, pulling her bathrobe tighter.

"Tucker's gone," Nina growled as Wanda wandered out into the living room.

"Where?" she asked sleepily, her normally elegantly styled hair smashed to one side of her head.

"We don't know!" Esther responded, grabbing her phone to see if there were any texts from Tucker, but there was nothing.

"Hold up," Nina said, grabbing her phone from the kitchen counter and scrolling until she pressed a button. "I'm calling Sam, we'll get him to track dumb-ass's phone, and when we find that moron, I'm going to rip his thick head off his shoulders."

As Nina paced the kitchen, her footie pajamas scuffing softly on the hardwood, Esther's panic rose. Where would he have gone so late at night, and why?

Wanda gripped her arm as she fought to catch her breath, her worry and fear rising with each passing second.

Fifteen minutes later, she heard Nina say, "Dude, I almost like you today. Thanks, man. Tell Phoebe and gang I love their little fucking guts." She ended the call and looked at everyone with a deadpan expression. "He went to the lake."

"So late?" Marty crowed the question, pulling her robe off and heading back down the short hall to the guest room. "I feel like we should check on him. Just in case. I'm sure he's perfectly fine. He's probably with Jessica, but it can't hurt to be sure, can it? And where's the damn aspirin? Why can't I ever find that stupid bottle?"

Arch appeared, seemingly out of nowhere, his aging brow furrowed, half-empty aspirin bottle in hand. "Mistress Marty, I worry about you. This bottle was almost full. I truly think you should see a doctor about these headaches."

She held out the palm of her hand and stuck her tongue out at Archibald. "It's just a headache and some aspirin. It's not like I'm popping Vicodin. Though, with this damn headache, I wouldn't mind some," she joked, and dropped a kiss on Arch's cheek. "I'm fine. It's just stress from this merger. Now scooch. I have to get dressed." She closed the bedroom door, leaving the rest of them to sort through what to do next.

"Do you think she's right? Do you think we should go to the lake?" Esther asked, now in full-on worry mode, already halfway to the door.

Wanda shook her head, stuffing her hands into the wide pockets of her baby-blue bathrobe. "I don't know, but how can it hurt? In the meantime, let's text him and see if he responds. I'll get my clothes while you do."

"The fuck you will," Nina said, planting her hands

on her hips, slim in the blue onesie. "If shit's not right, we can't take a chance you'll get hurt. Go back to bed and let the non-knocked-up handle this shit."

Wanda rolled her tongue in her cheek and rasped a sigh. "I'll stay in the car. Swear it. But you need a lookout if we're going to the lake where the community is *gated* and guarded by security. Also, I'm not exactly helpless. I'm crazy hormonal, which packs a mean punch. Besides, we don't even know if anything's going on."

Nina stuck her finger in Wanda's face. "You leave the car, I break your skinny chicken legs. Got it? Then you won't be going anywhere until this kid's born. Now make yourself useful and text Darnell. Tell him to meet us at the lake, just in case."

Wanda pinched her friend's cheek and blew her a saucy kiss. "I'll be ready in two seconds."

As Esther waited for Tucker to text her back, she fought a nagging feeling. Why would he have gone to the lake after what happened the other night with his father? And why had Tucker gone without somebody with him? He might have super strength under the water, but he was just your average guy on land. If he'd gone off to investigate on his own, and he ran into trouble, she'd kill him herself for leaving without a word.

As she gathered her jacket, she checked her phone again. Nothing from Tucker. Dead silence. She'd also texted Jessica, but silence from that end, too.

"You guys ready?" Nina asked, her eyes intense as she held the door open.

"Yep," Esther nodded, even if her voice sounded shaky. "Ready."

"We'll keep the midnight oil burning," Archibald assured, hugging the women one by one, giving Esther an extra-long hug she burrowed into, inhaling the scent of warm cookies still lingering on him. "Be safe, precious ones."

Nina kissed him on the top of his head, and headed out the door into the frosty night with the rest of them in tow.

As they climbed into the big SUV, Esther said a small prayer, her stomach twisting and churning. *Please let him be okay. Please.*

~

Esther's pulse raced in a tidal wave of sound in her ears. "How the hell are we going to get in here? Like Wanda said, it's a gated community." She hadn't given that any thought as they drove over, but now, looking at all the lights surrounding the lush homes, and the guardhouse with a guard, not to mention the big iron gates, she had no idea how they'd get inside.

Nina draped an arm around her shoulders and popped her lips as they stood on the outskirts of the mermaid compound beside the SUV. "Oh, Little Fish, you're such a newb. Get on my back."

"What?"

"You heard me. Get the fuck on my back and hurry it up. Big Fish is in there. I can smell him. So, I wanna know what the hell's going on. If he's just seeing his sister in the wee hours of the fucking morning, no harm, no foul."

After everything she'd seen, after a tail and fins and fangs and more hair than a zoo full of big cats, she suddenly felt afraid. "Get on your back? Wait… Do you turn into like a bat or something?" Oh, my God. Could she fly? Did she turn into a winged creature?

Nina flicked her arm—hard.

"Ow! Quit hitting the fish!" she squawked, rubbing her stinging skin with her palm.

"Then stop being an asshat. I don't turn into a bat. Get on my back before I doubt all this credit I've been givin' you and let's beat feet."

"You got her?" Marty asked, rolling up her sleeves and pulling her long hair up into a pony.

Nina nodded, pulling her hoodie on. "I got her. Wanda? Stay the fuck put. Promise on Charlie's life."

Wanda's eyes went wide as she swatted Nina's arm. "I will not swear on your child's life. There will be no swearing on *anyone's* life. You'll just have to take my word for it, you overgrown bat!"

Esther's finger flew up in the air in a shot. "You *do* turn into a bat!" she accused, now the one doing the flicking of arms as she pinged Nina's rock-hard biceps.

Nina rolled her eyes as though she'd just suggested madness. "I do fucking not. Wanda, stop scaring her and stay the hell put in this damn car. When Darnell gets here, send him the fuck in. Now, *you*. Get. On. My. Back!" she whisper-yelled.

Esther didn't question her this time. Instead, she hopped on her back, wrapping her legs around Nina's slim waist. As Nina pulled back on her foot like a slingshot, she said, "Hold on. *Do not let go*, or who knows where the fuck your uterus will land."

Her uterus? How had her lady bits gotten in the middle of this? Nonetheless, she tightened her grip around the vampire's waist and neck.

Marty looked at Nina with a cheeky grin, rocking back on her heels. "You ready, Dark One?"

"Like a Kardashian in front of a fucking camera," Nina replied, grinning back at Marty.

"Then onward ho!" Marty whispered into the velvety cool of the night.

After that, the only thing Esther was even capable of thinking about were Nina's words, and how many uteri had been lost before hers.

~

Nina grunted as she dug her heels into the hard ground to stop herself, their landing only a little bumpy as she came to a screeching halt in front of the big maple tree at the lake.

Esther—dazed, wide-eyed, freezing—silently screamed when Nina dropped her on the ground, where she crumpled against the tree in a heap.

Marty was just a hair behind them, skidding to a stop just inches from Nina, who slapped her friend on the back. "Slow as molasses uphill in the winter, werewolf." Then she cackled softly.

Marty flipped up her middle finger, bending forward at the waist and putting her hands on her knees. She gasped for breath. "Fuck off, Elvira," she hissed, making Nina laugh harder.

"And I had the mermaid on my back to fucking boot."

But Marty didn't answer, instead she kept breathing hard, making Nina stoop down. "Hey, you okay?" she asked softly, pushing a strand of Marty's loose hair from her face.

"Just gimme a sec to catch my breath. I'm just tired from work. I'm fine," she rasped, gripping Nina's fingers.

As Esther watched their exchange, her hand immediately went to her belly. Well, it felt like her uterus was still intact. And then it all came back to her. Nina, jumping the fence like some kind of superhero, then running through the woods at the speed of light, branches swiping at her cheeks as she ducked and dodged tree limbs. The ground, swelling up at her and virtually disappearing as Marty followed close on her heels, her puffs of air low and feral.

And here they were. At the lake, which, by the by, was dead silent. She used her body to inch her way up the trunk of the tree and refocus her still wobbly vision.

"You okay, Little Fish?"

Esther smiled, starting to come to grips with this latest leg of her journey. "I'm fine. My uterus is fine. I might have lost an ovary, but who needs one of those?"

Nina gave a soft chuckle before she scanned the lake and said, "We need to snoop around a little. Sam's tracking bullshit doesn't always give specific locations. Maybe he's up at Fish Daddy's house and they're makin' nice? Or at his sister's?"

Marty, breathing regularly now, planted her hands on her hips. "I don't see or hear a damn thing. You smell anything?"

Nina pushed her hoodie from her head and shook it. "Nope. *You* smell anything?"

Marty wrinkled her nose and spun around slowly. "Nope. Esther, check your phone in case you got a text while we were getting in here."

Pulling her phone from her jacket, Esther scrolled it. "Not a thing but from Wanda, checking in. Oh, she also says Darnell's on his way. So, what do we do now?" she asked on a shiver.

The lake was calm tonight, without the activity of so many mermaids swimming about. The surrounding areas, thick with various types of trees, sat ominously silent, their branches shedding piles of leaves.

"Y'all okay?" she heard Darnell whisper as he made his way toward them out of the inky blackness.

Esther smiled at him. She had a real affection for this big demon who grew each time she encountered him. "Hi, Darnell."

"Hey, little one. You okay?" he asked, pulling her into a quick hug, one she welcomed with a happy sigh. Darnell was the snuggliest demon ever.

"I'm fine. We haven't seen anything so far, but thanks for coming."

He grinned down at her, his wide smile a beacon in the dark night. "Always."

"Okay, let's scout this shit out. The shoreline's pretty long. I say we walk it and look everywhere," Nina suggested. "You stay near me, Little Fish. Got that? D, Marty? Pair up. Let's find us the other half of this surf and turf"

Just as they were about to split up, Esther noticed the edge of something under one of the picnic tables that looked out of place.

"Wait. Look under that table." She ran toward it, dropping to her knees and reaching underneath. Her fingers felt nylon fabric, like a backpack, maybe? Grabbing hold, she pulled it out onto the dying grass and looked closer. "It's Tucker's!" Then she reached under farther and pulled out a pair of sneakers and Tucker's boots.

Marty scratched her head. "Tucker doesn't wear sneakers, and I'm pretty sure Fish Daddy only wears chain mail, so what the hell?"

Esther gripped the sneakers, her heart in her throat. "Sneakers…" she whispered.

Nina pulled the backpack from her hands and unzipped it, sticking her fingers inside to root around. She pulled out his phone and pressed the button along the side. "Thank fuck he doesn't password protect," she muttered, scrolling the phone, the light from the face illuminating her concern. "He texted his father like a half hour ago and said he had to meet with him. Says it's something important. Then he grabbed an Uber. So maybe he *is* at Fish Daddy's house?"

"But which one is Fish Daddy's house?" Esther wondered out loud, looking at row after row of lush houses.

"Fuck!" Marty swore. "There are ton of houses. Though, I suppose we could go sniffing, right? We'll be able to smell him somewhere in mermaid suburbia?"

As Marty spoke, and her lips moved, all sound stopped for Esther, making her cock her head. Everything in front of her eyes swirled in circles, blurring and fading in and out, until all she saw was the water in front of her.

A vibration, low and deep, pooled in her belly, and the sudden, undeniable need to pull her clothes off compelled her to spring into action.

She thought briefly, just before she ran toward the water, almost totally naked but for her bra and panties, how funny it was that she felt compelled to take her clothes off in front of everyone.

As in, strip naked.

Like that had ever happened before.

CHAPTER 18

"Little Fish! Where the fuck are you going?" she heard Nina bellow, and gun to head, she wasn't sure she could answer.

All Esther knew was she had to be in the water. *Now. This second.* What force, or maybe even who was creating this tumultuous, aching need in her, remained unclear as she launched herself into the lake.

She didn't feel the cold air anymore. She didn't feel any fear. All she felt was this wild, unspoken whisper that said to get in the water.

Ignoring everyone's cries from the shore, she dove —she dove deep, popping her eyes open and pushing forward until her legs melted away and her tail propelled her forward.

As though on instinct, she headed to the same spot Tucker had taken her—the cavern, where its dark, wet stone and warm pools waited.

The beautiful scenery she'd been in such awe of

passed by without nary a glance from Esther. In her gut, as she swept past the ice-cream-colored castles and the conch shells the size of furniture, she drove forward with only one thing on her mind.

And it popped into her head as swiftly as she'd been compelled to take her clothes off and get in the lake.

Tucker.

Tucker was under here. She knew it, could taste it, and as she placed her arms by her sides and pistoned forward, that feeling became stronger, clearer.

As she careened past fish and tangles of seaweed, forced her way through strong currents and over groups of rocks, she headed straight toward the cavern.

Tucker needed help—she knew it—and as she grew closer, her heart speeding up, she ignored everything else, all the warning signs, all the vibrations of fear, and swam her way inside the cave.

~

"You lying bitch!" Tucker snarled, yanking at his arms, straining against the chains that held his wrists and rubbed his scales raw. He was partially submersed in the water to his waist, chained to a group of rocks.

"Tucker! Stop antagonizing her!" Chester whispered fiercely, he, too, chained to a rock deep within the cavern Tucker had taken Esther to just two days ago.

But Tucker was incensed; infuriated that he hadn't

figured this out sooner. That someone he loved and trusted had done this to him.

"Yeah, Tucker," Jessica mimicked, swimming around them, her fins flapping rapidly as she held the gun steady. "Stop antagonizing. But it won't matter anyway. You have to die, brother. I didn't think you'd figure it out, but you're smarter than I gave you credit for."

Still, he had to know why, and in his anger, all the questions that had pinged around in his mind as Jessica had tied them up at gunpoint, spilled out. "I don't get it, Jess! *Why?* Why would you do this? How did you get production to agree to this? Shelly would never have approved—"

"Shelly was bought and paid for. It's amazing how a little cash will make a bitch turn the other cheek. Shelly was happy to help me with that bullshit memo."

His anger ratcheted up a notch. "Why not just come to me? If you needed money, why not ask to borrow it from me? Why do you need so much damn money, anyway? Why kill people? Why kill Gomez?"

She scoffed at him, her pretty features turning hard and ugly. "Well, I wouldn't have killed *anyone* if they'd just stopped poking around. But that Dr. Sanchez just couldn't quit until he found an answer. Somehow, he figured out I'd hacked into his email. Know how I know that?"

"How?" he seethed, still in disbelief.

"Because I know *everything* he did on that computer. I know everything you do on *yours*. All your tech—your phone, your laptop, your desktop at work—all hacked by yours truly. I can watch your every move, see every communication. Ask Chester—*he's* the one who taught me. That's how I knew you were coming to see Father tonight. That misogynistic, sexist *bastard*!" She waved the gun around to emphasize just how much of a bastard she thought their father was.

Tucker swiveled his head to look at Chester with an angry question in his eyes. "Why? Why would you help her?"

But Chester immediately cowered, his eyes searching Tucker's, sweat beading on his brow. "I swear to you, Tuck, I had no idea this was what she was doing. Swear it! I just showed her a thing or two. How to look at a competitor's internal memos. Stuff like that. Not in a million years would I have ever believed she'd do this! I swear on my fucking life, I had no idea she was behind this!"

Tucker tightened his jaw and narrowed his eyes at Jessica, so irate, he wanted to throttle her. "You killed Gomez to shut him up about those bad tests. Gomez knew the water was bad. He never sent me a test that said otherwise. That's why he called me the night everyone thinks he killed himself—because he figured it out. He figured out that somehow, your email address was involved. PrincessFish@Gmail.com! I saw the note he scribbled, Jessica. I saw it—his assistant had it! But you know that, don't you? You know because you tried to kill Armand, too! An old man, for Christ's sake! You knew the water was bad and you threw me under the bus!" he thundered.

Smiling at Tucker, she winked. "Well, I didn't *know*-know, Tuck. I mean, Gomez was easy. I just threw some sleeping pills in his food and it was done. But Armand? I heard about the ruckus he created the day he was let go. I have spies, by the way. Anyway, it was too much of a risk to take a chance he had something I didn't know about. When I found out they shared another apartment together, I did what I had to do. As one does when they don't want to go to jail for murder."

Christ, he'd been so stupid. So damn stupid. Jessica. His own *sister* had betrayed him so deeply, he felt a tear in his soul. Never in a million years would he have suspected her—which made her the most likely suspect, didn't it? With her boyfriend's background in IT, all of this had been a cakewalk.

And those sneakers—those fucking sneakers. He knew he'd seen them somewhere. On his sister's feet. That's where. She'd snuck into Gomez's office and rifled through his email, and he'd never once noticed it was her, dressed in a suit. But he'd known those sneakers.

"*Why?*" he raged. "Why did you do this? Why would you frame your own flesh and blood for murder? Why would you let people get sick—die—for a *buck*? Why? You have plenty of money, Jessica!"

"Oh, Tuck. Poor, poor blind Tuck. Here's why—because *father*," she spat, letting the word drip with derision, "would never have let me get anywhere at H2O-Yo but right where I am as we speak. I'll always be nice Jessica, the underrated, overworked, always-trying-to-prove-herself, bullshit marketing director! Know why?"

His eyes went wide. She'd gone mad. Utterly and totally mad, but he went along with it anyway—because he had to know. "Why?"

"Because, you bloody fool—I'm not your sister! I'm your *half-sister*. The product of an affair mother had many years ago!"

~

Holy fucking deception, Batman! As Esther peered into the cave, listening to everything Jessica confessed, her stomach churned, and if she didn't do something fast—if she didn't get that gun from Jessica—Tucker and Chester would be dead.

Closing her eyes, she tried to remember how to communicate with Tucker via her mind, but she couldn't remember if there were any details to it. So, she just kept her eyes closed and called his name.

"Tucker! Tucker, I'm here!"

And then, as she listened, as she prayed, hoped against hope he'd answer back, she heard nada. Not a damn thing.

Oh, Jesus in a sardine can—what now?

Try again, Esther. Try again. She heard her grandfather's voice in her head when he'd encouraged her to get in the water.

Okay, try again, she would.

"Tucker! Tucker, listen to me. I'm here. Answer me, Tucker!"

Clinging to the cave's wall, she prayed harder and tried once more. *"Tucker. Goddammit, answer me! I'm out here by the cave's opening and I'm doing everything you taught me to do like a good little mermaid and it's damn well not working. Answer me, you fathead fish!"*

"Esther?"

"Yees!" she screamed in her mind. *"Yes!"*

"Get out, Esther! Go get help!"

"Are you insane? She'll kill you before I have the chance to get anyone. We have to get the gun!"

"Esther, get the fuck out of here nooow!" he roared in her head.

"The fuck you say," she answered back, her chest so tight, she almost lost her breathing skills. *"Shut up and distract her. Work with me, Tucker. I can help!"*

"Esther, she's crazy! And you're too unskilled to take her on. Just get away!"

Unskilled-unschmilled. She'd show him unskilled—his head was on the chopping block and he was tit for tatting her mermaidness.

Jerk.

Hands touched her from behind—hands that weren't unfamiliar, but she jolted anyway, spinning around, trying to keep all her mermaid balls juggling in the air at once.

But there was Nina, her long dark hair making her beautiful face look as though it were peeking through a dark cloud. How the hell had she…

And then she remembered. Nina didn't breathe!

Gripping Nina's shoulders, she pulled her into a hug, the water between them creating a small wave. Thank God for Nina.

She grabbed Esther's shoulders and frowned before she pointed to the inside of the cave and motioned she'd go in first. Esther hoped she meant she was going to be Jessica's distraction, but she wasn't sure. However, it was a gamble she was willing to take.

Esther nodded and gave her a thumbs-up. And then she told Mr. Critical, *"Hang on just a minute longer, Tucker—we're coming in!"*

~

As his mind raced and Jessica's latest revelation sank in, he fought disbelief. Their mother'd had an affair?

"How do you know Mother had an affair?"

Jessica rolled her eyes at him and floated toward the ledge of the rocks they were chained to. "Because I found their letters, stupid. Their *love letters,* so to speak. It was disgusting. But you know Serafina. Always doing the right thing. She broke it off with him after Father found out. I have to tell you, I don't really blame her for cheating. I mean, he's a total douche. But he raised me sort of like his own—except for when it comes to H2O-Yo. Oh, that's all pretty-boy Tucker's baby, now, isn't it? He was never going to let me get anywhere. So I decided to take matters into my own hands. Once you were in jail, he would have given me VP of Production. He'd have no choice anymore, because I'm the most qualified!"

"How could I have never seen how much you hated me?" he asked, praying Esther had given up the foolish notion of tangling with Jessica and gone off to find some help. She was no match for Jessica.

Jessica rolled her eyes and wrinkled her pert nose. "I don't hate you, Tuck. I hate Father, who isn't even really my father, is he? And when the opportunity presented itself, and I had a chance to show him I was worthy, you were going to nip that in the bud, weren't you? You ass-kisser!"

"People were going to get sick from that water, Jessica—people *did* get sick, one died! How could you be so heartless?" he spat.

But she just shrugged her shoulders nonchalantly. "Collateral damage and all. Mining from that spot in Australia was my idea, remember? The new line was *my* idea, and you screwed it all up. So I screwed *you* all up. You dig?"

"You should have come to me, Jessica," he said sadly. "I would have helped."

"Fuck you, and fuck your help! All you big corporate assholes and that damn glass ceiling! Anyway...you gotta go, brother, and so does your weasel of a friend. Sorry it had to end this way."

Just in that moment, as Jessica raised the gun and aimed it at his chest, there was an explosion of water so fierce, so powerful, he thought surely his father had somehow found them.

Ah. But no. It was the vampire—with the newb mermaid hot on her heels. And him helpless to do anything to prevent their deaths.

Shit.

CHAPTER 19

Nina flew out of the water like some kind of actor from *The Matrix*, her hands in claw-like position, her legs spread wide apart to help her land on the cavern's ledge.

Water sprayed everywhere, blinding Esther for a moment before she stood her ground and did what Tucker taught her—she rolled with the force of the water until she was just behind Jessica's shoulder.

And as she swam up behind her, she balled her fist, looking directly into Tucker's eyes, filled with surprise, and let 'er rip, hurling a ball of water.

Which didn't go quite as planned—or at all, really. It ended up swiping Jessica's shoulder like a water balloon—which, in hindsight, wasn't terribly effective.

"Little Fish, look out!" Nina screamed, diving into the water again as Jessica swung toward her and pulled off a shot.

But Nina knocked Esther out of the way, the bullet

missing her by mere inches. As they dropped to the bottom of the cavern, deep into its beautifully blue depths, Esther righted herself and headed straight back upward toward the shadow that was Jessica's gorgeous fin.

She propelled toward her at an alarming speed, almost losing control as she rammed into Jessica's tail, using her own to swat at her.

And that swat was weak and slow, but it gave her enough time to see Nina get hold of Jessica's wrist and make her drop the gun. As they fought and fell to the depths of the lake, Esther raced upward, hoping to free Tucker and Chester.

Just as her head popped above the surface, and the cavern became clear, in all its sleek rock and warm pools, she remembered another mermaid superpower, and she prayed it would work—because bubbles could be like bullets, right?

As she focused on the chains that bound the men, she gathered water in her mouth, and rolled her tongue around, spitting it at the chains on Tucker's wrist.

"Esther, no!" he bellowed, ducking his head and wincing.

But there was a ping of satisfaction, and as she watched the water bounce off the rock, making part of it crumble, she at least knew she was on the right track. So, she did it again in an awkward spray, managing to nail the chain securing Tucker's right arm.

"Well done, Newb!" he yelled to her with a proud smile as he began to pull at the chains holding him.

"Get Chester!" she cried, before diving back downward to find Nina.

"Esther, no! Wait for me!" he shouted.

But Jessica had Nina, and after all the vampire had done for her, after all the coddling and soothing in her own crass way, Esther wasn't going to let anything happen to her without putting up a fight.

Zooming downward, she looked left and right, but couldn't see them anywhere—and then she spotted a length of Nina's hair, twirling in the blue water behind one of the ice-cream-colored castles.

Without thought, she went for it, racing toward Nina and coming around the corner of the fake castle at breakneck speed.

Unfortunately, maybe because she was nowhere near the master of deceit Tucker's sister was, she slammed right into Jessica, who had Nina wrapped up in her tail, squeezing until Nina's eyes bulged. Jessica laughed at Esther as Nina struggled.

Even knowing she couldn't drown, or maybe couldn't even die, that didn't stop Esther. This woman had killed her uncle. Her only relation left in the world. Had tried to kill her uncle's lover.

She had to go.

She didn't think about what she did next, she didn't consider the fact that she'd failed miserably just moments ago in her attempt—she just did it. Esther balled her fist, swung her arm wide, and just let go.

The result was a thunderous wave—one so powerful, it didn't just knock Nina from Jessica's deadly grip, it knocked over *everything* in its path, shooting them all forward, leaving Esther tumbling helplessly until she hit the bottom of the lake floor.

One wouldn't think they could crash to the depths with such force; it was, after all, just water. But somehow, she'd managed to whip up a mother of a doozy, because she fell to the bottom like a sack of rocks, smashing her back against a boulder and cutting the backside of her tail.

With a groan, Esther Williams Sanchez forgot how to be a mermaid for a moment, and when she opened her mouth to cry out her anguish, she let the water in. As it seeped into her lungs, the weight of it in her chest made her eyes roll to the back of her head.

Blood twisted and twirled upward in tendrils of crimson as her eyes began to bulge and her arms grew weak.

"Esther!" Tucker yelled in her head. *"Jesus Christ, Esther!"*

She heard him scream her name, felt his hands grip her, heard water rush past her until she almost passed out.

And then blessed air—cold, crisp air. She sucked it into her lungs, spitting out the water packed in her chest with a garbled hack.

"Esther!" Marty screamed, running into the water to help. She caught a glimpse of Darnell right behind Marty, splashing into the water to grab her from Tucker.

"Take her!" Tucker ordered. "I have to get Nina!" He

dove back in without looking back, and tears formed in the corners of her eyes as he went.

"Jesus!" Marty yelped. "She's bleeding! Help me get her out!"

But Esther struggled against Marty and Darnell, trying to sit up and reposition herself to dive back in—one thing and one thing only on her mind.

Kill the bitch.

The moment she'd managed to struggle upright was the moment Jessica popped up out of the water, holding what appeared to be a passed-out Tucker by his hair. Hovering almost above the lake, she stretched her arms out, and just like her not so Fish Daddy, she did the whirling dervish thing—and in seconds, everything and everyone in her path was hit by a wall of water.

Darnell lost his grip on Esther, and Marty flew back against the shoreline, whizzing behind them with a sound she heard rumbling in her ears.

"Esther! No!" Darnell shouted, his hoarse voice just barely heard over the roar of the water. "Duck, Esther, duuuck!"

Nah. She was tired of ducking. There would be no more ducking for Esther Williams Sanchez. This fuck-nuttery would stop *now,* because the guy she was really heating up to was dangling lifelessly in the air, and her uncle was dead.

All because of greed.

This one's for you, Grandpa, she thought before the wave came at her with the force of a tornado. Balling her fists—both her fists, Esther responded with some primal instinct.

She'd never be able to explain how she knew to do it just the way she did—or even how she'd managed to summon the power to do so while she bled and her body ached with agonizing stings to all her muscles. She couldn't even explain how she knew if she didn't do something at that very moment, Tucker would die either way. If Jessica slammed him down against the water, she'd crush him, and Esther wasn't going to let that happen.

But by God, this woman had killed her uncle to climb some damn corporate ladder, and with that angry thought behind her next move, she let her hands go. Just threw them out into the cold night air, aiming directly for Jessica.

The thunderous whoosh emitting from her hands took her by surprise. The power with which she threw her hands rolled like a bowling ball, gaining speed, roaring, rolling, screaming through the air and hitting Jessica square in the face. Her hands let go of Tucker, and as he fell to the water, Jessica crumpled, deflating much like a balloon, her body flailing as she hit the water with a loud splash.

Esther ducked under the madness she'd created, back into the water to race toward Tucker.

"Go left, Little Fish!" She heard Nina yell from somewhere far off, just as she reached Tucker and threw herself under his falling body.

There was a brief flash of Nina's face, her hair plastered to her head, moments before she rushed up underneath both of them and lobbed them at the shore in a rush of water, where they landed side by side, sprawled out on the grass beside—of all surprises—Chester, who Darnell knelt to help up.

Reaching out, she felt for Tucker's hand, prayed he'd grasp hers.

And when his fingers wrapped around her hand, she whispered, *"Thank God."*

Instantly, he popped up, his handsome profile filled with worry as he turned to her and cupped her cheek. "Are you okay? Jesus, Esther! You scared the hell out of me. Don't do that *ever* again. Please don't do that ever again."

She chuckled. Weakly, because, you know...bleeding. "Unskilled my eye," she teased as his lips grazed hers, and even in her sorry state, she was instantly warmed by his mouth on hers.

"And I liked your shoes, you heathen!" Marty yelled, making Esther pop up next to Tucker to find the werewolf had Jessica by the tail, dragging her toward the picnic table and slamming her facedown on the ground.

"Marty!" she heard Wanda call. "Put her down!"

Oh, Wanda was going to get it from Nina for leaving the car. But as she came into view, Esther saw she had towels in one hand, and her other arm looped through someone else's.

Getty Pearson's.

As their tails melted and their limbs returned,

Wanda threw towels at them while a sopping-wet Marty and Darnell kept an eye on Jessica. Nina rushed to the shore, ready to do more battle, but Getty held up his hand.

"Please," he said to Nina, his eyes sharp and clear. "Accept my apologies for my horrid behavior the other night."

Nina didn't say a word, but she nodded her head before she knelt to wrap Esther in towels, pinching her cheek. "Way to fucking do some damage, Little Fish," she praised, knocking Esther in the shoulder.

Shivering, Esther could only smile, because Getty Pearson terrified her—far more than Nina ever could.

But Getty held out his hand to her, his eyes almost kind. "Esther? May I help you?"

Eyeing his broad hand, she hesitantly placed hers in his palm and allowed him to help her up.

"You're bleeding, honey!" Wanda gasped, kneeling to inspect her wound, but Esther shooed her away.

"I'm okay, Wanda. It's nothing a bandage won't cure."

Getty shook his head, his white hair, shorter in her human form, bouncing under the moonlight. "Esther, I don't know where to begin. I—"

But Esther shook her head, ignoring the sting of her wound. "It's fine, Mr. Pearson. None of this is your fault...but none of it is Tucker's, either. I hope you know that, and you'll do your best to make it right."

Then Getty looked to Tucker, his eyes now full of sorrow. "I don't know the details yet. I only know I was wrong, and forever I'll regret the actions I took, son." Getty held out his hand, extending the olive branch.

Tucker's jaw clenched, his profile tight and angry, his wide chest puffing outward.

Oh, no, no, no. No posturing today. She drove a finger into his ribs. "Don't be a jerk. I think it's pretty obvious, your sister did a number on everyone. Your father's no different. Now make nice."

Tucker took his hand, holding on to it for a brief but substantial moment before he let go. "We need to talk, Father," he said, low and husky.

"Indeed, son. We do. For now, I have more pressing matters. Shall we meet tomorrow sometime? Maybe for breakfast? I know your mother would be delighted."

Tucker finally smiled at his father, and nodded. "Sure, Dad. Text me and I'll be there."

Getty smiled back, the first smile Esther had seen from him, and it was remarkably like Tucker's. "And now, those pressing matters," he said, moving off in the direction of Jessica, who Marty and Darnell still had a firm grip on.

She lay limp as someone else entered the scene and carried her off toward the exit to the lake, with Getty behind them, his face grim, leaving everyone cold and wet and in total silence.

Chester was the first to speak, his chattering teeth clacking together. "Tuck. I swear, I didn't know. I'll speak to council. I'll confess that I showed her some stuff. I'm sorry, but I'll take my punishment as council sees fit. And I'll tell them what happened tonight."

But Tucker shook his head. "It's okay, Chester. I guess she was just the last person I suspected. I never..." His voice drifted off, and then he squared his shoulders and slapped his friend on the back. "Go home, Chester. All will be well. Get a good night's sleep and we'll talk in the morning."

Chester took his leave quietly, likely lost in his thoughts about the night's events.

And then Nina narrowed her gaze at Wanda. "Didn't I tell you to stay in the GD car?"

"Well, if I'd done that, Getty never would have known what was going on down here. I had to do *something*. Also, you wouldn't have fresh towels. So there." She stuck her tongue out at Nina, who hissed at her before Wanda wrapped Esther in a floral-scented hug, kissing the top of her head. "You're a badass, young lady. So badass, I think we should call you Hurricane or some such superhero name."

Marty hugged both Esther and Wanda before she let them go and said, "Well, fish folk, I don't know about you, but I'm ready to hit the road and go back to the cottage. I have it on good authority Arch has, in his waiting-to-see-if-they-lived-this-time baking frenzy, made cake. Double fudge, chocolate-something infused with the petals of some rare flower from somewhere, and I think a win for the good guys deserves cake, don't you?" She secured the towel now wrapped around her head with a smile

"Aw, fuck you and your cake, Marty," Nina groused, scooping up towels. "You know I can fekkin' eat cake. Shit, I miss cake."

"You don't even know cake from a damn hole in your head, vampire," Marty teased. "You lived on Ring Dings and chicken wings for more than half your life. Now c'mon. I want a do-over. Race ya to the car!" Marty yelled, taking off.

As Nina tore after her, Darnell plopped a kiss on Esther's cheek and patted Tucker on the back before he offered his arm to Wanda. "May I have this dance?" he asked on his bubbling chuckle.

Wanda sighed, blowing a stray strand of hair from her eyes. "I thought you'd never ask," she teased, patting his arm as they made their way toward the exit, leaving Esther and Tucker alone.

He looked down at her and smiled his delicious smile. "That was really quite something, mermaid. The two-handed tidal wave. Well played—well played."

She smiled back at him. "I don't know where that came from. Panic, fear, I just saw you dangling there and it freaked me out so much, I reacted."

Pulling her closer by the towel wrapped around her shoulders, he winked. "I think that means you like me, Esther Williams Sanchez."

Her heart beat hard against her ribs, and the heat in her belly lurched and churned as they pressed against one another. "As merman go, I just think you're okay."

Without warning, he scooped her up, pressing his lips to hers, taking control of her mouth and making her forget her wound and her hesitations and pretty much everything else.

When he pulled away, he asked with a teasing grin. "Still just okay?"

"You know what we're doing here, don't you?" she asked, breathless and hopeful—so hopeful.

"Hysterically bonding, right?"

"Yes. That's what we're doing," she replied, but she wasn't so sure that was true anymore.

"Then I have a proposition for you. Wanna hear it?"

"Go."

"What say we go hysterically bond on a real-live date?"

"Like for food or something?"

"Don't push your luck. I save my food dates for the women who *like me*-like me, not just think I'm okay. Maybe some coffee? Or a drink?"

"Do mermen drink?"

"Like fish," he said, unable to hold back his laughter as his belly rippled with it against hers.

Esther looked up at him and smiled. "Then I say we go hysterically bond, Big Fish," she answered, the edges of her heart melting with more of that hope.

And then she pressed her lips to his and sighed, after which, hand in hand, they went off to hysterically bond.

Together.

EPILOGUE

Two months later, on an unseasonably warm day in November…

One little newbie mermaid who'd found a new family of merpeople to love, and a super-hot merman she was rapidly falling deeply in love with; a sexy merman who was working his way toward not just a less argumentative relationship with his father, but a new relationship with a newbie mermaid he couldn't keep his hands off of; a half vampire, half witch who's suddenly learned she's more than just the muscle of her group, she's also, much to her surprise, some of the very important glue; a pretty, blonde, faithful Spanx-wearing werewolf who's still in the process of a very complicated merger with her husband's cosmetic company, and continues to have the headaches to prove it; a very pregnant halfsie, who can't keep her eyes open but will dare you to say such; a manservant who is never happier than when he's cooking for a crowd of people —especially merpeople, who enjoy hearty appetites; a demon who has absolutely no intention of ever getting wet again; a snarky cat who's just returned from the realm after a much-needed visit with her fellow familiars; a kind, gentle zombie who's read *The Little Mermaid* at least twenty times in order to get to know his new friends; happy, healthy children gathering seashells and running amok on the shores of Oyster Hollow; volleyball-playing spouses; and a whole pod of merpeople, gathered together at the new mermaid's beachfront cottage to celebrate the joy of framily…

"Little Fish! Get the fuck over here!" Nina demanded as Esther rushed into her arms and gave her a sloppy kiss on the cheek, which the vampire managed to endure for all of a half second before she was squirming out of her embrace.

"Vampire!" she squealed. "Long time no see!"

"You just fucking saw me a week ago, dipshit. Remember the stupid outlet mall with these two morons?"

Esther snorted. It didn't matter the short length of time since she'd seen Nina. She was always thrilled to bits when she did—she hadn't just hysterically bonded with Tucker, she'd bonded with the vampire, and she was never going to let her go.

Wanda, still as pregnant as ever, waddled toward her, her beautiful face as flawless as her maternity dress with the pink bow around her waist. "Esther, honey! You look amazing. I see love agrees with you?"

Love. Something she'd had all her life in various forms, but not this particular kind of love. The kind that made her smile to herself during an ugly mediation. The kind that texted her in the middle of the day just to send her heart emojis. The kind she knew would pick her up after a long day and buy her a cheeseburger.

Kissing Wanda's cheek, she smiled back—in fact, there was hardly a time she wasn't smiling these days. "Everything agrees with me these days. Marty? How's the headache?"

Marty, in her form-fitting jeggings, oversized lavender sweater, thigh-high flat black boots and big hoop earrings, flapped a hand at her before she gave her a tight squeeze. "My head's fine. It's the pain in my ass I'm worried about."

Nina gave Marty a shove with a smile. "Fuck off, Ass Sniffer. I'll never be as big a pain in the ass as you."

"Wanna race? Whoever loses is the biggest pain in the ass!" she called as she took off down the sand and past the men, who'd begun a rousing, very boisterous game of volleyball.

But Nina didn't follow her, instead, she left Marty

spinning her wheels. "So, everything okay? Mermaiding good?"

Esther gripped her favorite vampire's hand and grinned, pulling her toward the long table where Getty and Serafina sat, sipping wine. "It's the best thing that's ever happened to me."

And it was. She was learning, growing, getting better every day at being a mermaid. She and Tucker swam every night at the beach together, laughing, kissing, making love.

When they'd finally decided the time was right to consummate their relationship, she was only a little disappointed to hear mermaid sex was a myth. But Tucker made up for it in spades.

In spades.

And now, they spent all their days together with Mooky and Marsha, and his cats Freckle and Fran, who'd all taken a little while to warm up to each other, but still kept a guarded distance apart, sprinkled with a healthy dose of respect.

"And the pod people? They're being nice? You're making lots of little mermaid friends?" Nina asked as the water lapped at the shore in the background.

Now she beamed. Once she'd met everyone, when Serafina had graciously introduced her as though she were one of her own children, her world grew even bigger. Nowadays, she managed at least an invitation a week from one merperson or another to some function or other, and her world was full—full of belonging somewhere and to something.

"The pod people are amazing," she answered, as Tucker, strong, handsome in his black turtleneck and low-slung jeans, wandered over and greeted Nina.

"Look who's here! The most laid-back vampire in the world," he teased, giving Nina a kiss on the cheek.

She gave him the finger with a grin. "Fuck off, Sharkbait." And then she laughed at her own joke before she squeezed Esther's shoulder and ran off down the beach toward the men, yelling, "Hey, you bunch of sissy-asses, lemme in on this game!"

"Did we ever thank her for helping to save our hides?" Tucker asked as he pulled her close to him, running his hands over her spine in that delicious way he had of evoking some serious heat in her loins.

"I think we did. I mean, if bringing her a blood basket isn't a thank you, what is?" Esther asked, kissing his lips.

"Today's a good day, wouldn't you say, brethren in hysterical bonding?"

Yeah, today was a good day. The sun was shining and the breeze had only a slight nip to it, making it perfect for Archibald's impromptu barbecue. Of which they'd been to many—impromptu celebrations, that is.

Arch was always cooking up something in that beautiful kitchen of Wanda's, and he was always inviting them to share.

And for the most part, the darkness of Jessica's betrayal had settled, if not passed. She and Tucker had talked long into the night on many nights about what had happened, and why she'd done what she did. They never really found any answers, and Jessica didn't help.

Tucker had tried to visit her in mermaid lockdown with permission from the council, but she'd refused to see him, and he'd come to accept that she might never want to talk to him—or his father, who, little by little, had begun to mend the broken bridge between himself and his son.

Serafina was the one who made Esther's heart hurt the most, in sympathy. Her daughter, so lost, so angry, had hurt her, and in one of her more emotional moments, she'd confessed to Esther those awful, helpless feelings, and they'd talked about it, and Esther had listened, and now, she hoped the woman was on her way to at least finding acceptance. What else was there when your child betrayed you so harshly, but accepting and moving forward?

Now, on this sunny day, with three long tables set with gorgeous fall floral arrangements, and wine and food in abundance, all their family and friends gathered around, laughing, eating, drinking, with her uncle's picture prominently displayed on the head table, alongside her parents' and grandparents' pictures. Esther tucked herself into Tucker's embrace and sighed. "Yeah, today's a good day, my fellow hysterical bonder. And as a matter of fact, I like you a lot. *A. Lot*," she joked, rubbing her cheek against his chest.

"I love you, Little Fish," he murmured against the top of her head.

"I love you, too, Big Fish. I love you, too."

And then Esther Williams Sanchez smiled, and cuddled with her favorite hysterical bonder ever.

The End

Thank you, thank you for joining me for *The Accidental Mermaid*! I so hope you'll come back for Marty's journey and for *The Accidental Unicorn* (yep. It's true!) coming soon!

PREVIEW ANOTHER BOOK BY DAKOTA CASSIDY

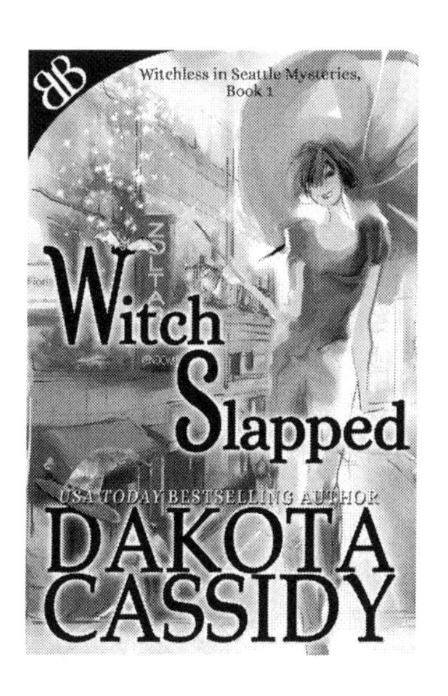

Chapter 1

"**L**eft, Stevie! Left!" my familiar, Belfry, bellowed, flapping his teeny bat wings in a rhythmic whir against the lash of wind and rain. "No, your other left! If you don't get this right sometime soon, we're gonna end up resurrecting the entire population of hell!"

I repositioned him in the air, moving my hand to the left, my fingers and arms aching as the icy rains of Seattle in February battered my face and my last clean outfit. "Are you sure it was *here* that the voice led you? Like right in this spot? Why would a ghost choose a cliff on a hill in the middle of Ebenezer Falls as a place to strike up a conversation?"

"Stevie Cartwright, in your former witch life, did the ghosts you once spent more time with than the living always choose convenient locales to do their talking? As I recall, that loose screw Ferdinand Santos decided to make an appearance at the gynecologist. Remember? It was all stirrups and forceps and gabbing about you going to his wife to tell her where he hid the toenail clippers. That's only one example. Shall I list more?"

Sometimes, in my former life as a witch, those who'd gone to the Great Beyond contacted me to help them settle up a score, or reveal information they took to the grave but felt guilty about taking. Some scores and guilty consciences were worthier than others.

"Fine. Let's forget about convenience and settle for getting the job done because it's forty degrees and dropping, you're going to catch your death, and I can't spend all day on a rainy cliff just because you're sure someone is trying to contact me using *you* as my conduit. You aren't like rabbit ears on a TV, buddy. And let's not forget the fact that we're unemployed, if you'll recall. We need a job, Belfry. We need big, big job before my savings turns to ashes and joins the pile that was once known as my life."

"Higher!" he demanded. Then he asked, "Speaking of ashes, on a scale of one to ten, how much do you hate Baba Yaga today? You know, now that we're a month into this witchless gig?"

Losing my witch powers was a sore subject I tried in quiet desperation to keep on the inside.

I puffed an icy breath from my lips, creating a spray from the rain splashing into my mouth. "I don't hate Baba," I replied easily.

Almost too easily.

The answer had become second nature. I responded the same way every time anyone asked when referring to the witch community's fearless, ageless leader, Baba Yaga, who'd shunned me right out of my former life in Paris, Texas, and back to my roots in a suburb of Seattle.

I won't lie. That had been the single most painful moment of my life. I didn't think anything could top being left at the altar by Warren the Wayward Warlock. Forget losing a fiancé. I had the witch literally slapped right out of me. I lost my entire being. Everything I've ever known.

Belfry made his wings flap harder and tipped his head to the right, pushing his tiny skull into the wind. "But you no likey. Baba booted you out of Paris, Stevie. Shunned you like you'd never even existed."

Paris was the place to be for a witch if living out loud was your thing. There was no hiding your magic, no fear of a human uprising or being burned at the stake out of paranoia. Everyone in the small town of Paris was paranormal, though primarily it was made up of my own kind.

Some witches are just as happy living where humans are the majority of the population. They don't mind keeping their powers a secret, but I came to love carrying around my wand in my back pocket just as naturally as I'd carry my lipstick in my purse.

I really loved the freedom to practice white magic anywhere I wanted within the confines of Paris and its rules, even if I didn't love feeling like I lived two feet from the fiery jaws of Satan.

But Belfry had taken my ousting from the witch community much harder than me—or maybe I should say he's more vocal about it than me.

So I had to ask. "Do you keep bringing up my universal shunning to poke at me, because you get a kick out of seeing my eyes at their puffiest after a good, hard cry? Or do you ask to test the waters because there's some witch event Baba's hosting that you want to go to with all your little familiar friends and you know the subject is a sore one for me this early in the 'Stevie isn't a witch anymore' game?"

Belfry's small body trembled. "You hurt my soul, Cruel One. I would never tease about something so delicate. It's neither. As your familiar, it's my job to know where your emotions rank. I can't read you like I used to because—"

"Because I'm not on the same wavelength as you. Our connection is weak and my witchy aura is fading. Yadda, yadda, yadda. I get it. Listen, Bel, I don't hate BY. She's a good leader. On the other hand, I'm not inviting her over for girls' night and braiding her hair either. She did what she had to in accordance with the white witch way. I also get that. She's the head witch in charge and it's her duty to protect the community."

"Protect-schmotect. She was over you like a champion hurdler. In a half second flat."

Belfry was bitter-schmitter.

"Things have been dicey in Paris as of late, with a lot of change going on. You know that as well as I do. I just happened to be unlucky enough to be the proverbial straw to break Baba's camel back. She made me the example to show everyone how she protects us…er, *them*. So could we not talk about her or my defunct powers or my old life anymore? Because if we don't look to the future and get me employed, we're going to have to make curtains out of your tiny wings to cover the window of our box under the bridge."

"Wait! There he is! Hold steady, Stevie!" he yelled into the wind.

We were out on this cliff in the town I'd grown up in because Belfry claimed someone from the afterlife—someone British—was trying to contact me, and as he followed the voice, it was clearest here. In the freezing rain…

Also in my former life, from time to time, I'd helped those who'd passed on solve a mystery. Now that I was unavailable for comment, they tried reaching me via Belfry.

The connection was always hazy and muddled, it came and went, broken and spotty, but Belfry wasn't ready to let go of our former life. So more often than not, over the last month since I'd been booted from the community, as the afterlife grew anxious about my vacancy, the dearly departed sought any means to connect with me.

Belfry was the most recent "any means."

"Madam *Who*?" Belfry squeaked in his munchkin voice, startling me. "Listen up, matey, when you contact a medium, you gotta turn up the volume!"

"Belfryyy!" I yelled when a strong wind picked up, lashing at my face and making my eyes tear. "This is moving toward ridiculous. Just tell whoever it is that I can't come to the phone right now due to poverty!"

He shrugged me off with an impatient flap of his wings. "Wait! Just one more sec—what's that? *Zoltar?* What in all the bloomin' afterlife is a Zoltar?" Belfry paused and, I'd bet, held his breath while he waited for an answer—and then he let out a long, exasperated squeal of frustration before his tiny body went limp.

Which panicked me. Belfry was prone to drama-ish tendencies at the best of times, but the effort he was putting into being my conduit of sorts had been taking a toll. He was all I had, my last connection to anything supernatural. I couldn't bear losing him.

So I yanked him to my chest and tucked him into my soaking-wet sweater as I made a break for the hotel we were a week from being evicted right out of.

"Belfry!" I clung to his tiny body, rubbing my thumbs over the backs of his wings.

Belfry is a cotton ball bat. He's two inches from wing to wing of pure white bigmouth and minute yellow ears and snout, with origins stemming from Honduras, Nicaragua, and Costa Rica, where it's warm and humid.

Since we'd moved here to Seattle from the blazing-hot sun of Paris, Texas, he'd struggled with the cooler weather.

I was always finding ways to keep him warm, and now that he'd taxed himself by staying too long in the crappy weather we were having, plus using all his familiar energy to figure out who was trying to contact me, his wee self had gone into overload.

I reached for the credit card key to our hotel room in my skirt pocket and swiped it, my hands shaking. Slamming the door shut with the heel of my foot, I ran to the bathroom, flipped on the lights and set Belfry on a fresh white towel. His tiny body curled inward, leaving his wings tucked under him as pinhead-sized drops of water dripped on the towel.

Grabbing the blow dryer on the wall, I turned the setting to low and began swishing it over him from a safe distance so as not to knock him off the vanity top. "Belfry! Don't you poop on me now, buddy. I need you!" Using my index and my thumb, I rubbed along his rounded back, willing warmth into him.

"To the right," he ordered.

My fingers stiffened as my eyes narrowed, but I kept rubbing just in case.

He groaned. "Ahh, yeah. Riiight there."

"Belfry?"

"Yes, Wicked One?"

"Not the time to test my devotion."

"Are you fragile?"

"I wouldn't use the word fragile. But I would use mildly agitated and maybe even raw. If you're just joking around, knock it off. I've had all I can take in the way of shocks and upset this month."

He used his wings to push upward to stare at me with his melty chocolate eyes. "I wasn't testing your devotion. I was just depleted. Whoever this guy is, trying to get you on the line, he's determined. How did you manage to keep your fresh, dewy appearance with all that squawking in your ears all the time?"

I shrugged my shoulders and avoided my reflection in the mirror over the vanity. I didn't look so fresh and dewy anymore, and I knew it. I looked tired and devoid of interest in most everything around me. The bags under my eyes announced it to the world.

"We need to find a job, Belfry. We have exactly a week before my savings account is on E."

"So no lavish spending. Does that mean I'm stuck with the very average Granny Smith for dinner versus, say, a yummy pomegranate?"

I chuckled because I couldn't help it. I knew my laughter egged him on, but he was the reason I still got up every morning. Not that I'd ever tell him as much.

I reached for another towel and dried my hair, hoping it wouldn't frizz. "You get whatever is on the discount rack, buddy. Which should be incentive enough for you to help me find a job, lest you forgot how ripe those discounted bananas from the whole foods store really were."

"Bleh. Okay. Job. Onward ho. Got any leads?"

"The pharmacy in the center of town is looking for a cashier. It won't get us a cute house at the end of a cul-de-sac, but it'll pay for a decent enough studio. Do you want to come with or stay here and rest your weary wings?"

"Where you go, I go. I'm the tuna to your mayo."

"You have to stay in my purse, Belfry," I warned, scooping him up with two fingers to bring him to the closet with me to help me choose an outfit. "You can't wander out like you did at the farmers' market. I thought that jelly vendor was going to faint. This isn't Paris anymore. No one knows I'm a witch—" I sighed. "*Was* a witch, and no one especially knows you're a talking bat. Seattle is eclectic and all about the freedom to be you, but they haven't graduated to letting ex-witches leash their chatty bats outside of restaurants just yet."

"I got carried away. I heard 'mango chutney' and lost my teensy mind. I promise to stay in the dark hovel you call a purse—even if the British guy contacts me again."

"Forget the British guy and help me decide. Red Anne Klein skirt and matching jacket, or the less formal Blue Fly jeans and Gucci silk shirt in teal."

"You're not interviewing with Karl Lagerfeld. You're interviewing to sling sundries. Gum, potato chips, *People* magazine, maybe the occasional script for Viagra."

"It's an organic pharmacy right in that kitschy little knoll in town where all the food trucks and tattoo shops are. I'm not sure they make all-natural Viagra, but you sure sound disappointed we might have a roof over our heads."

"I'm disappointed you probably won't be wearing all those cute vintage clothes you're always buying at the thrift store if you work in a pharmacy."

"I haven't gotten the job yet, and if I do, I guess I'll just be the cutest cashier ever."

I decided on the Ann Klein. It never hurt to bring a touch of understated class, especially when the class had only cost me a total of twelve dollars.

As I laid out my wet clothes to dry on the tub and went about the business of putting on my best interview facade, I tried not to think about Belfry's broken communication with the British guy. There were times as a witch when I'd toiled over the souls who needed closure, sometimes to my detriment.

But I couldn't waste energy fretting over what I

couldn't fix. And if British Guy was hoping I could help him now, he was sorely misinformed.

Maybe the next time Belfry had an otherworldly connection, I'd ask him to put everyone in the afterlife on notice that Stevie Louise Cartwright was out of order.

Grabbing my purse from the hook on the back of the bathroom door, I smoothed my hands over my skirt and squared my shoulders.

"You ready, Belfry?"

"As I'll ever be."

"Ready, set, job!"

As I grabbed my raincoat and tucked Belfry into my purse, I sent up a silent prayer to the universe that my unemployed days were numbered.

NOTE FROM DAKOTA

I do hope you enjoyed this book, I'd so appreciate it if you'd help others enjoy it, too.

Recommend it. Please help other readers find this book by recommending it.

Review it. Please tell other readers why you liked this book by reviewing it at online retailers or your blog. Reader reviews help my books continue to be valued by distributors/resellers. I adore each and every reader who takes the time to write one!

If you love the book or leave a review, please email **dakota@dakotacassidy.com** so I can thank you with a personal email. Your support means more than you'll ever know! Thank you!

ABOUT THE AUTHOR

Dakota Cassidy is a USA Today bestselling author with over thirty books. She writes laugh-out-loud cozy mysteries, romantic comedy, grab-some-ice erotic romance, hot and sexy alpha males, paranormal shifters, contemporary kick-ass women, and more.

Dakota was invited by Bravo TV to be the Bravo-holic for a week, wherein she snarked the hell out of all the Bravo shows. She received a starred review from Publishers Weekly for Talk Dirty to Me, won a Romantic Times Reviewers' Choice Award for Kiss and Hell, along with many review site recommended reads and reviewer top pick awards.

Dakota lives in the gorgeous state of Oregon with her real-life hero and her dogs, and she loves hearing from readers!

OTHER BOOKS BY DAKOTA CASSIDY

Visit Dakota's website at
http://www.dakotacassidy.com for more information.

A Lemon Layne Mystery, a Contemporary Cozy Mystery Series

1. Prawn of the Dead
2. Play That Funky Music White Koi
3. Total Eclipse of the Carp

Witchless In Seattle Mysteries, a Paranormal Cozy Mystery series

1. Witch Slapped
2. Quit Your Witchin'
3. Dewitched
4. The Old Witcheroo
5. How the Witch Stole Christmas
6. Ain't Love a Witch
7. Good Witch Hunting

Nun of Your Business Mysteries, a Paranormal Cozy Mystery series

1. Then There Were Nun
2. Hit and Nun

Wolf Mates, a Paranormal Romantic Comedy series

1. An American Werewolf In Hoboken
2. What's New, Pussycat?
3. Gotta Have Faith
4. Moves Like Jagger
5. Bad Case of Loving You

A Paris, Texas Romance, a Paranormal Romantic Comedy series

1. Witched At Birth
2. What Not to Were
3. Witch Is the New Black
4. White Witchmas

Non-Series

Whose Bride Is She Anyway?

Polanski Brothers: Home of Eternal Rest

Sexy Lips 66

Accidentally Paranormal, a Paranormal Romantic Comedy series

Interview With an Accidental—a free introductory guide to the girls of the Accidentals!

1. The Accidental Werewolf
2. Accidentally Dead
3. The Accidental Human
4. Accidentally Demonic
5. Accidentally Catty
6. Accidentally Dead, Again

7. The Accidental Genie
8. The Accidental Werewolf 2: Something About Harry
9. The Accidental Dragon
10. Accidentally Aphrodite
11. Accidentally Ever After
12. Bearly Accidental
13. How Nina Got Her Fang Back
14. The Accidental Familiar
15. Then Came Wanda
16. The Accidental Mermaid

The Hell, a Paranormal Romantic Comedy series

1. Kiss and Hell
2. My Way to Hell

The Plum Orchard, a Contemporary Romantic Comedy series

1. Talk This Way
2. Talk Dirty to Me
3. Something to Talk About
4. Talking After Midnight

The Ex-Trophy Wives, a Contemporary Romantic Comedy series

1. You Dropped a Blonde On Me
2. Burning Down the Spouse
3. Waltz This Way

Fangs of Anarchy, a Paranormal Urban Fantasy series

1. Forbidden Alpha
2. Outlaw Alpha